The Christmas Bookshop

DARCIE BOLEYN

The Christmas Tea Shop

CANELO

First published in the United Kingdom in 2019 by Canelo

This edition published in the United Kingdom in 2020 by

Canelo Digital Publishing Limited
31 Helen Road
Oxford OX2 0DF
United Kingdom

A CIP catalogue record for this book is available from the British Library.

Print ISBN 978 1 78863 978 1
Ebook ISBN 978 1 78863 121 1

Look for more great books at www.canelo.co

Printed and bound in Great Britain by Clays Ltd, Elcograf S.p.A.

For my husband and children, with love always.

Chapter 1

'Fran, did you hear what I just said?'

Fran frowned at her best friend, Holly Dryden.

'Uh… yes, yes I did. You said that you opened a bottle of wine last night, took a sip and it made you feel queasy.'

The two women stared at each other and Fran felt her jaw drop. Just moments ago, they had been chatting about paintings and Christmas plans and Holly's forthcoming wedding – all innocuous enough – and now…

This.

Fran had suspected that Holly had something on her mind, as Holly had seemed somewhat distracted, then she had confirmed Fran's suspicions when she'd blurted out her comment about feeling queasy when she'd taken a sip of wine.

'Fran, I think I might be pregnant.' Holly's bottom lip wobbled and her eyes filled with tears.

'Oh, Holly, it's okay, come here.'

Fran wrapped her arms around her friend and held her tight. This was clearly unplanned but it didn't have to be a bad thing. Holly's son, Luke, was still very young and he had been a surprise, but he had also brought everyone around him so much joy. Holly had experienced a difficult time when Luke was born, because she'd split up with Luke's father and left Penhallow Sands before finding out that she was pregnant, but on her return she had been reunited with Rich. Now, their relationship was stronger than ever. They made a delightful family and doted on their baby son, along with Holly's father and grandmother. Another baby hadn't been on the agenda so quickly, but if Holly was pregnant, then it wouldn't be the worst thing that could happen to them.

Fran gazed around the shop that Holly ran at Greenacres Vineyard, buying some time to let the realisation sink in, and to find the right words to offer Holly the support she needed right now. The shop's familiarity was comforting, with the counter and till, the shelves stocked with bottles of wine, a selection of Fran's handiwork including glasses, pottery bowls and goblets lining the shelves and a number of her paintings of local landscapes adorning the wall behind the counter.

'Look, Holly, you don't know for certain yet, so there's no point worrying. It could just be that you weren't in the mood for wine last night, or that the wine was... I don't know... a bit off.'

Holly shook her head. 'Our wine is good.'

'I know that, silly, but sometimes there's bound to be a bottle that's not quite right. It might have turned. Like... did it have that heavy raisin smell?'

Holly nodded. 'It didn't smell good, so I guess you could be right.'

Fran pushed Holly's blonde hair behind her ears. 'Have you told Rich?'

'Not yet. I'd prefer to know for certain and I don't know how he'll take it if I am.'

'Holly, that man adores you and would do anything for you. Along with Luke, you are his whole world. Don't underestimate him. He'll come through for you.'

'I know. But with the wedding just over six weeks away, we have so much to do and we were hoping to have a few days away at some point as a honeymoon, but that all depends on how Granny's feeling, and—'

'And none of that is a problem. You can still do all those things.'

'But also...' Holly sighed. 'With Granny being under the weather recently, I've been so concerned about her. I can see that she's struggling, yet she's trying so hard to help with getting things ready for the wedding and I just think that if I am pregnant, then she'll try to do even more because she'll be worried about me and... I can't bear to see her wear herself out. You know how she gets... She'll feel that she has to look after me but it's her who needs looking after right now.'

'Yes, I know Glenda well.' Fran nodded.

Holly's maternal grandmother would try to lighten Holly's load if she suspected that she was pregnant and taking more on wasn't a good idea right now. Glenda Morton hadn't fully recovered from a recent bout of flu, and between them, Holly, Rich and Holly's father, Bruce, were keen to ensure that Glenda got as much rest as possible. The elderly lady was strong willed, and even when the doctor had recommended bed rest, Glenda had been found mopping the kitchen floor and trying to clean the windows.

'So you understand why I want to keep this quiet for now. At least until I know for certain if I am pregnant and then... if I am... I'd like to keep it secret until after the wedding. Hopefully, by the time January rolls round, Granny will be feeling stronger.'

'That makes perfect sense.'

Fran glanced out of the window. 'But Rich is on his way over here right now, so if you're not ready to tell him yet, wipe your eyes, blow your nose and take a deep breath.'

Holly did as she'd been told.

'Let's meet later so we can talk properly, shall we?' Fran feigned interest in a leaflet on the counter about a Christmas market in Newquay. The jolly Santa on the front had fat rosy cheeks and an impossibly white beard.

'I can't today, but how about tomorrow?'

'Fine. You could come to mine or we could meet up at Rosewood Tea Shop? I have to deliver a few things there anyway, so it's as good an excuse as any to meet there and enjoy some of Audrey's finest. We can have cake, coffee and hopefully some peace and quiet.'

'Cake sounds good.' Holly smiled.

'That's better. Keep smiling because it will all be okay.'

Rich was almost at the shop now.

'One more thing though...' Holly leant over the counter and met Fran's eyes. 'Could you get me a pregnancy test, as I won't have a chance to go out and buy one and... I also can't be seen buying one in the village. You know how people talk.'

With her soft blonde hair, big green eyes and pale face, Holly looked so young and fragile that Fran wanted to wrap her up in cotton wool and protect her from the world. She loved her friend and would do anything to help her.

Fran nodded. 'No problem. I've never bought one before, so it'll be a first.'

'Never bought what?' Rich had entered the shop and he smiled as he approached the counter.

'Oh… um… she's never bought a… a…'

'A man-bun visor,' Fran blurted.

'A what?' Rich's face creased as he started to laugh. 'A man-bun visor? Why on earth would you want one of those? Although… I'm not sure if I know what one is.'

Holly's eyes widened and her lips twitched and Fran knew that she had to dig them out of this hole and quickly, otherwise Rich might become suspicious about the nature of their conversation before he had arrived.

'Because…' Fran ran a hand over her short hair. 'My hair's quite short and sometimes I'd like to have longer hair. And… I saw one of those man-bun visors online and it looked like the perfect solution.'

Rich nodded but his eyes had narrowed. 'Is it actually for Holly's hen night? Is that what's going on here? You two are planning something wild, aren't you?' He winked at Holly.

'Yes. Yes we are.' Holly nodded.

'I thought so.' Rich walked around the counter and slid an arm around Holly's waist then kissed the top of her head. 'Always up to mischief. You really don't need to hide anything from me, though. I don't mind what you want to do as long as you look after each other when you're out and about.'

'Yes that's us.' Holly held Fran's gaze with her bright green eyes and Fran could see that Holly hated deceiving Rich, but she also understood Holly's reasons for wanting to wait before she told him. Besides which, Fran really had seen a man-bun visor online the other day and it had both intrigued her and repulsed her, and now she wanted to go and take another look. It could well be something funny to purchase for Holly's hen night. But first she had to go and buy a pregnancy test…

—

Fran's heart was pounding and her palms were clammy as she marched away from the small village pharmacy. She felt like she'd just purchased something illegal or illicit and not a couple of plain old pregnancy tests, and that at any moment she'd feel the weight of a police officer's hand on her shoulder and be dragged in for questioning. But *oh*… it had not been as straightforward a task as she had imagined. The village of Penhallow Sands had been busy for a Friday afternoon in November, and when she'd entered the pharmacy, it had been filled with coughing pensioners and snotty-nosed toddlers, with people she knew from the village and some of the returning tourists who liked to visit the Cornish location during the quieter winter period. She had felt instantly uneasy, as if everyone knew why she was there, and her scalp had prickled and her stomach churned as if she'd eaten a hot chilli before leaving the house.

Fran had dawdled for a while, reading the instructions on conditioner bottles and toothpaste boxes, trying to absorb the information about colour protection promised by the conditioner and about a brighter whiter smile from the toothpaste. Then she'd shuffled along the aisles, picking up things she didn't need and dropping them into a basket until she reached the aisle with the desired product. As she ran her eyes over the shelves, she was horrified to find that there was a vast selection of tests available. She had not been prepared for that at all and a wave of panic had swept over her. From the bargain test that looked as though it might be some kind of torture device, to the test that told you how many weeks pregnant you were, to the one that predicted if you were pregnant even before your period was due, there was so much choice. How was the promise made by the latter test even possible? Was it somehow psychic?

It had occurred to Fran then that the pregnancy testing market was clearly lucrative. Fran loved Holly's son, Luke, and liked holding other friends' babies, but she hadn't planned on having children or really felt any desire to procreate at all, so to her this was an enigma. She had never been in a serious relationship, which could be linked to that lack of maternal yearning, but it could just be that she didn't have the biological desire to reproduce. As she stood staring at the shelves, she had shrugged. Her absence of maternal yearning wasn't important; what did matter was finding a test for Holly, so she'd grabbed a cheap one and one that could tell how many weeks pregnant a woman was, and dropped them into her basket. She had tucked them under her other purchases, hurried to the counter, then held her breath as the girl at the till had slowly scanned each item before loudly telling her that the one test had a buy–one–get–one–free offer on it so did she want two of the same? Fran had shaken her head furiously and the girl had raised her thickly drawn on brows and opened her mouth to protest at the stupidity of her declining the offer, but clearly thought better of it when Fran glared at her, injecting as much venom into her gaze as she could muster. It didn't come naturally to Fran, that kind of glare, but desperate circumstances had called for it. The girl had wrinkled her highlighted nose – why did people do that? – then scanned the rest of the items and deposited them into a paper bag before requesting payment.

'Fran!' A deep voice rumbled close to her ear now and she froze as if she'd been caught. 'What's the hurry?'

She turned on her heel and met the dark brown eyes of Jamal Wilson, the co-owner of the local salon Hairway to Heaven.

'Hi, Jamal.' She brought a smile to her lips but it felt more like a grimace. She'd usually be glad to see the handsome and kind hair stylist, but today was not the day for banter.

'I asked what the hurry was. You were hotfooting it along the pavement like you were being chased by rabid hounds.'

'Rabid hounds?' She frowned.

'Hounds that wanted to bite your bottom.' He laughed. 'Sorry... Bradley's had me watching this new series on Netflix and there were these rabid dogs and...' He shook his head. 'You know what, you'd have to watch it to understand.'

'Okay.' Fran nodded, the image of dogs chasing her to bite her bottom now emblazoned on her mind. What if they grabbed the paper bag off her and stole the tests? Then she'd have to go back to the pharmacy and experience the whole horrid process again.

'So why were you rushing? Everything okay?' He scanned her face, his eyes filled with concern. Fran felt her shoulders relax a fraction at his kindness.

'Yeah, I'm okay. I was just... lost in my own world.'

'We all have days like that.' He pushed his spiky dɪ locks back with his large hands and the diamond studs his ears sparkled in the winter sunlight. 'Do you know if Holly still wants me to do her hair for the wedding? She mentioned it a few weeks ago and I'd love to do it. She has fabulous hair.'

'I'm pretty certain that she does. Tell you what, I'll text her now and tell her to let you know. If I don't do it immediately, I'll forget and it's not fair to leave you wondering.'

Fran pulled her smartphone out of her pocket and swiped the screen. The bag from the pharmacy was heavy on her arm, the paper handles digging into her skin.

'Let me take that for you,' Jamal said, reaching for the bag.

'Thanks.' Fran was about to release it when she remembered what was inside. She snatched her hand back just as Jamal's long fingers gripped the bottom and the bag tore in half like a Christmas cracker. She watched in horror as the contents flew across the pavement, but there was no paper hat and joke along with some plastic trinket inside; instead, there was toothpaste, shampoo, facial oil and… two pregnancy tests.

Jamal's jaw dropped as he stared at the tests.

Fran stared at Jamal, then at the tests, then slowly raised her eyes to Jamal's face. Even though the air was clear and cold, her chest tightened and she struggled to suck in a breath. She glanced around them but people were continuing with their day, oblivious to the pregnancy test debacle currently unfolding for Fran.

She finally pulled air into her lungs then dropped to her knees and reached for the tests, stuffing them into her coat pockets. Jamal picked up the other things and handed them to her, so she put them into what remained of the paper bag, folded it over then tucked it under her arm.

'Jamal… it's not what it looks like.'

He raised his big hands, pink palms facing her, and cocked an eyebrow, looking more like Idris Elba than ever – just with more hair.

'None of my business, Fran.'

'No. You're right. But… uh… don't say anything about this to anyone, will you?'

'My lips are sealed.' He placed a finger over his mouth. 'Not a word. This is clearly very big news for you.' He smiled. 'And very exciting!'

Fran swallowed her dismay. She really liked Jamal and his husband Bradley, but she knew they enjoyed a bit of juicy gossip and wondered if Jamal would be able to keep this secret to himself, or if it would spill out as he chatted to a client. He wouldn't do it intentionally, but it was likely that it would slip out at some point. She took a deep breath and tried to steady herself. Whatever he did wasn't important. She needed to keep Holly's secret for now, and keep it she would. If the Penhallow Sands rumour mill decided that Fran was pregnant, then so be it.

'Right, let me send that text.'

She swiped the screen of her phone and typed the message to Holly, aware that Jamal was staring intently at her face and probably wondering who the father was. She could certainly have some fun with that mystery, although she didn't feel in the mood for playing around right now.

In fact, she needed a caffeine and sugar fix, and quickly.

Chapter 2

Ethan Clarke suppressed a sigh as he manoeuvred his black VW Golf around the country lanes. He'd forgotten how narrow these roads could be, having grown up in Bath and not visited Penhallow Sands since he was fifteen, and that was twenty years ago. He suppressed another sigh at the thought of how quickly those years had flown. He was five years off forty and certainly hadn't thought his life would turn out as it had. He'd been convinced that he was destined for success and that his future would be happy and healthy, that life would open up to him as he got older. Instead, his marriage had broken down, he'd been a single father for two years and now, to top it all off, he'd lost the job he loved as a chef, in a place where, although it wasn't high end, his colleagues were warm and friendly and the routine was comfortingly familiar.

But whenever he felt glum, all he had to do was look at his six-year-old daughter, Tilly, and know that nothing else mattered. Tilly was his world and all he cared about was keeping her safe and making sure that she was happy. His own happiness was something he'd put aside two years ago when his marriage ended, or even before that if he counted the years of uncertainty when he was with Melanie Tranter, never knowing if she was going to stay or go, if she loved him or felt that she was stuck with him.

He'd been a fool to fall in love with her and he knew why it had happened when it had: he'd been reeling from the loss of his mother and trying to find a salve for his pain. Unfortunately, Melanie hadn't been the soothing balm he'd hoped for and they'd married for the wrong reasons. But that was in the past, behind him now, and he'd never make the same mistakes again. Tilly was his focus and always would be.

The wipers cleared the windscreen of drizzle, revealing an opening in the hedgerows, and the grey sky opened out before him. The rain that was falling appeared cold and sticky and he didn't relish the prospect of getting out of the car and having to unload their belongings. It wasn't the best welcome to the place he'd once enjoyed visiting, and it didn't fill him with confidence that he'd made the right decision returning here, but his options had been limited. Something had needed to change in his life and a cross-country move had seemed worth a shot.

'Are we nearly there, Daddy?' Tilly asked from the back seat of the car for what had to be the millionth time since they'd left Bath that morning. The journey had taken over four hours with comfort breaks and a quick stop for some lunch, but his daughter had been incredibly patient and well behaved. He could cope with the question because he understood how she felt. All he wanted now was to stretch his legs, take a hot shower and sleep. He doubted that his afternoon and evening would follow that exact pattern, as he had family to catch up with, but he hoped that later on, after he'd put Tilly to bed, he'd be able to relax and gather his thoughts.

'Yes, angel, almost there.'

'Good because I need a wee.'

'Me too.' He wiggled his eyebrows at her in the rear-view mirror and she giggled.

He indicated left then turned and drove along a gravel road towards large open gates and a sign for *Rosewood Farm and Tea Shop*. The crunching of the gravel under the tyres and the wooden sign – with its painting of a black and white cow with a big pink rose tucked behind its ear – brought back a jolt of memories from his childhood. When he was younger, he'd come here with his parents in their old yellow Ford Fiesta, following what felt like an endless journey. The car had smelt of sun cream, his father's Brut aftershave and salt and vinegar crisps – because Ethan had opened a bag and the contents had flown everywhere. His mum had collected the crisps, dusted them off then shared them with Ethan while his dad drove. They'd sucked the crisps slowly to get all the flavouring off before chewing them up, treating it like a game to make the time pass more quickly.

Back then, his mum, Heidi, had been young and beautiful with long blonde hair, bright green eyes and an easy smile. She was one of life's dreamers, his dad always said as he gazed at her adoringly, and Ethan had loved to listen to her stories about the places she wanted to see and the things she wanted to do when they had enough money. As an artist, her income had been unreliable, so sometimes they'd had money and at other times, things had been tight. But his mum had always been cheerful and seen the positives in every situation, counted her blessings and refused to allow worries to darken her days. She had also been a wonderful cook and had taught him how to make healthy and delicious meals from scratch with just a few ingredients, and how to bake bread, cakes and puddings that made his mouth water and filled their house with amazing aromas. Even now, eight years after his mother's passing, the smell of baking could lift Ethan's spirits and bring his mum right back into his world.

He missed her so much.

'Are you sad, Daddy?' Tilly asked.

'What? No, Tilly, I'm not sad. Why do you ask?'

'I saw in the mirror that your mouth turned down and your eyebrows moved together. My teacher says you should always turn that frown upside down.'

He shook his head and laughed. 'I'll do my best.'

Tilly was the tonic to his grief that he had needed and whenever he felt himself sinking, she always managed to lift him into better spirits.

As he drove along the gravel lane, the farm buildings came into view and his stomach flipped. He hadn't seen his father's sister, Audrey Sanders, in years, and although they spoke on the phone every month and sometimes via WhatsApp, it was always about Tilly and his dad and nothing too heavy. Seeing Audrey now, as an adult with a child of his own, would be strange and he hoped that it wouldn't be too awkward, especially seeing as how he'd be living at Rosewood Farm for the foreseeable future.

At the end of the lane, a signpost pointing to the right announced Rosewood Tea Shop, while to the left was the farmhouse. He'd go there first because there was a good chance that someone would be home and because he didn't fancy walking into a busy tea shop and having to meet people just yet. He needed to settle in first and to find his feet.

'Are we there now, Daddy?'

'Yes, we're here!'

'Thank goodness for that!'

Tilly's comment made Ethan smile as he parked in front of the long stone building with its small-paned black-framed windows and slate-tiled roof and cut the engine. Smoke curled up from the wide chimney and disappeared into the air.

'This is Aunty Audrey's house,' Ethan said, as much to himself as to Tilly, as if confirming to himself that he was really here.

'Yay! Can I see the cows?'

Ever since he'd told Tilly that Rosewood was a dairy farm, she'd been asking about the cows. She'd seen cows in fields as they drove past them, but never up close, and he did wonder how she'd find them in real life. The first time he'd seen the cows at Rosewood, he'd found their size and strong countryside smell quite overwhelming, but he had soon come to enjoy helping out his Uncle Gary. Tilly had also been asking for a dog for years but with Ethan working and having no one around to help, he hadn't thought it was fair to have one as it would end up spending a lot of time alone. At least here on the farm, Tilly would have contact with a variety of animals, and he hoped that it would be an educational and enjoyable experience for her.

'You can, but perhaps later or tomorrow, all right? We have to meet Aunty Audrey and Uncle Gary first, as well as my cousins, Harper and Scarlett.'

'Okay, Daddy, but don't forget.'

'I won't. I promise.'

'Glitterbug says her tummy is fizzing.'

Ethan turned in his seat to find Tilly waving her brown dog toy in the air.

'Fizzing?'

'Like she drank too much coke.'

'Does Glitterbug need a wee?'

'She does but she said her tummy is fizzing because she's nervous too.'

'That's nice to know, Tilly. Tell Glitterbug that she'll be fine and doesn't need to worry.'

'Don't worry, Glitterbug.' Tilly kissed the toy's head. 'Can we get out now, Daddy?'

'Yes we can.'

Ethan got out of the car then opened the back door and helped Tilly out of her car seat. He scooped her up and whirled her around, which made her giggle, then set her down next to the car.

'Wait there for a moment while I get what we need, then we can go and knock on the door.'

'Yes, Daddy.'

Ethan smiled at her, his heart filled with love for the small girl with her long blonde hair just like his mother's and her soft brown eyes that were exactly like Melanie's – but without the coldness. Some days, he could barely believe she was his daughter because she was so stoic and funny; she took everything in her stride and he hoped she always would do. He'd hate for her to become a worrier like him, and his one main wish was that she'd never be hurt by anyone, ever. He knew that wasn't realistic but he could hope. Hope was something he could always do, even if it was simply hoping that he could cling on to hope.

He shook his head at his musings, grabbed the rucksack containing his laptop, wallet and glasses, then locked the car.

'Come on then, Tilly, let's see who's home, shall we?'

He held out his hand and Tilly took it, then they walked towards the farmhouse. Ethan wondered if Glitterbug's tummy was fizzing as much as his was, and if she was wondering how their new start was going to work out.

The door swung open and a short, stout woman squealed and clapped her hands.

'Ethan! Tilly! Hellooooo!'

She launched herself at them and hugged them both in turn, Ethan first then Tilly, leaving him breathless and Tilly wide-eyed.

'Hello, Aunty Audrey.' Ethan smiled.

'Oh, love, call me Audrey otherwise it's a right old mouthful.'

She beamed at him, her cheeks flushed and her green eyes the mirror of his own, except that they had a few more lines at the corners and her lashes were so fair they were almost white.

'And look at you, Tilly, you beautiful little girl!'

Tilly held out her toy dog. 'This is Glitterbug. She likes cows.'

'Does she now?' Audrey said, leaning over to Tilly's eye level. 'Well, there are plenty of cows at Rosewood for you to meet, Glitterbug. I'm sure you'll love it here and that you'll be able to get stuck in with milking and mucking out and… well… everything. Gary will be grateful for the help of an apprentice, no doubt.'

'Glitterbug says she will be glad to be an prentice.' Tilly peered up at Audrey shyly. 'What's an prentice?'

'An apprentice is someone who works with someone to learn something, like a skill. So if you were Uncle Gary's apprentice, you'd learn how to be a dairy farmer.'

'Okay.' Tilly grinned. 'I'll be Uncle Gary's prentice.'

'Look at me, will you?' Audrey shook her head. 'Here I am, keeping you on the doorstep, and with it being such a dreary day. Come on in and have a cuppa and some cake. You must be exhausted after that journey.'

Audrey stepped back and ushered Ethan and Tilly into the warm hallway that smelt of cinnamon and coffee, newspapers and woodsmoke. The dark flagstone floor was smooth and worn, and the walls were crammed with family photographs. It was how Ethan had always thought a home should be, a place where family ties ran deep and where there was a history that bound the lives of the inhabitants together. It was something he'd longed for at times, and something he wanted for Tilly, but it had always seemed out of reach for him as a single dad whose time was split between his young daughter and his job. In the time he had outside of work, he hadn't had much energy for anything other than taking care of Tilly.

Ethan scanned the photographs and saw a few of his mum and dad in amongst those of Audrey, Gary and their two girls. He suspected that he'd be on at least one of them, somewhere, albeit a far younger version of him. He'd have a good look later, although seeing his mum had already made his heart ache, so it was something he'd do discretely so no one saw him if he did get a bit upset.

Audrey closed the door then led the way through the hallway with its coat stand and rack of wellies and hats, and through to a large bright kitchen-diner. Everything was wooden, from the cupboard doors to the table and chairs, and Ethan thought it was exactly how a farmhouse kitchen should look – solid, warm and welcoming.

'Take a seat.' Audrey gestured at a sofa piled with plump feather cushions set in front of French doors leading out onto a small walled garden.

Ethan and Tilly sat down, sinking into the cushions, and Tilly wriggled along so that she was right next to Ethan then she slid her hand into his. He squeezed her hand and she squeezed back – their secret sign that said *I love you.* She was still clutching Glitterbug in her other hand.

'Right, that's the kettle on.' Audrey smoothed her wavy blonde bobbed hair back behind her ears. 'Can I get you anything to eat?'

Ethan turned to Tilly. 'Do you want anything?'

She looked at Glitterbug then back at Ethan. 'Glitterbug said can she have some cake?' she whispered, her eyes flickering sideways at Audrey.

'Could we have some cake, please?' Ethan asked.

'Of course you can.'

Soon, Audrey placed a tray on the small coffee table in front of the sofa. There were three mugs of tea, three small plates and a large plate with slices of carrot cake, chocolate cake and what Ethan suspected was lemon drizzle cake.

'Help yourselves.' Audrey gestured at the tray then took the chair opposite them.

'Thank you.' Ethan picked up one of the small plates. 'Which one would you like, Tilly?'

She poked out her tongue as she gazed at the cakes. 'Chocolate, please, Daddy.'

Ethan handed her the plate and she tucked in while he picked up a mug of tea.

'I forgot to ask if you wanted sugar,' Audrey said, rolling her eyes and pushing herself upwards.

'It's fine, thanks. Just milk for both of us.'

'Wonderful. How was your journey, my lovelies?'

'It was fine, thanks. We made good time. Obviously, it was long, but it's not like we're going to be commuting every day, is it?'

'Thank goodness for that! I'm so glad you've come to us at last.' She smiled warmly. 'Your uncle is out in the barn at the moment and your cousins are working in the tea shop, but you can meet them all later. They can't wait to see you again, Ethan, or to meet you, Tilly.'

'How old are they?' Tilly asked with the forthrightness of a child, and Ethan winced but Audrey didn't miss a beat.

'Well, Uncle Gary is fifty-seven, Harper is twenty-five and Scarlett is twenty-two.'

'That's a lot younger than my daddy.' Tilly frowned. 'Why are they younger?'

'Interesting question, Tilly. Your grandfather, who is also my brother, is five years older than me and I didn't have my first baby until I was thirty, so by then your daddy was already ten.'

'Oh.' Tilly nodded. 'So they were a bit young to be your friends when you were a little boy, Daddy.'

'Kind of.' Ethan smiled.

'I'm sure you'll all get on now, Ethan.' Audrey stood up and reached for a photograph that was on the sideboard. She handed it to Ethan and Tilly peered at it.

'The young woman with the long blonde hair is Harper and the other one is Scarlett. Her hair is bright red now, although a few weeks ago it was green, so I struggle to keep up with what colour it is.' Audrey shook her head.

'Do they still live with you?' Tilly took the photo from Ethan and ran a finger over the silver-plated frame.

'Yes they do and they both work in the tea shop. Harper intends on going away travelling with her girl-friend soon so she's been saving up, and Scarlett likes her home comforts so I can't see her moving out any time soon.'

'It's funny, living with their mummy and daddy when they're grown-ups.' Tilly laughed. 'I don't think I will live with my daddy when I'm that old.'

Ethan placed a hand over his heart and blinked rapidly. 'Why not? You mean you're going to leave me all on my own?'

Tilly frowned, placed the photograph on the table then took his hands. 'I won't leave you, Daddy, don't worry.' She turned to Audrey. 'Daddy doesn't have anyone else, so I can't leave him, see. Sometimes I forget that when I'm thinking about being a grown-up.'

'Tilly, I will be fine. One day, when you're older, you will move out and have your own life and your own family.'

'Your daddy is right, Tilly.' Audrey smiled. 'My girls have stayed here for so long because it's an expensive world and because they work here, but I don't expect them to live at home with me for ever.'

'But you have Uncle Gary to keep you company,' Tilly said. 'Daddy doesn't have a wife.'

Ethan met Audrey's eyes and smiled to try to show her that he was fine with how things were, but the smile felt more like a grimace. Knowing that Tilly had concerns about him being alone made him sad, because he wanted her to have a carefree and fulfilling life, not to be worrying about him and how he'd manage without her. He had to ensure that she knew he'd be just fine, and that he would always be happy as long as she was happy. He couldn't deny that the thought of having a special someone in his life would have been nice, but Tilly was his priority and he was doing his best to be a good dad to her.

'Don't you worry about your daddy.' Audrey waved a hand at Tilly. 'He will be just fine as long as you are fine. Isn't that right, Ethan?'

He nodded his agreement and his thanks.

'So let's have tea and cake, then I can show you the cottage where you'll be staying. I've lit the log burner and the Aga and made up the beds, so it'll be warm and cosy for you tonight.'

Audrey made the cottage sound extremely appealing and Ethan found that he was looking forward to seeing it. 'Thank you so much. That sounds perfect.'

Ethan was warmed right through. It had been such a long time since someone had done anything for him, so to be shown such kindness was quite overwhelming. In fact, apart from hugs from Tilly, he couldn't remember the last time he'd been hugged by an adult, so his aunt's big hug on the doorstep had been very nice indeed.

'Glitterbug misses her friends.' Tilly placed her empty plate on the tray then perched her toy dog on the end of the table. 'She's scared she won't have any here.'

Audrey shook her head. 'There's plenty of children in the village and the most wonderful school where you'll love to go, I'm sure. My girls went there and loved it, and the deputy head teacher, Miss Catherine Bromley, is very nice. You'll meet her soon. Then there's Ms Jowanet

Tremayne, the head teacher, and she's strict but she's also very kind.'

Ethan smiled his thanks at his aunt again. He'd been worried about uprooting Tilly from her home, but after he'd lost his job two months ago, he'd felt more isolated than ever. With his mother gone, his father jetting off regularly to Majorca and no one else around to turn to, Ethan had wondered what to do next. Then Audrey had phoned to wish Tilly happy birthday a few weeks earlier, and she'd been so kind and caring on the phone that Ethan had poured everything out to her. She'd told him that it was fate as their chef had just accepted a job on a cruise ship, and that if Ethan took the post, he'd save her from having to go through the rigmarole of finding another one. Apparently, the first chef had been difficult to find as not many chefs seemed to fancy the idea of working at a small farm tea shop in the Cornish countryside, preferring the towns and cities with their busy pubs and restaurants. But to Ethan, it sounded perfect. It would be time away from Bath with its vortex of painful memories and a fresh start for him and Tilly. So he'd accepted the job on the spot and made arrangements to leave Bath. He'd put the house he'd bought with Melanie on the market, packed up their furniture and put it into storage, and brought only what he and Tilly needed with them to Cornwall. Anything else could be moved later on when they were settled here. If they settled here. He hoped they would because moving was a big wrench and more than anything he longed for security for him and, more importantly, for Tilly.

'Do you think she will like Glitterbug?' Tilly asked quietly.

'Miss Bromley will love Glitterbug, and she'll love you! How could she fail to adore you both, you little cherub.' Audrey gazed at Tilly and Ethan saw his daughter flush with pleasure. She'd been a bit quiet recently and he was worried that not having a mother around was affecting her, so being around a positive and loving female role model like Audrey would surely be good for Tilly.

'Can I have more cake?' Tilly asked.

Ethan took in her chocolatey mouth and chin, and was about to say that perhaps one piece was enough for now, but then he relented. They'd just arrived and another piece of cake wouldn't hurt for once.

'What's the magic word, Tilly?' Ethan asked.

She pouted, then her eyes flashed as if taking up a challenge, and he held his breath. There was mischief rising in her now, he felt sure, and whenever she got mischievous, she always made him laugh.

'Abra... cadabra!' she exclaimed, sending Audrey into fits of giggles.

'I meant the other magic word, Tilly. You know... *please*, but you got me there, didn't you?' Ethan shook his head.

'Ha ha, Daddy, I did. I got you.'

'You must play that joke on Uncle Gary, Tilly. It's very funny. More tea, Ethan?' Audrey stood up and reached for his mug.

'That would be great thanks. I'm parched.'

He handed his mug to his aunt then relaxed into the squidgy sofa, feeling some of the tension in his body ebbing away. They'd been here less than half an hour but his aunt's warm welcome meant that his daughter was relaxed enough to start teasing him. It wasn't a side of his little girl that he'd seen for a while and it lifted his spirits.

This move could well be exactly what he and Tilly needed.

—

Fran settled back on the sofa and closed her eyes. It had been a busy day and she was glad to finally put her feet up. She'd given the bearded dragons their salad, fed the cats and the dogs and picked up after them all in the garden, then deposited the waste in the bottomless buckets where it would drain into the soil.

The patter of dog paws on flagstones made her smile. Seeing as how her golden lab, Crosby, was snoring in front of the log burner and her mongrel, Dust Bunny, was on the sofa at her side, it must be her whippet, Scamp, who'd got up to visit the kitchen. She hoped he'd only gone for a drink of water.

Fran reached out and ran a hand over Dust Bunny's fluffy white fur, enjoying how soft it felt under her palm, and the dog gave her hand a lick of thanks. The pitter patter of feet returning to the room made Fran open her eyes, and Scamp dropped to the rug in front of the log burner near Crosby. The dog was chewing something.

'Decided to clean your teeth, did you?' Fran asked, assuming that it was one of the dogs' chew toys. But as she looked more closely, she saw that Scamp actually had a box and was pulling something thin and white out of it.

'What the hell have you got there?' Fran jumped to her feet. 'Have you been in my bag, Scamp?'

The dog looked at her as if surprised at her tone, then continued chewing.

'Give me that!' Fran lurched at the dog and grabbed the box. 'You bloody mischievous dog.' She held out what was left of the pregnancy test box then reached down and took the test from Scamp's mouth. 'What made you think this would be tasty? Or that it was yours to take?'

Scamp peered up at her, his brown eyes pleading innocence, but then he started rubbing his face with his paws, suggesting that he knew he'd done wrong.

'This wasn't even mine, Scamp; it was for Holly. And... why did you have to take the more expensive one?'

Scamp let out a whine and Fran immediately felt guilty for scolding him. He didn't know that it wasn't for him and she had left her bag hanging on the back of a kitchen chair. Scamp had come to her as a rescue dog with some issues and one of them was that he stole things from bags and chewed them up. He was calm and happy now, but his old habit sometimes reappeared, especially if something smelt particularly interesting.

She leant over and rubbed his ears then kissed his soft head. 'It's okay, boy. I'm not angry, not at all.'

He wagged his tail then flopped onto his side next to Crosby and closed his eyes. Clearly, after all the excitement, it was nap time.

Fran went to the kitchen and threw the remains of the test in the bin then washed her hands. She glanced at the clock. Her parents and Nonna were due to Skype her soon from Italy, so she'd make a cuppa to drink while she spoke to them. After that, it would be a baked potato for one with cheese and beans and something on Netflix, along with doggy cuddles.

It sounded like the perfect evening.

Ethan tiptoed down the stairs and into the lounge of the stone cottage at Rosewood Farm. A smaller version of the farmhouse, it was located on the opposite side of the yard from his aunt and uncle's home and just behind the tea shop. It had a small private garden and a wonderful view of the fields that stretched out for what seemed like miles. The coast was just visible in the distance, with flashes of blue-grey sea reflecting the November weather.

He'd put Tilly to bed in the single room where the pretty pink and lilac bed linen smelt of floral fabric softener, and where Tilly had clung to Glitterbug as if her life depended on it. That had worried Ethan so he had stayed with her, reading her stories and stroking her hair until she'd fallen asleep. It was daunting enough for him being in a strange cottage, let alone for his six-year-old child. He'd left a nightlight on and her door open so he could hear if she called for him. It was clear that his aunt had bought the pretty bed linen especially for Tilly and she'd added touches like some books on the white shelves and a small lamp that matched the bed linen. It all looked and felt fresh and new and he appreciated her thoughtfulness. Tilly had looked around the room in awe when they'd come to take a look around, but at night, when darkness fell and bedtime arrived, it was harder to be so positive. However, he had reassured himself that she would soon adjust and that this cottage could easily become home, as long as they were together.

Now, he sat on the damask velvet cushioned sofa and curled his legs up under him. The room was warm and cosy with the curtains drawn and the log fire burning in the hearth. There was a large flat-screen TV in the corner and the cottage had Wi-Fi, so he knew he'd be able to sign up to Netflix or Sky or some other form of relaxing distraction. To survive the long winter nights, plenty of good TV would be essential, although Audrey had told him that he and Tilly would always be welcome to join them at the farmhouse.

He'd eaten dinner there this evening and met his uncle and cousins again for the first time in years. They had been warm and friendly and Tilly had responded well to them. Dinner hadn't been a long affair, as his uncle still had jobs on the farm to complete and his cousins, Harper and Scarlett, had prior social engagements. Being a fair bit younger than Ethan, they still lived at home and weren't yet settled with children or partners. Like most twenty-somethings they seemed to have an active social life, which they chattered about throughout the meal. Tilly had been quiet at first when everyone was introduced, but she'd soon come out of her shell with gentle coaxing and some strawberry ice cream. She'd also been fascinated by his cousins' names and kept repeating them, emphasising the syllables and smiling each time. In turn, his cousins had found Tilly's behaviour amusing and they'd seemed enchanted with her. Ethan could only hope that this would be a good thing for Tilly. She'd gone from having no female role models around – other than teachers and classroom assistants – to having three female family members.

He wriggled down so that he was lying flat and he watched how the glow from the fire created shadows on the wall. It would be nice to have a partner now, to have a woman to snuggle up to and to talk with, to plan with, even to sit in comfortable silence with. It would be soothing to have the reassurance of another adult around. But then, if he had that, he'd also have the fear and the vulnerability that came with being in a relationship. He didn't think he'd be able to handle all that again, especially now that it wasn't just him he had to worry about. Tilly needed to have a stable home life, she needed to know that she was loved and cared for and he could never allow someone to come into her life in case they left it again. His baby girl had lost one mother; he couldn't bear for her to lose another. She deserved far better than that and Ethan would ensure that she was never hurt again.

Chapter 3

Fran pushed open the door to the tea shop at Rosewood and stood back to allow Holly to enter before her with the pushchair. She closed the door behind them, appreciating the warmth inside after the icy bite of the wind swirling around the yard outside. They headed for a table near the log burner and removed their coats before sitting down. She'd picked Holly up after delivering some pottery olive bowls to Greenacres, and she'd been worried when she'd seen how pale her friend was. The first thing they needed to do was to get some tea and cake into Holly, then they could continue their discussion about whether or not Holly was pregnant and, if so, what her next move would be.

Audrey Sanders approached the table with a small notepad and pencil. 'Hello, ladies.'

Fran met the woman's kind green eyes and returned the smile. 'Hi, Audrey. How are you?'

'Very good, thanks.'

'I have a box of mugs in the car for you so you can check out the sample designs. I'll bring it in before we leave.'

'Thanks, Fran.' Audrey smiled. 'How are you, Holly?'

'I'm fine, thanks, Audrey.' Holly smiled at the older woman but Fran noticed that her eyes were guarded.

'Glad to hear it. And how's this beautiful little boy of yours?' Audrey asked, leaning over the pushchair and smiling at the sleeping Luke, who hadn't even stirred as he was transferred from car seat to pushchair.

'He's an absolute joy.' Holly nodded. 'Rich and I are very lucky.'

'I don't doubt you'll want a little brother or sister for him at some point,' Audrey said, still cooing over Luke.

Holly blanched and pushed her chair back then stood up. 'Excuse me for a moment.'

As Holly hurried to the toilets, Fran met Audrey's concerned gaze.

'Must've been a sleepless night,' she suggested. 'Luke's probably teething.'

Audrey nodded but Fran wasn't certain that she was convinced.

'I remember losing lots of sleep with my two girls when they had teeth coming through. Thankfully, it passes. Although then you lose sleep for all sorts of other reasons, like worrying about their school reports, if they're eating enough vegetables, if they're spending too much time on social media and if they're safe when they go out on the town with their friends.' Audrey shook her head. 'Being a parent is wonderful but, between you and me, it's incredibly stressful too.'

'I can only imagine,' Fran said as she pushed her glasses up her nose, hoping that Holly wouldn't reappear in time to hear how having more than one child doubled the stress and worry.

'Do you know what you'd like to order or shall I come back when Holly returns?'

'I'll order for us, thanks. She always goes for your delicious lemon drizzle cake, so I doubt she'd choose anything else.'

After Audrey had gone to make their drinks, Fran looked up to see Holly returning. She sat down slowly and placed shaky hands on the table in front of her.

'Sorry about that. I think it could be just anxiety or it could be anxiety making the morning sickness worse, but I've been sick three times this morning already.'

'Oh god, Hols.'

'I know.' Holly grimaced. 'It's exhausting. I went off wine when I was expecting Luke and I had some queasiness early on in the pregnancy, but I thought I had a bug or something and had no idea I was pregnant. This time though… if it definitely is because I'm pregnant… I feel even worse.'

They fell silent and Fran made a point of tidying the sachets of sugar in the small purple bowl on the table. When they were all neatly lined up, she took a deep breath.

'Are you still unsure about whether this could be a good thing?'

Holly worried at her bottom lip and her eyes darted from side to side before she replied. 'Yesterday, I was worried it was a possibility, then last night, I was sitting next to Rich on the sofa as he gave Luke his bottle and watching the two of them together just filled my heart with so much love. Granny and Dad were there too, and we're such a happy family unit now. It all feels so secure and settled and I know how lucky I am. It made me think that having another baby wouldn't be a bad thing at all. Yes, it's true that the timing could have been better but then, it doesn't make that much difference really. I mean… a new baby would surely bring more joy with him or her?'

Fran nodded then reached across the table and took Holly's hand. 'Of course it would. And yes, this is a bit of a surprise… as Luke is only just ten months old, but at least he and his sibling will be close in age.'

'True.' Holly nodded as she gazed down at her sleeping baby.

'Hello.'

Fran turned to find a little girl with long blonde hair and big brown eyes standing next to her. She was wearing jeans embroidered with flowers and a long-sleeved pink top and she had a purple headband in her hair. Clutched in her hand was a brown toy dog with white spots on its fur.

'Well, hello there.' Fran smiled. 'Who are you?'

'I'm Tilly.' The little girl stared down at her glittery blue trainers.

'I'm Fran and this is Holly. We're very pleased to meet you.'

'Pleased to meet you too.' Tilly smiled shyly at them.

'I really like your trainers,' Fran said.

'Thank you. I like glittery things, which is why my dog is called Glitterbug.'

'You have a dog?' Fran asked. 'I like dogs.'

'Not a real dog.' Tilly held up her toy dog. 'This is Glitterbug.'

'Ah, I see. Well hello, Glitterbug.' Fran smiled at the toy.

'Is this your baby?' Tilly stepped closer to the pushchair.

'This is Holly's baby, Luke.'

'He's very small.' Tilly sniffed. 'Glitterbug says she likes him.'

'I'm sure he'd like her too,' Holly said.

'Can I wake him up to find out?' Tilly asked.

'No!' Holly exclaimed. 'What I mean is… please don't. He's taking his nap and if you wake him he'll be grumpy.'

Tilly giggled. 'Like my daddy when I wake him up too early.'

Fran smiled. Tilly was so cute. 'Who's your dad, Tilly?'

'Ethan. He works here.'

'Does he?' Fran frowned. 'I don't think I've met him. How long has he been here?'

Tilly shrugged. 'Since yesterday. We came from our home in Bath. I like it here but I do miss my home and my friends from school.'

Fran didn't know what to say. 'Are you staying here then, Tilly?'

Tilly nodded. 'I'm going to the school to be with Miss Brom… Miss Brom–w–ley.'

'Miss Bromley?' Fran asked.

'Yes. My aunty said she's very nice.' Tilly returned her attention to the pram and lowered her face so her nose was almost touching Luke's.

'Tilly!'

She jumped at the sharp tone and Fran looked up to see a man hurrying over to them. He was tall and broad-shouldered with floppy blonde hair and a strong square jaw. In jeans and a grey T-shirt, he was casually attired but with that effortless style that only really handsome men seemed to pull off.

'Tilly, I told you not to harass people. You'll scare Audrey's customers away.'

Tilly stepped away from the pushchair and hugged her toy dog to her chest. 'I was just saying hello,' she replied, her brown eyes so wide they seemed to dominate her tiny face.

'She really was just saying hello.' Fran stood up. 'She wasn't doing any harm, honestly.'

The man's eyes darted to Fran's face and she almost gasped at how green they were, reminding her of spring-time ferns and freshly cut grass and sparkling rock pools all at once. Her heart pounded in her chest and she opened and closed her mouth as she struggled to take a breath.

'She certainly wouldn't have meant any harm,' the man said, 'but she was told not to wander around.'

'She's only young,' Fran retorted, feeling a bit irritated now by this handsome stranger's insensitivity. 'And curious. Besides which, she was very polite.'

He blinked hard then sighed. 'I'm sorry. I just... I was in the kitchen and I looked up and she'd wandered off and I... I panicked.'

Fran watched as his expression softened. Her own irritation faded away and was replaced with curiosity and a hint of compassion.

'I'm okay, Daddy. See?' Tilly held out her arms and turned around. 'No harm done.'

The man smiled as he gazed at his daughter, then he swept her up in his arms and kissed her cheeks. 'Yes you are, thank goodness. Now let's go and sieve that flour or the scones will never be ready.'

'Yes, Daddy!' Tilly giggled.

'Sorry.' The man, who Fran guessed was Ethan, flashed an apologetic look at Fran then at Holly before carrying his daughter away.

Fran watched him go, wondering why her heart was still hammering in her chest. It was like she'd had too much caffeine today or like she'd just gone for a run, which she didn't do that often because she rarely had time and she wasn't that keen on running anyway – too much jiggling up and down. She'd prefer a good brisk walk or a bicycle ride any day.

'Was that Alexander Skarsgård?' Holly asked.

'Who?' Fran asked, meeting Holly's eyes.

'You know, the actor from *Big Little Lies* and *True Blood*.'

'Ahhh…' Fran nodded. 'Yes, I guess he does look a bit like him.'

'Very nice.' Holly smiled, her queasiness apparently forgotten – for the moment at least.

'And he has an adorable little girl.'

'He does.'

'So he's likely got a beautiful wife or partner some-where too.' Fran chuckled. 'Don't they all?'

'Do you fancy him, Fran?'

Fran lowered her gaze to the table and cleared her throat. 'Absolutely not. I've no time for men, Holly, and you know that well enough.'

When she raised her eyes again, Holly was staring at her with her arms folded across her chest and her eyebrows raised.

'One day, Francesca Gandolfini, you will fall head over heels for someone. You mark my words.'

Fran rolled her eyes. 'Whatever. I'm not fussy on doing forward rolls or cartwheels, so I very much doubt it.'

'Ha ha!' Holly shook her head.

Audrey arrived then with their tea and cake, changing the direction of the conversation that had started to make Fran quite uncomfortable.

'Here you go, ladies. Can I get you anything else?'

'No, this is perfect, thank you.' Fran's mouth watered at the thick golden slices of lemon drizzle cake with the crusty lemon-sugar topping. Audrey's lemon drizzle cake was always a delicious mix of lightweight sponge and incredible flavours, both sweet and sour, zesty and tangy.

'Uh… Audrey?' Holly placed a hand on the tea shop owner's arm.

'Yes, Holly?'

'We were wondering who the tall man is.'

Audrey frowned.

'The one with floppy blonde hair and the little girl. I think his daughter said his name is Ethan?'

'Oh!' Audrey beamed at them and nodded. 'That's my nephew, Ethan Clarke, my brother's boy, and his little girl, Tilly. They've come to live here at Rosewood. He's had a…' Audrey grimaced. 'I probably shouldn't say too much but he's had a tough few years, my nephew. After our chef quit, I offered him a job here and thankfully, he accepted.'

'So has he moved here with his daughter and partner?' Holly asked.

Fran glared at her and shook her head.

'Oh no.' Audrey folded her hands in front of her. 'It's just him and Tilly, the poor loves. But they're with family now so we'll take care of them both.'

'I'm sure you will.' Holly nodded.

'Yes, they need some proper old-fashioned Cornish TLC.'

'They've come to the right place,' Fran said, knowing how much Audrey adored her family.

'Thank you, Fran. I'm relieved to have them here at last. I was worried about them being alone in Bath all that time. Anyway, just call if you want more tea or anything else.' Audrey headed back to the counter.

'Why did you ask if he was here with a partner?' Fran sighed, horrified at her friend's behaviour.

'It was an innocent enough question.' Holly picked up her cup and blew on the hot tea.

'No, it wasn't. It seemed really nosy and like you had an ulterior motive.' Fran sipped her own tea, hoping it would help to soothe her.

'What ulterior motive could I possibly have?' Holly pouted at Fran.

'Oh, whatever. I know you too well, Holly Dryden, and you were plotting something then, and seeing as how you're about to marry the man you love, Audrey probably realised that you were asking for more information with your very single friend in mind.'

'Perhaps I was, perhaps I wasn't. But I really don't think Audrey even raised an eyebrow. She's just happy to talk about her family.' Holly smiled. 'Do you... do you have the... the thing?' Holly asked, her voice softer now.

'The test?'

'Yes.'

Fran nodded then reached into her bag and pulled out a small foil packet. She'd taken the test out of the box so it would be easier to tuck into her bag.

'Here you go.'

She handed it to Holly under the table.

'It looks like we're up to something untoward.' Holly blushed. 'I hope no one noticed anything.'

'Are you going to do it now?'

'I'll just eat my cake first.'

'That's procrastinating.' Fran winked at her friend.

'I know, but I'm nervous.'

'That it will be positive?'

'That it might be and also… that it might not be.'

'There's only one way to quieten those doubts.'

'I know, but it feel like Russian roulette. Either way, the so-called bullet could be the one that floors me.'

'Try not to worry, Holly. If it's meant to be…'

'It's meant to be.' Holly nodded. 'I know and I certainly can't change the outcome now.'

After Holly had eaten her lemon drizzle cake, chewing each mouthful slowly, she stood up. 'Here goes…'

'Holly?' Fran reached out a hand and Holly took it. 'Good luck, sweetie. You've got this either way.'

Holly looked as if she might cry and Fran wanted to hug her, but knew that if she did in the middle of the tea shop, Holly might burst into tears and people would stare, and ask questions, and neither of those would be helpful right now.

—

Ethan helped Tilly to wash her hands then he settled her on a stool at the island in the centre of the tea shop kitchen. They were both wearing hairnets and aprons and Tilly kept laughing at him, telling him he looked funny. She had never been to work with him before, so this was quite a novel experience for them both. Her tongue poked out of her mouth as she used the star shape to cut biscuits from the dough they'd made. Ethan was in charge of the scones for the tea shop but he'd given Tilly her own task to get on with and she was taking it very seriously.

'Daddy?' Tilly asked without looking up.

'Yes?'

'Would you like another baby?'

He coughed in surprise. 'Pardon?'

'Well… I was looking at the baby with the two ladies and he's so cute and I thought, does Daddy want a baby too?'

'I don't need a baby, Tilly, I have you.'

'But we could have a baby brother for me, couldn't we?' Tilly looked up now and smiled at him so innocently that he thought his heart would break.

'Uh… Tilly… a baby needs… uh… a mummy too. We… you and me, that is… can't have a baby without a mummy.'

She tutted and shook her head. 'I know that, silly, so you'll have to find a new mummy to have a baby for you, won't you?'

She returned her attention to the cutting of stars and Ethan swallowed hard. He worried so much about Tilly not having a mum around and yet she constantly surprised him with her resilience. The problem was that she still had such a simple perspective on it all, and for Ethan, as an adult who'd had been hurt and disillusioned, nothing was simple any more. Nothing at all…

And the last thing he wanted was for his pain to seep out into all aspects of his life. Look at how he'd behaved out in the tea shop when Tilly had wandered off and he'd seen her with the two women and the baby. His first concern had been that Tilly was safe, his second that she was bothering the women and his third that he had reacted so snappily. That wasn't who he was, but sometimes the worry and the pressure of being a single dad and now moving and starting a new job mounted up, and he wondered where it would all go. He'd been rude and he regretted it now. All he could do was hope that it didn't deter his aunt's customers from coming to the tea shop again.

Especially the petite woman with the short red-brown hair and trendy black-framed glasses. She'd had unusual coloured eyes, some deep purplish-blue shade that had made him falter when he met them full on. Her lips had been a bold bright red and she'd been wearing some kind of black floaty top with jeans and boots. She was certainly very attractive and she had that air of self-confidence that suggested that she knew her worth and could take care of herself. Since Melanie, Ethan rarely noticed if a woman was good-looking. In fact, he hadn't found himself drawn to any woman in any way, because he'd been unable to see past his hurt and his concerns for Tilly. But for some reason, today he had felt a flutter in his chest when he'd met the woman's eyes and he'd even admired the way she'd stood up to him in defending his daughter. Not that he'd been annoyed with Tilly at all, just worried about where she'd gone and then concerned that she was disturbing customers, but even so... In the very short time he'd been near the stranger, he had seen fire and strength in her and it had briefly ignited something inside him, as if a part of him had remembered something he used to feel, something he used to know.

He sighed.

It was gone now, whatever it was — a flicker of physical attraction or a primal recognition of a kindred spirit, or possibly just admiration of her pretty eyes and confident demeanour. It was surely natural to notice other human beings and it didn't have to mean anything.

'Daddy?' Tilly cut through his thoughts.

'Yes?'

'Can I eat these now?' She picked up a floppy star, making him laugh.

'Not yet, Tilly, we need to pop them in the oven for a bit first.'

'Okay.' She nodded. 'But then I'm having five.'

'Five?' He feigned mock horror.

'Okay, four, but only so I have some room leftover for a scone.'

'Deal.'

He looked at his little girl, wearing a white apron that was too big for her, with her long hair held back in a hairnet and her innocent brown eyes, and his heart ached. She was his whole world and he would do anything for her.

Anything at all.

Chapter 4

Fran picked up her cup but it was empty, just like the last time she'd looked. She didn't know whether to order more tea now or to wait until Holly came back to their table. Because Holly had been gone for quite some time. Twenty minutes to be exact. Thankfully, Luke was still fast asleep, oblivious to the clinking of cutlery, the clattering of dishes, the whir of the frothing machine and the murmuring and laughter of the tea shop's customers.

She couldn't go and check on Holly because that would mean leaving Luke or taking him, which might wake him up, and she didn't want to risk that in case Holly needed some time to come to terms with the result of the test.

Instead, she tried to focus on the smell of freshly baked cakes and the aromatic scent of coffee and spices. Each one took her back to the autumn when she'd come here with Holly because her friend told her she had exciting news. Over pumpkin-spice lattes and gingerbread, Holly had told her that Rich had proposed as they'd strolled around the vineyard. He'd intended on waiting for Christmas, but then had realised that a Christmas wedding would be magical, so instead he'd proposed as they'd taken a walk in the autumnal air, as their feet had crunched through fallen leaves and as the sky had turned a burnished copper,

43

laced with purple and gold. Fran had been delighted for them both and agreed that a festive wedding would be wonderful.

Finally, the toilet door opened and Holly emerged. As she walked to the table, Fran scanned her face for clues, but Holly kept her eyes lowered and her hands in her pockets. She was giving nothing away.

When she sat down, Fran held her breath for a few moments to resist asking if it was positive. Under the table she dug her nails into her palms, hoping that Holly would be happy with the result.

'Fran.' Holly broke the tense silence then cleared her throat.

'Yes?' Fran croaked out. She was a jumble of nerves and felt like a coiled spring. If Holly didn't tell her soon, she thought she might bounce off into space.

'It was... It was...' Holly's eyes widened. 'Oh shit, there's Lucinda!'

Fran turned around and saw Holly's fiancé's mother, Lucinda Turner, at the doorway to the tea shop, along with two other women. Lucinda's brown hair was covered by a pink beret that matched her puffy pink and purple coat.

'Why isn't she at the bakery?' Fran asked. 'It's Saturday. You'd think she'd be busy, wouldn't you?'

'It's one of her friend's birthdays. She told me in the week that they were going out for tea and cake, possibly to Rosewood, but it must have slipped my mind.' Holly pulled a face. 'Quick, take this.'

Holly nudged Fran under the table so she put out her hand. When she looked down she saw a white plastic stick.

'Holly!' She recoiled. 'You've peed on this.'

'Of course I have. How else would it work?'

'But... eugh.' Fran held it gingerly between finger and thumb under the table. 'What am I going to do with it?'

'Hide it quickly! Lucinda's coming over.'

Fran grabbed her bag and stuffed the test into it. She didn't have time to look at what it would be touching in her bag because Lucinda was upon them in no time.

'Girls!' Lucinda hugged them in turn, squishing them against her duck-down jacket, her sweet floral fragrance washing over them, followed by the aroma of cakes and pastry that always clung to her from all the hours at the bakery. 'And my darling grandson.'

Fran smiled up at Lucinda as she removed her beret. With her brown bobbed hair with its sweeping side fringe, her cute freckles and brown eyes, she was very pretty and looked younger than her fifty-eight years. For a long time, Lucinda had seemed sad, broken even, after losing her one son in a tragic accident, but since becoming a grand-mother, she had seemed happier, as if she was somehow healing.

Lucinda leant over the pushchair and Fran saw Holly stiffen. She was clearly worried that Lucinda would wake the baby, but Lucinda just smiled at him then straightened up. 'He's such a cherub. I feel blessed every time I look at him. Can I get you two anything?'

'No, we're fine, thanks.' Holly shook her head. 'We won't be long as I need to get back to Greenacres to go over some figures with Rich.' She rolled her eyes then grimaced. 'You know how I love numbers, especially when Rich gets all excited about them.'

Rich worked as an accountant and for as long as Fran had known him, he had enjoyed working on things that

45

involved numbers. Fran didn't mind maths but she'd rather read or walk the dogs.

'Well, I shall see you later then.' Lucinda turned to head over to her friends then paused and looked at Holly again. 'Holly, are you all right? You look a bit... peaky.'

Holly blinked hard and her left eyebrow twitched. 'I'm fine. Luke just... was a bit restless last night, so I'm tired. I didn't sleep well.'

'Okay, then. As long as you're okay. You know where I am if you need me.' Lucinda nodded, squeezed Holly's shoulder then walked away.

'That was close,' Holly muttered.

'Indeed.' Fran shifted on her chair and held her hands out. 'And I'm desperate to go and wash my hands after holding your pee stick.'

'I don't know why that bothers you, Fran, you pick up dog poo all the time.'

'But not with my hands!' Fran shook her head. 'Anyway, I didn't get a chance to look at the test. What was the result?'

Holly licked her lips and took a deep breath, then picked up her tea cup, saw it was empty, so placed it back on the saucer.

'It was... It was...' She exhaled then nodded.

'Positive?'

'Yup.'

'Right. Okay.' Was Holly pleased? She couldn't tell. 'The thing is, though... I did buy two tests but bloody Scamp ate one so you had to have the cheaper one. It could be wrong.'

'Do you think?' Holly leant forwards, her eyebrows raised.

'I'm sure they're not one hundred per cent, are they?'

'I guess not.'

'So if it is incorrect, how will that make you feel?'

Holly sat back and rolled her shoulders as if she had the weight of the world on them. 'I'd be… disappointed now, I think.'

'Well it's probably correct, so try not to worry.'

Holly nodded. 'I will try, but it's just so difficult.'

'I know. I suspect I'd feel that way too. You know… if I was in your situation… uh… Do you need to get back to Greenacres now?'

'I should get home. Things to do and all that. Plus if we stay here, Lucinda will end up coming over again, and as much as I love her… I don't feel up to chatting much right now. She'll guess that something's up with me.'

'What are you going to do about Rich?'

'I need to tell him.' Holly twirled a strand of her blonde hair around her forefinger.

'I'm so glad you said that. He'll be fine about it. In fact, I suspect he'll be delighted and you need his support right now more than ever.'

'But I don't want anyone else to know at the moment. With the wedding and Christmas approaching and us being so busy at the vineyard, I don't want to have to share this yet. And, of course, with Granny being so run-down. I want to hold it close so we can come to terms with it first, if that makes sense, then Rich and I can tell Granny and Dad together.'

'I won't say a word.'

'Promise?'

'Holly, you know I won't. When have I ever betrayed you by telling someone your secrets?'

'I do know that and you have always been such a loyal friend to me. I know I could trust you with my life. I just like seeing the exasperation on your face whenever I ask you to promise me something.'

Holly smiled and Fran smiled back.

'I'll go and pay.'

Fran picked up her bag and approached the counter. Audrey was serving another customer and her two daughters didn't seem to be around, so she occupied herself by eyeing up the delicious cakes on offer in the glass display in front of the counter. There were slices of chocolate cake with fat round cherries on the top, squashed into the rich chocolate fondant icing, thick slices of carrot cake topped with silky white cream cheese icing, then blueberry muffins with cracked tops where fresh blueberries had burst, flooding the muffins with their purple-blue shade. Her mouth watered and she decided to purchase a few to take home.

'Can I help you?' Audrey was back.

'Yes, I'll take one of each of those, please, and I'd like to pay for our tea and cake.'

Audrey nodded. 'Of course.'

She boxed up the cakes then placed the card machine on the counter and Fran touched it with her credit card.

'This chip and pin lark is so easy that it's not even like spending real money.'

'I know.' Audrey nodded. 'Gary worries every time I go shopping that I'll forget that I'm actually spending from our account.'

'It would be easy to do.'

Fran picked up the box then tried to put her purse in her bag but she couldn't do it with one hand. She shook her shoulder to lower the strap but her hairbrush seemed to be stuck in the lining, preventing the bag from opening. She put the box back on the counter then tugged at her hairbrush, and as she did so, the small white pregnancy test flew out too and landed on the tiled floor then spun away. Fran stared at it in horror before stuffing her brush back into her bag along with her purse and picking up the cake box, ready to flee.

She turned to see Audrey looking across the floor at the test.

'You dropped something, Fran. What is it? One of those e-cigarettes or something?' Audrey frowned. 'I can't see far without my glasses.'

'No... uh... it's... uh...'

Just then, the man from earlier, who Audrey had named as her nephew, Ethan, emerged from the kitchen with his little girl.

'Ooh, look, Daddy. Someone's dropped their lollipop!'

Tilly hurried over and picked the stick up then frowned at it. Fran hovered anxiously, watching in horror, not knowing whether to go over and grab the test or to run away. Ethan's smile faded as he took the stick from his daughter and peered it, before realisation dawned on his features. Fran glanced behind her to see Holly hovering near the door with Luke, her eyes wide as saucers as she watched the scene unfold.

Ethan looked up and saw Fran staring at him, then he turned to his aunt. 'Who dropped this?'

Audrey nodded at Fran. 'What is it, Ethan? I can't see from here.'

He approached the counter. 'It's a pregnancy test.'

'Is it now?'

'And it's positive,' he added.

Audrey took the stick from him, peered at it, then turned to Fran.

'I believe this is yours.' She beamed as she handed Fran the test and Fran's cheeks flooded with heat. She wished the ground would open up and instantly swallow her whole and save her from this horrible experience. This couldn't really be happening, could it? It was the stuff of nightmares.

'Yes… uh… thank you.'

Fran took the test, stuffed it into her bag then pushed her shoulders back. She couldn't deny that it was hers because she had promised to keep Holly's secret, but now Audrey and her nephew thought Fran was pregnant, and anyone in the tea shop who'd overheard and witnessed the scene would do too.

She had to be grateful that her parents now resided in Italy, because the way news spread around Penhallow Sands, they'd have known she was pregnant before she even got home. She loved the village, but at times like this, she wished she lived somewhere more isolated like the wilds of Norway or even the North Pole. Either might be preferable to the village right now.

'Thanks again, Audrey. I'll get that box of mugs from the car for you.' She forced a smile onto her face, flashed it at Ethan and Tilly as if she hadn't a care in the world, then turned and followed Holly out of the tea shop. Her legs felt stiff as blocks of wood and her neck ached as if her head had become too heavy to support, but she had to get out to the safety of her car and to escape the curious gazes of Audrey and her family.

'I'll come with you, love, and get the box.' Audrey hurried behind Fran to the car park. She didn't say another word about the test but Fran could feel her bubbling with questions and knew that this would not be the end of the matter. Audrey gave a warm smile as she took the box from Fran, gently patted her hand then took the box inside, and Fran released a deep sigh.

As Fran helped Holly to get Luke into his car seat, she realised that if she had to keep Holly's secret until after the wedding, it was going to be a very long six weeks indeed.

Chapter 5

The following morning, Fran stood on the shore, watching as the sky turned slowly from navy to purple to pink. She shivered in the cold morning air, in spite of her bobble hat, scarf, thick coat and gloves. Following yesterday's incident at Rosewood Tea Shop, she'd had a restless night and barely slept. She had tossed and turned for hours, worrying about what Audrey would be thinking, wondering if the news of her fake pregnancy would spread across Penhallow Sands like a Mexican wave overnight, and everyone she encountered today would cast a knowing smile her way.

Her stomach churned. This might be an awful situation but she had to remember that she was doing it for the right reasons; she was protecting Holly, her best friend in the whole world.

The sea lapped at the toes of her cerise wellington boots, grey and frothy in the dawn light. The breeze nipped at her nose and cheeks, but she breathed deeply, wanting to feel the chill filling her lungs, cleansing her from the inside. Everything would be okay, she just had to keep breathing and keep focused.

Behind her on the beach, her dogs raced around, delighted to have time off the lead. In the summer, dogs were only allowed off their lead in the early morning and in the evening, but in the winter months the hours were relaxed. However, if Fran was going to bring her dogs down to the village, she preferred to do it at quieter times and sunrise was just perfect. It meant that the dogs got to burn off some energy before breakfast and then they relaxed through the day.

She turned and watched as they ran in circles, flashes of different-coloured fur, pink tongues lolling from open mouths as sand and droplets of water flicked up in the air. They'd need a good brush when they got home, possibly even a shower, but it was worth it just to see them having so much fun.

Fran found peace in the company of her dogs. They lived so much in the moment, focused purely on enjoying the here and now, and there was a lot to be learnt from that. She did her best to give them a good life and they rewarded her with their easy company, their devotion and their loyalty.

'Come on you lot,' she called as she started to walk along the sand. 'Let's get home and have some breakfast.'

She listened to their paws pounding the sand as they changed direction, to the foaming of the sea on the shore, to the cries of the hungry gulls as they soared across the sky and far off into the village and the spluttering of an old car engine as someone tried to start it in the chilly air. Simple things, but precious things, filling her with optimism that everything would be okay in the end, and Fran laughed as her dogs raced on ahead, watching as they ran in and out of the water, simply enjoying being alive.

–

'So you've told Rich?' Fran asked Holly as they stood in the kitchen at Greenacres that evening.

'Last night when we went for a walk.'

'How did he take it?'

'Really well. At first, he was a bit surprised, but as the news sunk in, he was delighted. He admitted that there was that one time… about two months ago when we were… uh… a bit…'

'It's okay, I get the picture. No need for specifics.' Fran smiled.

'I know it's unreliable but I thought I was past my so-called fertile time and…' Holly shrugged. 'Perhaps it was a subconscious thing and we both wanted this to happen, or at least didn't mind if it did.'

'That sounds plausible.' Fran nodded. 'I'm glad he's happy.'

'Yes I am!' Rich entered the kitchen still in his suit and tie, looking every inch the professional accountant. 'Hi Fran.'

'Hi Rich.'

'Thanks for supporting Holly with the whole pregnancy test thing.' He smiled as he took a seat at the table.

'It's no problem.' Fran met Holly's eyes, hoping that Rich was okay with the fact that she knew before he did.

'It's okay, Fran. I told Rich that I ran it by you first because I wasn't sure if I was pregnant, and anyway, he knows what we're like.'

'Yes I do. Years of being the partner of a woman with a BFF means that I expect Fran to know most things before me.' Rich laughed. 'It's fine, honestly. I'm just glad that Holly has your support. Sometimes I get so wrapped up in work stuff that I miss what's happening right under my nose.'

Holly went to him and slid her arm around his shoulder. 'I love you just as you are, Rich.'

'I know, and I'm a very lucky man and I love you right back, Holly.'

They kissed and Fran smiled at them. They were so loved up and she was really happy for them. Physically, they were very different, as Rich had dark hair and eyes and was over six foot tall, whereas Holly was blonde with green eyes and was just five foot five. But they were so compatible in so many ways and complemented each other perfectly. Fran enjoyed being around them because she could bask in their happy glow.

'Where's Luke?' Fran asked, always keen to grab a hug with the baby boy whenever she could.

'Napping.' Rich pointed at the ceiling. 'I just popped up to check on him. It's not the ideal time for him to nap and he probably won't sleep well tonight because of it, but he's been a bit restless the past few nights and I think he needs to catch up.'

'A bit like Granny really,' Holly said. 'She's napping a lot at the moment but I figure that sleep is healing, so she's doing what she needs to do to recover from the flu.'

'Poor Glenda.' Fran shook her head. Flu was awful when you were young but as an elderly person, it could be extremely debilitating and dangerous.

'Cup of tea?' Holly asked.

'Well, I wasn't going to stay long, but why not?' Fran sat down at the table. 'How're you feeling now, Holly?'

Holly wrinkled her nose up. 'I've been better. It's as if since I saw the positive test, my symptoms have worsened.

Everything smells funny and I need to pee more and the nausea this morning was vile. It lasts all day but is at its worst first thing.'

'I'm sorry.' Fran pulled a face. 'I hate feeling sick and I'm certain that I couldn't cope with it all day. You're doing really well, Holly.'

'Thanks, but I'm okay.' Holly opened a cupboard and pulled out a packet of biscuits. 'I'm on the ginger nuts now, and who doesn't mind an excuse to munch on plenty of biscuits?'

She placed the packet on the table and Fran helped herself to one.

'Holly told me that you covered for her at the tea shop.' Rich reached for the biscuits and took one out.

'I had no choice, really.' Fran shook her head. 'What else could I do?'

'I can't believe that the test flew out like that. It's one of those cringeworthy moments.'

'Tell me about it.' Fran rolled her eyes. 'It was like something out of a movie or a TV comedy.'

'And people believe that you're the one who's pregnant?' Rich raised his eyebrows.

'So it seems.' Fran bit into her biscuit and munched thoughtfully.

'Are you okay with that?' Rich's voice was filled with concern.

'Well, I neither confirmed nor denied it, so I'm not exactly lying about it, am I? Therefore, it's not a big moral dilemma for me. Anyway, if it gives you and Holly some peace to come to terms with everything and protects Glenda from too much excitement when she's recovering, then that's great.'

Rich nodded slowly.

'Fran also said that Jamal saw the tests in the village just after she bought them, so he probably thinks she's expecting too.' Holly brought three mugs of tea to the table then sat down.

'Oh, Fran, this is probably going to escalate.' Rich rubbed a hand over his eyes. 'In a small village like Penhallow Sands, how could it not?'

'Probably.' Fran inclined her head. 'But it's only until after the wedding, isn't it?'

'I'm so grateful.' Holly reached for Fran's hand. 'At the moment, with the wedding planning and the fact that Granny has been under the weather, I'd really prefer to keep it quiet until we have it confirmed by the doctor, and until we're past the three-month mark. If we told her now and then something happened... I'd hate to put her through that.'

Fran squeezed Holly's hand then reached for her tea. 'That's very wise.'

'I'll probably tell Dad before the wedding, but first Rich and I want to digest the news ourselves.'

'Of course you do,' Fran said. 'Besides which, if I am currently fake pregnant, I get to eat more ginger nuts, right?'

'Right!' Holly laughed and handed Fran the packet.

–

Ethan held Tilly's hand tight as they walked into the school on Monday morning. He suspected that he might be even more nervous than she was. The deputy head teacher he'd spoken to previously had suggested that he bring Tilly to school mid-morning to give the other

57

children a chance to settle and to give Tilly a chance to prepare for her first day.

The reception area smelt of paint, musty textbooks, disinfectant and chips. It was a smell loaded with memories and one that he thought must be inherent to educational establishments, because every school he'd been in had smelt the same. It was a heavy smell, but not unpleasant; its familiarity was almost comforting.

He gave their names at the reception desk and Tilly gazed up at him, her big brown eyes filled with uncertainty. She was chewing on her lower lip in a way that made his shoulders tense.

'It's okay, Tilly. It will be fine, you'll see.' He wished he sounded more convinced than he felt.

'Okay, Daddy.' Tilly nodded, causing her blonde ponytail to bob.

Ethan wanted to scoop her up and take her out of there, back to Rosewood where they could turn on the TV and drink chocolate milkshakes while snuggling on the sofa with Glitterbug. This was his baby girl, his whole reason for being, and he hated to see her anxious and vulnerable. He'd do anything to avoid that. But he knew he couldn't keep her away from school indefinitely. The sooner she got into a routine, the better for her. Waiting to start school would be far worse than actually doing it. She needed to socialise and to integrate, to learn and to experience life.

The door to his left buzzed and a woman he estimated to be in her thirties came through. She had bright blue eyes that emanated kindness, blonde hair loosely pulled into a bun and her skin was very clear, devoid of any makeup. That was something that his mother would have noticed and highlighted for him and it was a habit that had stayed with him. He wasn't a fan of heavy makeup on anyone; he always felt that it was like they were trying to cover something up. This woman looked fresh-faced and honest and when she smiled, Tilly's grip on his hand relaxed a bit.

'Hello, are you Tilly?' Her voice was warm and welcoming.

'Yes, and this is my Daddy, Ethan.'

'Well, I'm Miss Bromley, the deputy head teacher, and I'm very pleased to meet you both.'

Ethan held out his hand. 'Pleased to meet you too.'

She gave him a firm handshake then gestured at the door behind her.

'Shall we go on through? I always think it's easier to get these things over and done with. Delaying it will only increase your nerves and that's the last thing I want because there is absolutely nothing to worry about. Your class is ready and waiting for you, Tilly. You have a peg for your bag and coat, and a chair at a table with some friendly children and a tray for your work. How does that sound?'

'Good, thank you, miss.'

Miss Bromley nodded then buzzed them through to a long corridor.

The aromas from reception were stronger here, especially the smell of food, as if the cooking that had been done over the years had seeped into the paint on the walls, the rough nylon carpet on the floor and the plaster on the ceiling.

'Cottage pie for dinner today,' Miss Bromley explained. 'With carrots and broccoli, of course.'

Tilly looked up at Ethan. 'I like cottage pie, don't I, Daddy?'

'Yes you do. It's a good job you said you wanted to have school dinners.'

'Yes, or I'd have missed out on it.' Tilly nodded, a smile playing on her lips.

'Your classroom is just along here, Tilly.'

The woman led them along the corridor then stopped in front of a classroom. The door was open and excited chatter spilled out into the corridor, along with the sounds of chairs scraping on a tiled floor, laughter and an adult's authoritative voice.

'Your teacher is called Mrs Thomas and she's very nice. She'll keep an eye on you today and you can speak to her about anything. Are you ready to go in?'

Tilly peered up at Ethan and he thought his heart was going to leap out of his throat. This was one of the hardest things he'd ever had to do.

Tilly closed her eyes for a moment then released a slow breath. 'I'm ready, miss.' She nodded then released Ethan's hand. 'See you later, Daddy. Be brave.'

Ethan inclined his head, unable to reply because he had a feeling his voice would crack, then Miss Bromley took Tilly into the classroom. He watched through the internal window as Tilly crossed the room to a circular table. Miss Bromley showed her to a seat with her name printed on a sticker on the back of it. Tilly glanced around at the other children before pulling the chair out and sitting down. She kept her little chin up and her shoulders back, as if she were trying with all her might to be brave and to hold it together. She would be fine, his strong little girl; she was tougher than he gave her credit for.

Ethan turned away and gazed out of the windows that opened onto a square patio at what seemed to be the heart of the school. He forced himself to focus on the pots with their trees bereft of leaves, stark brown fingers of branches pointing to the sky. Then he moved his gaze to the greenhouse, where someone had stored a variety of garden tools, presumably until the spring months. Tilly would enjoy it here, he reassured himself. The place had an atmosphere of warmth and security about it and that was what any parent would want for their child.

When he turned around again, he found the deputy head standing there smiling at him.

'Are you okay?' she asked.

He nodded. 'It's just… it was difficult seeing her having to do that.'

'She was very brave and will, no doubt, have ten best friends by mid-morning. They were all very excited to meet her and want to know all about her. She'll be fine, Mr Clarke, I promise.'

'Please, call me Ethan.'

'And I'm Catherine.'

'Thank you, Catherine.'

'Would you like a cup of tea or coffee?'

'That would be fabulous, thanks.'

'I know I gave you the basic details last week on the phone and you've filled in all the forms online, but we can have a proper chat and you can ask any other questions you might have.'

Ethan released a sigh of relief.

'My office is this way.'

She led the way back towards reception and Ethan glanced into the classroom as they passed it, and was gladdened to see Tilly chatting animatedly to another little girl. Moving her to another location and to a new school was never going to be easy, but little things like friendly children and an understanding deputy head teacher could make all the difference. His aunt had told him that Penhallow Sands was a wonderful place to raise a child and he was starting to believe that she was right.

–

'Thank you, Fran. That was an informative and inspirational talk.' Jowanet Tremayne shook Fran's hand firmly. 'And it was especially kind of you to come in and speak to the children late in the morning, as this close to lunchtime they start to get a bit... restless, shall we say?'

Fran smiled at Jowanet in the reception of the primary school, trying to appear confident but feeling like a little girl as she stood in the presence of her former head teacher. Jowanet had been a formidable presence at the school for as long as Fran could remember, and with her severely cut white hair, small square glasses and beady hazel eyes, she hadn't changed since Fran was a child. She had always seemed to look this old and this intimidating, although Fran knew that she must have looked younger when Fran attended the school twenty years ago. It had been surreal but an honour to be asked to come in and talk to the children about her work as an artist. She could have stayed all day if it hadn't been for the head pointing out that it was almost time for the children to have their lunch.

'It was a pleasure, Ms Tremayne.' Fran shook her head. 'The pupils had so many good questions.'

'They're inquisitive young minds and keen to explore possible career avenues, which is a very positive thing as we want them to know that there are plenty of options available to them.' Jowanet nodded and her jowls wobbled. 'We've had some wonderful female role models delivering talks, from a heart surgeon to a tree surgeon to an engineer to a beekeeper. Having you come to talk about your creative career was very enlightening and it's good for them to understand that being self-employed is an option open to them too.'

The door behind Jowanet opened and a tall man stepped into reception. With him came the scent of citrus and spice and Fran's eyes travelled from his broad shoulders to his strong jaw to his handsome face and her heart flipped over.

It was Ethan Clarke from the tea shop.

What was he doing here?

'Ah, Mr Clarke, is it?' Jowanet turned and shook his hand. 'Catherine did say you were bringing Tilly in for her first day. How did it go?'

'I left her with her class about an hour ago and Miss Bromley has kindly, and very patiently, answered all of my questions.' Ethan gestured behind him. 'Tilly was very brave and seemed quite happy to be left.' He rubbed the back of his neck. 'Which is a good thing, you know, because... uh... well, I just want her to be relaxed and settled.'

'Of course you do, and she will settle here, Mr Clarke.'

'I hope so. Thank you.'

'It's probably more difficult for you than for her.'

'I think you're right.' He nodded.

He looked past Jowanet and met Fran's eyes. Her legs weakened and her stomach clenched. She locked her knees tight and pressed a hand to her belly, confused by her visceral reactions to this man's proximity. Was he carrying too much static electricity around with him or something? Perhaps it was to do with his shoes and the nylon school carpets and if he touched her, an electric spark would shoot between them and stun them both…

'Hello, Ethan.' Fran lifted a hand.

'Hi, uh…'

'Fran.'

'Yes, Fran. Hi.'

He looked as awkward standing there as Fran felt.

'Okay then, Jowanet, I'll be on my way.' Fran hooked her bag over her shoulder.

'Yes, me too.' Ethan smiled at Jowanet. 'Thanks again. Any problems, call my mobile and I can come straight back.'

'Try not to worry, Mr Clarke. All will be well.'

Fran pushed open the heavy school door and stepped outside then held the door for Ethan. He blinked hard in the morning light then thanked her for holding the door.

'Are you all right?' Fran asked, concern filling her at how pale he was.

He sighed. 'Yeah… I guess so. It's just that I brought Tilly in for her first day and it was quite difficult leaving her.' He chuckled. 'Not for her so much, but for me.'

Fran nodded. 'It must have been hard but she will be fine. I went to Penhallow Sands Primary and I loved it there.'

'Did you?'

'Jowanet was the head teacher back then.'

'Really?' He raised his eyebrows. 'How long has she been there?'

'A looooong time.' Fran nodded. 'Back to times of yore, I believe.'

'Of yore, eh?' He grinned and his eyes crinkled at the corners. It softened his face and made him even more attractive. 'Were there Vikings here then?'

'Probably... and dinosaurs.'

They laughed and the air between them warmed a few degrees.

'Do you have a child at the school?'

'What?' Fran heard the incredulity in her tone.

'Have you got a child there?'

'No, I heard what you said, but I was surprised. Then again... at thirty-one it's possible that I could have a child there. But no. No child... at the school. I was there to give a talk about my work.'

'Oh, right! I see.'

'Yes.' Fran realised that she'd almost effusively denied any link to children at all, when doing so would betray the whole story she'd agreed to maintain for the next six weeks for Holly and Rich's sakes. 'I'm an artist and a ceramist. Jowanet asked me to come and speak to the children about what I do and about being self-employed.'

'Wow, really? That's brilliant.'

'I think so. I enjoy my work and I love the freedom of being my own boss.'

'I bet.' He tucked his hands into his pockets. 'And to work in the creative sector is pretty special.'

'Aren't you a chef?'

'I am.'

'So you must be creative too.'

He smiled. 'I like to think so. My mum was an artist, so I guess I get that side of things from her.'

'Wow! Do you have any of her work? I wonder if I've seen anything she's done.'

'Not with me. Most things are in storage. But she was very talented.'

Was…

Fran picked up on his use of the past tense. Had he lost his mother then?

'I'd like to see her art someday.'

'I'd like to show you.'

They stood in silence for a moment.

'I'd… uh… better get back to Rosewood, I guess.'

'Are you working today?'

'Later on this afternoon. My aunt gave me most of the day off to settle Tilly in school, and, if I'm honest, I think she knew I'd need some time afterwards to recover.'

'So you're free now?'

'I am.'

'Would you like to… grab a coffee… or… something?'

Fran winced. Why had she said 'or something'? Did that make her offer sound suggestive?

'By *something*, I meant coffee or cake or tea or whatever you like really.'

Shut up, Fran!

Heat crawled up her neck and into her cheeks as he stared at her, then a smile spread across his lips.

'I'd love to grab a coffee with you. It would be nice to have some company and you can tell me more about your talents.'

'My talents?'

'Yes, your painting and pottery.'

'Okay. Right. Of course.'

What other talents would he have been referring to?

'Lead the way!' Ethan waved his arm at the school gates.

Fran nodded then walked ahead of him, hoping that the gentle breeze would soothe her hot cheeks and fade the blush that burned there. She had no idea why she was blushing; she didn't blush easily but for some reason this man was stirring her body to do things she wasn't familiar with, making her a bit tongue-tied, and he was also creating feelings inside her that she hadn't experienced before.

She laughed inwardly at herself as she opened the school gate. It probably had nothing to do with him at all and was either due to something that she'd eaten or possibly she was going through early menopause. Yes, that was probably it.

After all, what else could it be?

–

Ethan looked around the establishment that Fran had brought him to and admired the eclectic interior. Shell's Shack had low ceiling beams draped with fishing nets and a variety of shells that were looped together with blue string, and shiny dark wooden floorboards. There was a large open fireplace to the right of the counter with a driftwood mirror on the wall above it, carved with seahorses. There were lobster pots and an anchor on the hearth next to a small purple Christmas tree that twinkled with fibre-optic lights. Dried lavender and rosemary bouquets filled seaglass vases on the small round tables and the air was rich with their sweet, medicinal scent.

Against one wall was a two-seater sofa draped with a festive-themed patchwork quilt, and in front of it was a driftwood table bearing an evergreen and holly wreath. It was a cosy, pleasant cafe and the aromas of cakes and pastries were making his mouth water. He'd have to bring Tilly here soon; he knew she'd love it.

Over at the counter, Fran was speaking to a woman with big blue eyes and a head of blonde curls. She was very pretty, plump and rosy-cheeked with a kind smile. Ethan took the opportunity to take a good look at Fran. He'd been shocked to see her in reception and was also battling his emotions at seeing Tilly going into class, so he probably hadn't been as polite as he should have been. Also, coming here for coffee with Fran might not have been his best move, but then it was only coffee and he could do with catching his breath before he went back to Rosewood. He liked the hustle and bustle of the farm and the tea shop, but he was still getting used to it after living alone with his daughter for so long. Having an aunt, uncle and cousins around was enjoyable but also a bit overwhelming and it would take some getting used to – although Tilly seemed to have settled into their new home quite well and she was already fairly relaxed with Audrey and her daughters. Perhaps it was easier to adapt to a move when you were younger.

Fran glanced across at him and caught him smiling at her, which she returned. She had such a warm smile and her indigo eyes were an absolutely captivating shade, somewhere between navy and purple, reminding him of a deep tropical lagoon and a sunset all at once. He wondered if they changed with the light and if they would be different out on the beach with the open horizon spread out before them. Would they seem lighter then? What if she was in the water, perhaps at twilight, with her white skin contrasting against the dark of the sea, as it lapped gently at her shoulders, caressing her skin and…

He shook himself. Where had that come from? The poor woman had invited him for a coffee, during the day, no less, and here he was picturing her scantily clad in the sea, even down to the goosebumps on her arms and legs. Ethan hadn't had anything other than the most cursory of thoughts about women and sex since things had gone wrong with Melanie, so thinking something like he just had was not familiar any more. But Fran was very attractive and the fact that she seemed nice had obviously triggered his latent libido and reminded him that he did still have some urges in that department. A smile spread to his lips, accompanied by a blush that flooded his cheeks.

'What're you smiling about?' Fran had returned to the table.

'Oh… uh…' He met her eyes and his blush deepened. 'I was just remembering something. Nothing to worry about.'

'Okay…' She cocked an eyebrow and it made her look even sexier, as if she could somehow read his mind and echoed his thoughts. But that would be impossible, wouldn't it? 'I've ordered for us and Shell said it will be ready in about ten minutes.'

'Wonderful, thank you.'

'How're you feeling now?' she asked as she pulled her chair closer to the table.

'I'm okay. It helps knowing that I'm just minutes away from the school, so if Tilly does need me within the hour, I can get there immediately.'

'I'm sure it does.'

'Although Rosewood isn't exactly miles away.'

'No, but I understand what you mean about being closer for now.' Fran ran her finger over the bouquet in the seaglass vase on the table and the sharp aroma of lavender intensified. Ethan realised that her eyes reminded him of the colour of the lavender flowers, but slightly darker. Then he imagined her lying on a bed of lavender and the heat that had seeped from his cheeks started to return.

'Uh... what's your story, Fran?' he asked, keen to distract his errant imagination from any more flowery Fran-based fantasies. It really wouldn't do, especially when he was sitting right here with her. Besides which, there was another issue with his attraction to her: she was pregnant. Perhaps it was the pregnancy hormones that were giving her that wonderful glow that made her skin almost luminous and her hair so shiny. Surely there had to be a reason for her almost ethereal beauty, for the sparkle in her eyes, for the plumpness of her inviting lips?

'My story?'

'Yes... how long have you lived here? How did you find out that you're an artist? What has led you to this point in your life?'

'Wow!' Her eyes widened. 'That's a lot to tell.'

He lowered his gaze to the table. 'Sorry. I'm not an accomplished conversationalist and I never really know where to start. I spend most of my time in the kitchen, so I'm usually kept away from people, which is... believe me... probably a good thing.'

Fran snorted. 'I'm sure you're not that bad.'

'Oh I am. Dreadfully inept at socialising. I lack an entire skills base and it wasn't the type of thing they taught at school.'

'Noooo. You're doing fine.' She chuckled. 'Okay, let me think.'

She rested her chin on her hands and he eyed the rings on her fingers. All silver, some with stones, but the ring finger on her left hand was bare. So she wasn't married or engaged then. But she was pregnant. Was there a man on the scene? There didn't have to be, but then her situation would be even more complicated if there wasn't. Of course, she could be gay and have been artificially inseminated or something like that. Did sperm banks even exist now? Hadn't there been something about the donors losing their anonymity so fewer men were prepared to donate these days? There were many possibilities and explanations and really, it was none of his business, but for some reason he found all possible explanations left him with a sense of disappointment.

'Right, okay, Ethan... I'm thirty-one, I like animals and take in strays then try to rehome them, I'm very creative and always have been and used to draw and paint even as a toddler, so my parents tell me. My dad is Italian and met my Welsh mum when she was taking a gap year in Italy and they've been inseparable since. They had one of those instant passions and fell madly in love, knowing from day one that they could never bear to be apart. It's always seemed a bit... romantic to me, but they're as much in love now as they were when they first met, so they weren't wrong about their feelings. Mum and Dad moved to Penhallow not long after they got married because they wanted to live by the sea, and during a camping holiday

71

when they toured around Cornwall, they fell in love with the location. They told me that it had everything they wanted in a place to raise a child. They now spend most of the year out in Verona with my little old nonna, as she's getting a bit frail and they want to be there for her, and I live in their cottage not far from the village with my animals. It's kind of mine anyway, as I doubt they'll return to Cornwall for any length of time, and I pay all the bills these days. To make ends meet, and because I love what I do, I paint, I make a variety of pottery items and I sell online and to local businesses.'

'A potted history of your life then?' Ethan smiled at his own joke.

'Ha! Yes.'

'And now you're about to start a new chapter.' Ethan smiled, knowing how drastically parenthood did change someone's life.

Fran frowned for a moment, seemingly puzzled.

'With your pregnancy.'

Her eyes flickered, then she looked down at her hands.

'Yes. I guess I am.' She coughed. 'What about you? How did you come to move to Penhallow Sands?'

Shell arrived then, with toasted cheese and chutney paninis and two frothy lattes, so Ethan thanked her then waited for her to leave before resuming the conversation.

'Well...' How much did he tell someone, even someone as kind as Fran seemed to be? 'I'm a single father to a wonderful little girl.'

'Tilly is adorable.'

'She is. I'm very lucky.' Goosebumps rose on his arms. He was lucky to have Tilly and he acknowledged it every day. 'She's an amazing child.'

'Is her mother... around?' Fran asked before taking a bite of her panini. She winced as she did so and the cheese stretched out and flopped onto her chin. 'Hot!' She waved a hand in front of her mouth.

Ethan laughed as she pulled it away then wiped her chin with a napkin.

'Something else to know about me, I guess... I'm a messy eater.' She rolled her eyes.

'No worries.' Ethan shook his head. At least if he ended up with cheese on his chin, Fran wouldn't be bothered. Melanie had been so uptight about things like that. Some of the tension in his shoulders loosened; he had a feeling he could relax with Fran, even become her friend. 'So... uh... I was a chef in a restaurant chain but there were cutbacks and I was made redundant, and, being the bread-winner, what with Tilly being far too young to work and all that...' He winked at Fran. 'I had to look for work that I could fit around the school run and school holidays. And... you asked about her mother, well, no, she's not around and hasn't been for two years. She does support Tilly financially, but rarely puts in an appearance.'

'Oh my goodness, I'm so sorry.' Fran put her panini down and wiped her hands on her napkin. 'That must be so hard on Tilly and you.'

He shrugged and moved his own panini around the plate, then broke the end off and watched as the cheese stretched out between the pieces. 'It's been challenging at times but, hey, you know... you just have to get on with it.'

That old chestnut!

If only it was that simple. He did get on with it but it still hurt. It was exhausting being the sole carer of a young child, being both mum and dad and worrying that if anything ever happened to him, then Tilly would be alone because he couldn't imagine Melanie ever stepping forwards to care for her child. It just wasn't Melanie. And his father wasn't exactly grandfather of the year, so that wasn't a viable option either. When his mind started racing along this path, it made him feel ill, so he usually tried to put a halt to it immediately.

And it was far too much to share with Fran when they barely knew each other.

'Well, I really admire you.' Fran reached out and touched his hand, then her eyes widened a fraction and she pulled her hand back. 'You're clearly doing a great job. I couldn't do it.'

Ethan looked at her curiously and she straightened in her chair.

'What I mean is… I'm going to be… uh… a mum, but… uh… being single and that as a parent and managing as you do must be hard. Well done, though, because Tilly is wonderful. Of course I can do it, though, I mean… I have to do it now. Don't I?'

Ethan nodded in spite of his confusion at Fran's comments, then bit into his panini. Warm cheese and spicy ginger and lime chutney teased his taste buds and he moaned with pleasure.

'Good, right?' Fran asked.

'Really good.' He nodded.

'Where is Tilly's mum? If you don't mind me asking.'

'Dubai.' Ethan wrinkled his nose. 'A long way from Tilly. She Skypes and texts and calls but that's about the extent of her maternal contact. She's very busy with her career and ambition to take over the world.'

'But you're in Penhallow Sands now and I'm sure you and Tilly will be happy here.'

'I hope so, Fran, I really do.' He took another bite of panini and chewed.

'Didn't you have family in... was it Bath?'

'Yes, we lived in Bath. My father lives there some of the time but he also spends a lot of the year in Majorca. Ever since my mum passed away, he's been unable to sit still for long. I think that being in perpetual motion stops him dwelling on his grief.'

'Sorry about your mum,' Fran said softly.

'Thanks.' Ethan blinked hard, not willing to allow himself to feel that sadness right now. 'At least here, I have my aunt and uncle and my two rather loud, warm and ostentatious cousins.'

'Harper and Scarlett!' Fran giggled. 'They're lovely girls.'

'So you know them? I guess everyone knows everyone around here. Yes, they are lovely, but when they're nearby, you certainly know it. Especially Scarlett because she likes everyone in a ten-mile radius to know she's around.'

'Yes, you're right about it being a small village. Everyone knows everyone or at least someone who knows them. I'm older than they are, so wasn't in school with them, but I've gone to the tea shop at Rosewood for years and I can remember Harper and Scarlett at about eight and five, running around the farmyard chasing each other, and if I think right back, I remember when they were both babies. I even babysat for them a few times when I was sixteen, on the rare occasions when your aunt and uncle went out. I'm glad you'll have company now, Ethan. It's hard being alone.'

He met her warm gaze and nodded. 'It really is a close village, isn't it? And thank you. I'm glad to be here.' Did Fran always say what was on her mind? It was refreshing to speak to a woman who didn't play games. Fran didn't seem like a player at all. He could be wrong, of course, as he barely knew her, but she didn't seem to be hiding anything. There must be a partner on the scene because he couldn't imagine anyone finding Fran, making love to her then leaving her. She was just... too good for that.

'Are you... uh... do you have a...' He shook his head. 'Of course you do. What am I thinking?' He tapped his forehead with the palm of his hand.

'Do I have a what?'

'It doesn't matter. When are you due?'

Fran had been taking a sip of coffee and now she spluttered and coffee shot from her mouth and out of her nose. She grabbed her napkin and covered her face while she coughed.

'Sorry! Are you okay?' He handed her some more napkins.

She waved a hand. 'I'm fine,' she murmured from behind the napkin, then coughed some more. She wiped her face then screwed up the napkins and put them onto her empty plate. 'I told you I'm messy. I... uh... don't have a due date yet. It's too early to know.'

'That early, eh?'

'Yes.'

'It's all estimated anyway. They can't tell exactly when baby will arrive.'

'No.' Fran picked up her mug and slowly took a drink, clearly worried about a repeat performance of choking. 'They can't.'

He wanted to ask about her partner or the baby's father, but he also felt as if that was intrusive, as she hadn't volunteered any information about it. Also, he was worried that it would seem as though he was interested – he was so unfamiliar with speaking to strange women and hadn't dated since way before Melanie – so he didn't know what was appropriate and what could be misunderstood. Better not to ask that question and to wait and see if she told him anyway. Not that it mattered, because even if she was single, she was pregnant and Ethan was not looking for romance, even if she was – by some strange coincidence, or by way of a miracle – attracted to him. And he had Tilly and no intention of bringing anyone into his daughter's life if there was the slightest chance that they wouldn't be sticking around. On days like this, more than ever, he wished his mum was still alive because he could speak to her about all of this; she always knew the right thing to say and do and he missed her sage advice and her reassurance badly.

He finished his lunch then drained his coffee and wiped his hands on his napkin. It was probably time to go and that thought filled him with disappointment. He didn't feel ready to say goodbye to Fran just yet.

'I don't suppose you have some room left for dessert, do you?' Fran asked, pulling a menu from under the seaglass vase. 'Shell bakes the most amazing cakes and makes the best knickerbocker glories, and I know it's winter, but I can eat ice cream anytime.'

'The most amazing cakes, eh? As a chef who's now local to the village, it's important to check out the competition. And yes, I do have room,' Ethan said, patting his flat stomach. 'I always have room for dessert… especially ice cream.'

Fran's eyes twinkled behind her glasses.

'That's what I like to hear.' She winked at him. 'Me too!'

—

Fran gazed at the festive knickerbocker glory on the table in front of her. The tall glass was filled with cinnamon cherry sauce, kirsch-soaked cherries, cream, vanilla, ginger and chocolate ice cream and was topped with chocolate sprinkles and two triangular gingerbread biscuits. It looked amazing.

'Are you going to eat that or just stare at it?' Ethan said from behind his own knickerbocker glory.

'Oh, I'm planning on eating it but I wanted to prepare myself first,' Fran replied.

Ethan closed his eyes as he tasted the first spoonful of the dessert and festive flavours danced on his tongue. 'It's soooo good.'

'Isn't it?' Fran spooned some of her own into her mouth and smacked her lips. 'Shell makes the cinnamon cherry sauce and gingerbread herself and they're just divine.'

Ethan nodded, his mouth too full to speak.

Fran had really enjoyed her time with Ethan at Shell's Shack. Seeing him at the school had been a surprise but she'd been glad when he'd agreed to come for a coffee, mainly because he'd seemed quite low leaving Tilly at the school and Fran hated to see anyone struggling. If she could help in any way, she would, and helping Ethan came with the bonus fact that he was gorgeous and – she now knew – a very nice man. They'd talked a lot since they arrived at the cafe and Fran found that Ethan was easy to talk to, she felt relaxed with him and she could be herself. Of course, there was no pressure like there would be if it was a date or anything like that. Yes, she was attracted to him, but had no idea if that was reciprocated, and anyway, it wouldn't matter because he was a single father with what sounded like a significant amount of baggage and, more specifically, he thought Fran was pregnant.

She sighed inwardly as she spooned more fluffy cream into her mouth. Thank goodness for comfort eating! And the cream was comforting, as was the ice cream and the rich, dark cinnamon cherry sauce.

'What's your favourite fruit?' Ethan asked, dragging Fran from her musings.

'Uh… probably cherries and strawberries. I adore them both.' She nodded.

'Have you ever been strawberry picking?'

'Not since I was a teenager.'

'Me neither but I'd like to go again and take Tilly.'

'I don't think you'll find anywhere this time of year.' Fran looked out of the window at the bright sky, but she knew that it was cold and that the wind was icy today. When it blew in off the sea, it could numb your fingers and nose in minutes and make your eyes water. Of course, it could also clear your head just as quickly, and Fran had always enjoyed that part of living at the coast, especially on her early morning dog walks.

'Ha! No, I doubt that too, but perhaps in the summer we could go together.' His eyes widened. 'I mean… that is if you'd like to go.'

'I'd love to! It's so much fun getting out in the fields and picking your own food with the sun on your head and shoulders and the scent of fresh fruit on your sticky fingers. There's nothing like the taste of fresh strawberries. We could make a day of it and have a picnic. As long as you're still here.'

'Why wouldn't I be?' He frowned.

'Oh… I don't know. You are planning on staying here long-term then, are you?'

He nodded. 'I can't keep moving around because that's not fair on Tilly. She needs stability so I'm aiming to settle here close to family.'

Fran smiled, warmth filling her at the thought that Ethan would be in Penhallow Sands in the summer and beyond.

'You'll be quite far along by the summer though, won't you?' he said, dragging her from her vision of wandering through strawberry fields with Ethan holding her hand, red strawberry juice on her lips and chin, sweet and fragrant, ready for him to kiss it away. 'You might not fancy traipsing around a field in the baking heat then.'

'That's true.' Fran swallowed hard. Of course, if she were pregnant, she would indeed be heavily pregnant by then. She wanted to tell this sweet and kind man that she was not expecting, that she would be free to roam around a field with him and his daughter picking strawberries that they could then eat with thick, golden-crusted clotted cream, but she couldn't. Telling Ethan the truth now would be a betrayal of her best friend and that was the last thing she wanted to do, because if word got out that it was Holly who was pregnant, then she knew Holly would have her own problems to deal with and Fran would feel terrible. They wouldn't be end-of-the-world problems, but Holly's granny, Glenda, would suffer a terrible shock if it all went wrong, Holly's wedding would be over-shadowed and Fran would feel like the world's worst best friend. It was no sacrifice really, not at all, or it wouldn't be if she didn't have to deceive Ethan. Not that she thought there was a chance of anything growing between her and the handsome single dad, because that wasn't how things worked, was it? Or did they? Other people met someone they liked and found attractive, dated them and that some-times led to a relationship, but it had never happened for Fran up to this point, so she didn't see how or why it would happen now. And that was fine; she was happy being footloose and fancy-free. Eating her strawberries and cream alone.

Wasn't she?

If someone had asked her if she liked being single last year, last week, hell, even yesterday, she'd have said she loved her life exactly as it was, but Ethan Clarke had thrown something into the equation that she'd never come across before: major attraction. She was finding herself drawn to him and his story, wanting to know more about him and to – hopefully – spend more time with him.

'That was incredible.' Ethan licked his lips and sat back in his chair. 'I'll have to bring Tilly here to try one of these as I'm sure she'd love it.'

'I'm sure she would.'

Something passed over his face then and Fran's stomach clenched.

'What is it?'

'I was just wondering how she's getting on. Here I am enjoying myself and I can't help but feel a bit guilty because my little girl is at school, possibly feeling anxious and insecure, trying to settle in…'

'There won't be any *trying* about it.' Fran shook her head. 'She'll have at least two best friends already and probably about ten invites for tea. People around here are like that and Tilly will have no problem settling in. That's the thing with a small village… all the mums and dads will want to make Tilly – and you – welcome. Heck, Ethan, you'll probably have invites for tea too!'

He laughed.

Fran could understand Ethan's concerns and knew that it must be difficult for him bringing his daughter up alone. How Tilly's mother could have walked away from her, Fran didn't know, but she also didn't want to judge a woman she didn't know. However, Tilly and Ethan seemed lovely and there must have been something wrong for Ethan's ex to decide that she couldn't be with her family. Or perhaps it was a matter of choosing her career over her husband and daughter. There would be far more to it than Fran had been told, no doubt, and every story had two sides to it. After all, Holly had fled Penhallow Sands last year after having her heart broken and she hadn't even told Fran (her best friend since they were small) and when she returned she had a baby. People went through their own difficulties and had to navigate life in the way that was best for them. Sometimes that meant running away.

And yet, looking at Ethan now, seeing his concern for his little girl, made something in Fran flutter. He was kind and caring, quite shy in some ways and also sweet, and she knew she would find it very difficult to leave him if he was hers.

Not that that would ever become a reality, of course. Men like Ethan went for leggy blondes with perfect hair and nails and witty conversation, didn't they? Fran was a Welsh-Italian girl, with her heart firmly grounded in Penhallow Sands, and she was happier in her pyjamas, snuggling with her dogs on the sofa and watching a TV series than she'd be out in a fancy restaurant dressed up to the nines. She was content with herself and her way of life, and didn't need to have her comfort zone upturned – not by a man, not by a child, in fact, not by anything.

Fran finished her dessert then set her spoon in the glass.

'I really enjoyed that.' She felt certain that her waistline must have expanded in the last hour and rested her hands on it, as comfortable with her feminine curves as she had always been.

'Me too.'

'Are you full now?'

He raised an eyebrow. 'I think I am. Well done, Fran, that has to be a first!'

'There's a first time for everything, right?'

He held her gaze over the table and smiled. Something crackled between them like an electric spark. Goosebumps rose all over Fran's body.

'Absolutely.'

And Fran found herself sinking into the depths of his green eyes as she would into a warm swimming pool. There was a first time for everything, and right now, being here with Ethan, was the first time she could ever remember feeling just like this.

Chapter 6

Ethan rubbed the butter and flower lightly between his thumbs and fingertips, creating the breadcrumb texture that pastry required. He was careful not to let the mixture settle against his skin, aware that heat would ruin it. There was a very fine line to creating perfect pastry or ending up with a heavy, sticky mess.

'Once that's ready, pop it in the fridge and we'll have a cuppa, shall we?' Audrey said, peering at him over the tops of her glasses. Ethan had noticed that she didn't wear the glasses all the time, but needed them for reading and close work.

'That sounds good.' He nodded.

'Will you want some lunch too?'

'Oh, no thanks. I ate in the village after I dropped Tilly off.'

After returning to Rosewood, he hadn't had a chance to speak to his aunt about where he'd been, as there had been a rush at the tea shop when a tourist bus had arrived, so she'd been out front serving while Ethan had got straight to work in the kitchen. His cousins had flitted in and out, helping with orders then taking them to tables. Now it was the middle of the afternoon and in just over an hour, Ethan would be able to go and pick Tilly up from school. The thought of seeing his little girl and finding out how her day had been made his insides vibrate with joy. He couldn't wait to hug her and listen to her stories.

He poured some cold water into the flour and butter then deftly mixed it in until he had a smooth ball. He lifted it out of the bowl and set it on the cling film he'd cut ready, wrapped it up, then set it in the fridge.

After he'd washed his hands, he accepted a mug of tea from his aunt.

'Thank you.'

'You're welcome.' She smiled. 'We might not have long, so drink it while it's hot. Some days we don't stop here and before I know it, I've gone all day without a warm drink or anything to eat. But I'm not complaining because it's wonderful to run a successful business and to work so close to home. I'd have hated to endure a long daily commute to work.'

She perched on a stool at the island in the centre of the kitchen and stretched out her legs.

'Oh, that feels good. My poor old legs ache some days from being on the go.'

Ethan sat opposite her and cradled his mug between his palms.

'I know that feeling well.' He nodded. 'I had a nice chat with Fran Gandolfini this morning after I'd dropped Tilly off.'

Audrey nodded. 'She's great, isn't she?'

'Very nice. I found her quite down to earth and easy to talk to.'

'We've known Fran since she was a baby. She even babysat for our girls when she was a teenager.'

'Yes, she told me.'

They sipped their tea in silence for a bit, appreciating the familiar taste and warmth of the drink.

'I'm so glad you came to stay with us, Ethan. I was hoping that the job would appeal to you. I've been worried about you for a long time.'

'You have?' He met her gaze and she inclined her head.

'Knowing that you were alone, without family around you and Tilly... other than my older brother, that is, but I know Lewis hasn't been much help, has he?'

Ethan chewed his bottom lip.

'Ethan, darling, I know you don't want to say anything bad about your father, but I also know that after he lost your mother, he really struggled with things.'

'He did. He's never... been the same.' Ethan swallowed hard as his father's face appeared in his mind. His skin bore the deep grooves of grief around his mouth and eyes and he sighed regularly, as if carrying around a pain that would never lift.

'Eight years is a long time to grieve so acutely and yet... after a lifetime with someone you love, it's no time at all. Lewis loved Heidi deeply and she was always the strong one in their relationship.'

'She was his rock.'

Ethan thought of the times he'd seen his mum support his dad, the times she'd taken a deep breath and seemed to prepare herself to be the backbone of her family. She had been a brave woman and he had admired her for it every single day. Losing someone like that, the woman who held her family together, was bound to leave a lasting hole. Ethan had a hole there that he'd been unable to fill, an ache that had never gone away, and it had been one of the reasons why he'd rushed into his relationship with

Melanie. But, of course, Melanie hadn't been the one – or wanted to be the one – to fill that hole, and neither should she have been expected to do so. Ethan could see both sides of that issue and sometimes wondered if he'd put too much pressure on her to be everything that he needed; no one could ever be everything to someone else. And Melanie had chosen not to be anything to him at all.

'How are you doing with everything else?' Audrey's voice was soft, her tone inviting confidence.

'I'm okay.'

'Are you?'

He sighed, pushing out a breath that he hoped would carry away the tension that seemed to be forever present, sitting inside of him like hardening clay. 'I have to be.'

'She was a fool that Melanie.' Audrey shook her head.

'She... she had things she needed to do.'

'You're a good man, Ethan, I know you are, but you don't have to defend her. Aren't you angry?'

He sipped his tea then set his mug on the island.

'I have been... at times.' And he had. He had ranted and raged to himself, pounded the treadmill and cycled for miles in virtual spin on the exercise bike in his bedroom – both because he couldn't go out at night to exercise because of a lack of childcare – but he had never allowed his anger to emerge in front of Tilly. He didn't want her to see him like that. In fact, he had hidden most of it from Melanie too, hating the thought that she would see his raw pain, his anguish and his yearning for a stable family life. It was embarrassing and humiliating to be rejected by someone as he had been, and overwhelmingly sad. 'But more than anger, I feel sadness. I never thought I'd end up divorced.'

Audrey slid off her stool and walked around to him, then she opened her arms. Ethan stared at her for a moment, uncertain, then he leant forwards and she hugged him tight. She smelt of flowers and baking and her hairnet scratched against his cheek. But the hug was good. It was warm and caring and he squeezed her back, his anxiety at the prospect of human contact drifting away like a grey storm cloud blown away by a summer breeze. Audrey was his aunt, she cared about him and she was letting him know that.

When she released him and stepped back, she took his hand.

'Ethan... has there been anyone else since Melanie left?'

He shook his head.

'You've been alone for what... two years?'

'I had Tilly.'

'You're a young man and you're entitled to have relationships.'

'I haven't been ready.' His voice wavered.

'That's understandable, love, it really is.' She squeezed his hand. 'But don't leave it too long because you are a good person and you deserve to be happy.'

'Tilly is my priority.'

'Of course she is.' Audrey nodded. 'She always will be. But she will be happy as long as you are and that might mean finding love again. You'll see if you just give your heart a chance to open to the idea again.'

Ethan lowered his gaze to the floor, not wanting his aunt to see the doubt in his eyes. He didn't think he'd ever be able to let another woman into his life. How could he trust someone with his heart, let alone Tilly's?

Ethan sipped the gin and tonic that his cousin, Harper, had made for him and settled into the sofa in the lounge at the farmhouse. Tilly was in the kitchen with his aunt and uncle and his two cousins had suggested that they go and sit in the lounge and watch a documentary about a band that Scarlett's boyfriend knew. Ethan had been glad to go and sit down after a busy Saturday at the tea shop and he'd left Tilly in the kitchen drawing portraits of Audrey while Gary chuckled into his glass of beer. Tilly definitely had an artistic flair like his mother, but it needed some refining, and at times Ethan found the way her sketches exaggerated certain aspects of someone's face and body quite amusing. Whenever Tilly drew him, he had ridiculously long legs and a very floppy fringe, and he'd said to her more than once that he looked like some kind of wig on legs. That always made Tilly giggle and he suspected that she did it deliberately now, just to get him smiling.

'What do you think?' Scarlett asked from the other side of the sofa, as she pointed at the TV screen where a group of five twenty-somethings cavorted around on a stage, shaking their heads, shouting into microphones, strumming instruments, pushing each other and performing chest bumps and high fives. The music was loud, raw and energetic.

'It's certainly... uh... lively.' Ethan smiled, hoping that he was being diplomatic.

Scarlett cocked a heavily drawn on eyebrow at him then flicked back her flame-red hair. The last time Ethan had seen her before returning to Rosewood, Scarlett's hair had been light blonde, long and silky. Now it was shoulder length, dyed bright red and messy – waved and backcombed to create something that made Ethan think of a bird's nest. Her blue eyes were lined with black kohl and her lips were the same shade as her hair. If she had any freckles, they were hidden by the thick foundation that she'd painted onto her skin.

'Look at you showing your age, cuz!' Scarlett poked out her tongue and the stud in it caught the light. Every time Ethan saw the piercing, he winced, wondering how anyone could bear to have something put through their tongue. Surely it must have hurt at the time as well as afterwards, and what if it caught on something as she was eating?

'Oh leave him alone, Scar!' Harper shook her head from the chair in the corner. 'Just because he's over thirty doesn't mean he's over the hill. Besides which, Camomile Motion are a bit of an acquired taste.'

'Just because lawyer Lottie doesn't like them.' Scarlett rolled her eyes. Lottie was Harper's partner and Ethan had only met her briefly when she'd picked his cousin up the previous evening. She was short with big brown eyes, and cropped dark hair that exposed tiny ears and a very serious expression.

'Lottie has good taste.' Harper winked at Ethan.

'So does Pip and this is one of his favourite songs.' Scarlett nodded her head along to the music and Ethan took another sip of his drink, hoping the music video would be over soon. The band wasn't terrible but they weren't his cup of tea either and he was worried that his smile would soon slip and betray his discomfort, which could be mistaken for disapproval. The last thing he wanted was for either of his cousins to feel that he disapproved of them or their music taste. He wanted to develop solid relationships with his family now that he was here.

'How are you settling in, Ethan?' Harper asked.

He met her green gaze, so much like her mother's, and watched as she twirled strands of her poker-straight long blonde hair around her fingers. She was exactly how he remembered her looking when she was younger: slim, pale-skinned and quieter than her sister. A lot quieter.

'All right, thanks.' He nodded. 'The cottage is very comfortable and you've all been really welcoming.'

'Mum is just delighted to have you and Tilly here.' Harper smiled. 'She loves having a little one round the place again. It'll be good for her when Lottie and I head off.'

Harper had told him about her plans to go travelling around Europe with Lottie in the new year. Lottie was taking a month off work to go with Harper, then she'd return to her job and Harper would continue travelling for another two months with some friends. It was something she'd always wanted to do and she said she intended on doing it now, before she settled down. At twenty-five, she was still young, and a tiny part of Ethan envied her freedom to pack a bag and set off to see more of the world. He had been abroad on holidays but never actually set off to see more than one destination at a time, and now, as a single father, it was unlikely to happen. But the flicker of envy soon faded as thoughts of Tilly filled his head. How could he ever want anything else when he had such a wonderful child to spend time with? Freedom was overrated and not something he needed to feel fulfilled. What he did need in order to feel fulfilled though was beyond his understanding.

'We're glad to be here.' He tilted his head as he heard laughter from the kitchen — the deep booming laugh of his uncle and the light tinkling of Tilly's giggle. She must be creating some amusing artwork to have Gary laughing that heartily. He hoped she wouldn't offend Audrey, although knowing that Audrey had lived with Scarlett for twenty-two years made him think that she could handle a slightly unflattering portrait drawn by a six-year-old. He wondered what she'd create if she decided to draw Scarlett and shuddered at the thought of how she would draw his cousin's eyebrows and hair and whether she'd include the tongue piercing. How exactly would she get that into a portrait?

'So, Ethan…' Scarlett wriggled closer to him on the sofa and peered at him over her glass. 'Are you in the right place for dating?'

His throat tightened. 'S-sorry… What?' He coughed.

'Well, you've been single for quite some time now, therefore… would you like me to set you up?'

He stared at her as a chill spread through his body, prickling under his armpits and curdling the drink in his stomach.

'No. No, thanks.' He drained his glass then set it down on the side table. 'Not at all.'

'No? Really?' Scarlett raised her eyebrows.

'Really.'

'But why?' Scarlett tilted her head. 'You're gorgeous, Ethan, and you're wasted being single. I know so many delightful ladies who'd be happy to go out with you. It doesn't have to lead to anything serious, but you could have some fun. In fact…' She pulled her smartphone from her pocket and started scrolling through her contacts list.

Ethan watched in horror as images rolled up the screen. Scarlett appeared to have photos of everyone next to their phone numbers. 'There we are!'

His cousin held out her mobile and he peered at the screen. There, next to the name Georgina Donovan, was a photo of a young woman with long brown hair and big blue eyes framed by impossibly thick, dark eyelashes. The photo was small but he could see that the woman was attractive. Even so, he had no interest in getting to know her at all.

Suddenly, Scarlett moved her finger and pressed video call, and a dialling tone filled the lounge. Ethan froze as the call was answered and the woman's face filled the screen. She certainly was very pretty and had a warm smile punctuated by bright white teeth.

'Hey, Georgie, what's up?' Scarlett sang into the phone.

'Hello, girl, I'm good. How're you?'

'Good, baby. I just wanted to check if you're doing anything next Friday evening.'

'I don't think so.' Georgie chewed her lip thoughtfully. 'Why, you want to go somewhere?'

'Nah, but my cousin would love to take you out.'

Ethan's stomach lurched. This was absurd. He was being put on the spot by a cousin he barely knew and in front of the very woman she had decided she wanted him to date. He pushed himself up from the sofa and started to back away on shaky legs.

'Ethan!' Scarlett patted the sofa next to her. 'Come back and say hello to Georgie.'

He shook his head and glanced at Harper. She looked as horrified as he felt.

'Cut it out, Scarlett,' Harper whispered. 'He clearly doesn't want to go.'

'What's going on?' Georgie asked from the phone.

Scarlett looked from Ethan to her sister then back at the phone.

'Gosh, sorry, Georgie, my mistake... he... uh... has something on.'

'Hey wait, is that the dishy cousin you were on about? The one who cooks?' George asked, her tone softening as it filtered out into the room. 'The one who's working at Rosewood? I've heard about him from some of the girls who saw him in the village. They said he's *gorgeous*. Please set me up! I'd love to go on a date with him.'

Scarlett looked at Ethan but he shook his head again, then turned and fled from the room. He could hear Scarlett muttering something to Georgie but he couldn't make out what she was saying and he didn't care to know. She would have to explain this to her friend as best she could because it wasn't his problem. Ethan was certainly not in the right place to be set up on blind dates and he never would be. The very thought chilled him to the bone.

Chapter 7

Fran pulled up in front of Rosewood and cut the engine. The sky was leaden with fat grey clouds and she wasn't looking forward to leaving the warmth of the car and venturing into the biting winter wind again. With just one week of November remaining, winter had settled into Penhallow Sands with a vengeance. There hadn't been any snow yet, but the farming forecast had said there was a likelihood that they'd see some over the next few weeks. She wondered if it would arrive in time for Christmas and stay for Holly's wedding, which would be nice but also troublesome in equal measure, as it could make proceedings difficult and was never a good thing for the local farmers.

Fran had had a busy week delivering Christmas stock to local shops, as well as trying to finish a landscape that she'd decided upon as the perfect wedding gift for Holly and Rich. Added to that, Shell from the village had arrived two nights ago with a very small and malnourished Westie that had been found wandering just outside the village. No one had claimed it, so they'd put up a notice at the vet's and in the local shops, but with Christmas approaching, it was suspected that the dog might have been abandoned by its owners as they welcomed a new pup in time for Christmas, or possibly by a breeder as it was completely deaf. It wasn't chipped either, so there was no way of tracing where it had come from. The vet had estimated the dog to be no more than a year old and it was very timid. Fran had left the dog in the care of her pack at home, knowing that they would keep the poor thing company. Their introduction had shown no ill will between them and no conflict of personalities, but then her dogs were as laid-back as they came and were used to Fran having waifs and strays of the canine and feline variety staying at their home for varying lengths of time. They took it all in their stride and Dust Bunny in particular liked to mother any new arrivals.

Fran wrapped her woollen scarf tightly around her neck, pulled on her red bobble hat then opened the car door. A gust of wind tugged at the door and she had to hold on tight as she got out then used her bodyweight to push the door closed. She went around to the rear of her car and opened the boot, then lifted out the box of festive mugs she'd made for the tea shop. She balanced it on her hip then reached up for the boot and closed it. Audrey had loved the samples and ordered three boxes. There were two more in there but she'd have to take them in one at a time.

She carried the box to the tea shop, peering around it because it was obstructing her forward vision, and pushed open the door. The warmth from inside met her along with the scents of coffee and cake and her mouth watered instantly. The tea shop always smelt so good and homely and she loved the delicious aromas of baking and beverages.

'What on earth are you doing?'

The voice, filled with concern, came from behind the box in her arms and she looked up to find Ethan staring down at her.

'You could hurt yourself, Fran.' He shook his head. 'Let me take that.'

He lifted the box from her arms and she could see again.

'Thanks, Ethan.' She pulled her bobble hat off, suddenly warm. 'I could have managed, though.'

'Not in your condition.' He carried the box over to the counter and Fran followed him.

She frowned at him. 'My condition?'

'Yes.' He nodded and she realised what he meant. 'You're not supposed to carry heavy things or to stretch too far or do anything strenuous. It could hurt you or the baby.'

'Of course,' she forced out through gritted teeth. Damn this fictional pregnancy and the issues it was creating – especially when she forgot about it and had to be reminded. Although, it had sent Ethan to help her, so it wasn't all bad.

'Are there more in your car?'

'Yes, two more.'

'Give me your keys and I'll get them for you.' He held out his hand.

'It's the blue Escort.'

'Okay.' He flashed her a smile then left the tea shop.

'Hello, Fran.' Audrey appeared from the kitchen. 'This the Christmas order?'

'Yes, and Ethan's getting the rest of the boxes from my car.'

'He's such a gentleman, isn't he?' Audrey beamed.

'He certainly is. I did tell him I could have managed to bring them in but he insisted.'

'He's very thoughtful. While you're here would you like a drink?'

'I'd love a hot chocolate, please.'

'Cream and marshmallows?'

'You know me too well.' Fran giggled.

As Audrey went about making the drink, Fran gazed around her at the Monday morning customers enjoying their warm drinks and respite from the cold outside. Even thought it was only just after nine, the tea shop was busy with groups of young mums nursing babies and wrestling toddlers, and a few elderly couples enjoying breakfast tea cakes and scones. The gentle hum of conversation and the tinkling of cutlery was punctuated by the odd squeal from an irritable infant, reminding Fran – as if she could have forgotten – that she was supposed to be expecting her own baby and making her shiver.

Just as Audrey placed a glass mug of hot chocolate on the counter, Ethan reappeared with both of the other boxes. He carried them effortlessly, his strong arms wrapped around the boxes that Fran had struggled to carry out to the car individually. Fran was fit and healthy and thought of herself as relatively strong, but she was petite and her arms hadn't quite fit around the boxes, so seeing how easy Ethan held them made her aware of how muscular he was. How broad his shoulders were. How feminine she felt next to him. She had to tear her eyes away from his frame and fix them on her hot chocolate.

'There you go.' Ethan paused in front of the counter. 'Where do you want them, Audrey?'

'In the back room will be best, thanks, love.'

'No problem.'

He carried them through to the kitchen and Audrey winked at Fran. 'Although Ethan spends most of his time in the kitchen, I swear he's increased custom this past two weeks as word has spread that the new chef is quite a dish. Pardon my pun.'

Fran smiled but her stomach plummeted. Of course Ethan would attract attention; he was a very handsome man and also friendly and chivalrous with it. Why wouldn't other women want to meet him and eat the delicious food he made? Why wouldn't they come here, hoping to find out more about the gorgeous single dad? There weren't many single men in Penhallow Sands, so any time a new one arrived, he was bound to create a stir.

'We're going to put the festive decorations up on Friday, Fran, as we usually do on the last Friday of November. But you'd know that, of course. Will you be joining us this year?' Audrey asked.

'Yes, I'll be here.' Fran nodded. 'I adore your traditions. It wouldn't be Christmas without them and I look forward to the decorating in particular.'

'There will be mulled wine and mince pies and gingerbread. I'm so excited this year because we'll have Ethan and Tilly here too. It's lovely to have children around for Christmas. It just makes it extra special, doesn't it?'

'I expect it does.' Fran smiled.

She enjoyed the build up to Christmas even though she didn't have any children and she always had done. She liked making festive mugs and goblets, listening to carols on the radio and eating mince pies. It probably was nice to have family around, but since her parents had gone out to Italy, she'd got used to spending Christmas Day either with Holly and her family at Greenacres or at home with the animals. She didn't mind her own company at all, and she never felt particularly lonely, but she could understand how some people might do, especially if they were used to having others around.

'How're you feeling anyway, love? You know… what with…' Audrey raised her eyebrows and lowered her gaze to Fran's middle.

Fran tucked two fingers between her neck and her scarf and pulled it away from her skin. Had the wool always been that scratchy? Had it always made her so uncomfortably warm?

'I'm okay, thank you. Just getting on with it. You know how preg… *it* goes.'

Heat rushed into her cheeks. This was getting worse by the day. She hated deceiving anyone and wondered if the lovely Audrey would understand when the truth was finally revealed. The thought made her feel weary and she had a sudden urge to go home to bed and hide under the duvet until January.

'Glad to hear it. This time next year, you'll have a little one to enjoy Christmas with! All being well, of course.' Audrey hugged herself and rocked from side to side. 'How exciting! What do your parents think?'

Fran's jaw dropped. Her parents! Of course, they would need to know just in case they spoke to someone from the village and the news was delivered to them first.

'They don't know yet, Audrey. It's very early days and I didn't want to raise their hopes in case it doesn't… uh… work out. I had hoped to keep it completely private, so I'd really appreciate your discretion in this, if you don't mind.'

'Very wise, love, and I understand completely. My lips are sealed.' Audrey reached out and covered Fran's hand. 'Now you take a seat and enjoy that drink. Plenty of rest is what you need. Put your feet up whenever possible and be kind to yourself because before you know it, you'll have another person to care for and little babies can be very demanding indeed.'

Fran forced a smile to her lips. 'I'll do my best.'

She'd drink her hot chocolate and leave as quickly as possible because she didn't want to get any deeper into this lie than she already was. It was like sinking in quicksand; every time she moved a fraction, she got dragged deeper down and before long she worried that it would swallow her up completely and the Fran she knew would be gone for ever. It made her want to bite her fist and screw up her eyes and hope it would all go away.

—

Ethan had put the boxes from Fran into the back room, then realised he still had her car keys. She'd been about to leave when he returned them to her and he'd been concerned at how pale she'd looked. After drinking one of Audrey's rich hot chocolates, Fran should've had rosy cheeks and a chocolate high, but instead she looked tired and strained. He hoped she was looking after herself or that someone else was looking after her. It was more important that she had people around who cared during her pregnancy than at any other time in her life.

He opened the oven door and slid the tray of cheese and asparagus tartlets inside then set the timer. As he straightened up, Audrey appeared from the back room with red cheeks and wide eyes.

'Are you all right?' he asked.

She nodded then worried at her bottom lip as if she were trying not to laugh. 'I think so, but uh… I think Fran has given us the wrong order.'

'How come?'

'Well, we have two boxes of festive mugs, which is exactly what I ordered, but the third box contains some… uh… rather… un-festive novelty… uh… things.'

'Yeah? Like what?' He couldn't imagine what Fran could have made that would get Audrey into such a state.

'Come and have a look!' Audrey gestured for him to follow her and as she walked away, he heard her chucking.

On her desk, in the back room that doubled as an office, stood an array of mini figures. From a distance they looked like festive elves, but as Ethan stepped closer and peered at them, laughter burst from him.

'What on earth?'

'Exactly.' Audrey giggled loudly now and a tear escaped her eye and ran down her cheek.

Ethan reached for one of the small figures and held it up. It appeared to be a naked and rather well-endowed man.

'Bloody hell!' He turned the figure around to show his aunt, feeling quite embarrassed about looking at it in her company.

'I know, right?' She grinned. 'And look at this one.'

She held up a goblet that had a colourful painting on the side. As Ethan looked closer, he could see that it was of a naked couple entwined in what he assumed was a position that probably featured in the Kama Sutra.

His cheeks flooded with heat that seeped into his ears and down his neck. Not only had Fran created these things, but he was now going through them with his aunt. It was as embarrassing as watching a film with his parents when a sex scene had come on and they'd been forced to sit there together, trying not to make eye contact, longing for it to be over.

'I can't wait to show these to Gary.' Audrey seemed to have recovered from her initial shock and was now finding it all highly amusing.

'Really?' Ethan frowned.

'He'll think they're fabulous. Might even give him a few ideas.'

'Please don't say any more.' Ethan turned his head, trying not to laugh at how mischievous his aunt was being.

'Actually, love, might be best if we get these back to Fran as quickly as possible. I know she said she has a busy week delivering stock before December starts, so she might be worried when she realises she's missing these. They have to be for a hen party or something, don't they? Or for one of those fancy shops that sells all manner of figurines and trinkets.'

'That would make sense.' Ethan turned the goblet around in his hands. 'It could be a fertility goblet or something.'

'Yes, love. Most likely. Although I'm not sure what the chances of conceiving are in that position.' She snorted and Ethan did too then they both surrendered to their mirth and laughed until they were drained.

Audrey started to put the figures back in the box on the chair and Ethan helped her.

'I could take it to Fran, if you like.'

'Would you mind?' Audrey squeezed his arm.

'Of course not, and I'll be back for the lunchtime crowd, but you'll need to keep an ear open for the oven timer. Those tartlets won't be long.'

'No problem. Now let me write Fran's address down for you so you know where to go.'

While she grabbed a pen and paper and wrote down Fran's details, Ethan gazed at her flushed cheeks and shiny eyes. He'd forgotten how amazing it felt to have a good laugh with someone, the kind that made you hot and sweaty but that left you with an endorphin high. He could tell that he was going to enjoy being around Audrey; she was good fun and had a great sense of humour and it added to his growing belief that that he'd made the right decision in their move to Cornwall.

–

Fran tilted her head. Was that a car pulling up outside her cottage?

The sudden scurry of dog paws from the lounge and into the hallway suggested that it was. The dogs loved a visitor, even if it was just the postman.

She closed her emails and got up from the kitchen chair and made her way out to the hallway. The dogs were already clamouring at the door, keen to find out who their visitor was, all except for the new arrival, that was. The small white dog hung back in the lounge doorway looking anxious. Being deaf, he wouldn't hear the excitement of his companions, so he'd have to read their body language, and he didn't seem to be very accomplished at that. Fran gave him a gentle ear rub as she passed, hoping to reassure him, then she pushed through the dogs in front of the door and gave them the order to sit and stay.

Fran opened the door and flashed the dogs a warning glance.

'Oh! Hello, Ethan.' She heard the shock in her voice.

'Hi, Fran.'

'This is a pleasant surprise.'

'Thank you. Sorry to come unannounced, but I wanted to get here as soon as possible. I think... well, I know, actually, that you gave us one wrong box.'

'I did?' Fran frowned.

'I'll just get it from the car.'

'What was in it?' Fran asked, trying to think what she might have given them.

'Uh...' Ethan cleared his throat as he walked away. Fran watched while he opened the boot and lifted a box out then brought it back to her. 'Some rather interesting items.'

Fran lifted the lid and peered inside.

'Ooooh. Oh dear...' She bit her lip. 'That wasn't meant for Rosewood.'

'Audrey was very surprised.'

'I hope she wasn't offended.'

'Not at all. She thoroughly enjoyed having a look at the contents.' Ethan was smiling and there was a glint of mischief in his eyes.

'They're for an online shop,' she explained. 'It stocks things for hen and stag nights and I meant to take that box to the post office. The other one for Rosewood must still be in my workshop.'

'Shall I take this through for you?'

'That would be lovely, thanks.'

Fran stood back and Ethan stepped into her hallway. Then he froze.

'Ethan? What is it?'

'D-dogs.' He stepped backwards.

'Yes, they're fine. All very friendly and tame.' She laughed.

He shook his head. 'Uh... no...'

He stepped back out of the door and onto the path.

'Ethan, it's fine, I promise. They're all quite sweet and the worst they'll do is lick you into submission.'

Ethan stared at her in horror over the top of the box.

'What is it?' Fran was confused by his reaction and now very worried.

'I'm just not a... a dog person, Fran.'

'Really?' Fran stared at him as if he'd grown another head.

'Really. They just...'

'They just what?'

'They're so unpredictable.'

Fran shook her head. 'I'll have you know that my dogs are friendly, welcoming and loyal companions.'

Just then, a low growl came from the hallway.

Fran turned in shock to see which of her dogs could be growling. But it wasn't one of hers. It was the small white newcomer.

The Westie was in the middle of the hallway now, his body taught with energy, his tiny mouth open exposing his yellow teeth as he growled long and low.

'They're obviously not as welcoming as you think they are.' Ethan leant forwards and placed the box on Fran's step, moving slowly as if he thought that any fast movements might provoke an attack. 'I would have taken this in for you, but I'd rather not have to try to pass the hound from hell.'

'Hound from hell?' Fran placed her hands on her hips. 'That tiny little thing is not only deaf but he was abandoned by his owner and left to starve. The poor little mite has been terrified and traumatised and... and...' Fran blinked hard. Her throat had closed over and she was surprised to find that her eyes had filled with tears as she tried to explain the dog's tragic history. 'He's just a poor little dog. All he wants is love and security, to know that human beings are not all bad and that many of us can provide love, security and a safe home.'

Ethan moved his gaze from the dog to Fran and something shifted in his eyes. 'I didn't know. I'm sorry. But regardless of that... he doesn't seem to like me very much.'

With that, the dog rushed to the doorstep and gave a loud bark. Ethan jumped, turned and raced down the path and through the gate. Only when he'd closed it behind him did he stop.

The dog hadn't even left the doorway and now it settled down to a sitting position and looked up at Fran. She shook her head in dismay.

'Ethan... He was just copying the others. When you arrived he didn't know how to behave but he watched my dogs and tried to copy what they did. He doesn't realise how loud his bark is.'

'He has a pretty sinister growl too.' Ethan's tone was filled with doubt.

'He can't hear himself. That's the first noise he's made since I brought him here.'

'Fran?'

'Yes?'

'Sorry but I really can't stay.' He ran a shaky hand over his eyes. 'So... uh... Do you have the other box of festive mugs for Audrey?'

'Yes... of course. I'll just go and grab it.' Fran ushered the dogs inside and closed the door to stop them running out as soon as she turned her back, then she went through the cottage to her studio and got the correct box for Rosewood. She locked the dogs in the kitchen before returning to the hallway and opening the front door.

'Here you are.' She handed the box to Ethan over the gate. 'I'm sorry that the dogs startled you.'

He shrugged. 'It's okay. You weren't to know.'

'No, I wasn't, but the last thing I want is for you to feel that uncomfortable at my home. Please... uh... apologise to Audrey for me, will you?'

'Of course, but I'm sure there's no need to apologise. You made Audrey laugh. A lot.' He gave her a tight smile but it didn't reach his eyes.

'I'd best get back inside then,' Fran said. 'I need to finish checking my emails and to get back on the road if I'm going to manage to deliver the rest of the orders.'

'Right. Okay. Well, see you soon. Be careful lifting the boxes, won't you?'

Ethan gave her a nod, placed the box in his boot then got in and started the engine. Before he drove away, he held Fran's gaze through the window. A peculiar sadness filled her heart, as if she was losing something that had given her hope and it was slipping through her fingers like grains of sand. It was ridiculous really, as what could she possibly be losing? So Ethan wasn't a fan of dogs. What did that matter to her? *Why* did it matter to her?

As she trudged back up the path and went inside, she knew why she was disappointed. She liked Ethan. A lot. Yet she loved her dogs and couldn't imagine life without them. She would always have dogs. Any man who might be a part of her life in any way would need to like dogs too. Ethan clearly didn't. So that was that.

She closed the door behind her and released a deep sigh, attempting to expel the regret that bloomed inside her, spreading to her limbs and making them heavy.

Nothing could have happened between her and Ethan anyway, but knowing that he felt this way was like another sure sign that it was never meant to be.

Chapter 8

'Daddy, I don't like sprouts.' Tilly patted Ethan's arm.

'No, I know, sweetheart, so just leave them on the side of your plate.'

'But they're making my gravy taste funny. It's like the smell of a ten-pence bit in my mouth.'

Ethan gazed down at his daughter and had to bite the inside of his cheek to avoid laughing. She looked so serious and her big brown eyes were framed by a small, indignant frown.

'What's wrong, Tilly?' Scarlett leant towards her.

Tilly glanced at Ethan then back at Scarlett. 'It's these bloody things.' She pushed the two dark green orbs around her plate. 'They're like balls of snot.'

'Tilly!' Ethan shook his head. 'You can't say that.'

'Sorry, Daddy. They're like bloody balls of boogies.'

Ethan met Audrey's eyes over the table and saw that she was shaking with laughter. A snort escaped him, then another, and soon the entire family was laughing.

'Tilly, love, leave them. It's fine.' Audrey waved a hand. 'I forgot that most children don't like sprouts, so don't worry about eating them.'

'They're making my gravy taste funny.' Tilly pouted.

'Here, I'll take them.' Ethan lifted the sprouts with his fork and set them on his plate. 'How's that?'

'Much better, Daddy, thank you.'

Tilly resumed eating her dinner, now the picture of innocence and good behaviour.

'Aunty Audrey?' Tilly piped up again and Ethan held his breath, wondering what was coming next.

'Yes?'

'Why are we having Sunday dinner on a Thursday?'

'Well, it's not Sunday dinner today, Tilly, is it? It's just a cooked dinner.'

'A cooked dinner?' Tilly frowned. 'But aren't all dinners cooked?'

'Yes, love, a lot of them are, but not all.'

Tilly nodded. 'Some are cold like salad and ham.'

'That's right.' Audrey inclined her head.

'Are you excited about tomorrow?' Gary asked.

'What's tomorrow?' Tilly frowned.

'Decorating the tea shop and the big tree in the yard ready for Christmas.' Scarlett wiggled her thick black brows, making Ethan think of fat caterpillars or slugs as they moved across the ground.

'Wow!' Tilly looked up at Ethan. 'Did you hear that, Daddy? Christmas decorations! It will be… amaaa–zing.' Her excitement was clear in the way that she elongated the vowel sound.

'It will.'

'And Santa will know exactly where to come this year, won't he, Daddy? And he will tell Mummy and everything and she'll know how to find us.' Tilly's words poured out in a torrent, revealing her thought process and her main concerns about the festive season.

Ethan's heart squeezed. 'Mummy knows where we are, Tilly, if she needs us.'

'I wish she was coming for Christmas.' Tilly pushed a potato around her plate. 'Glitterbug says she wishes Mummy was coming too. Mummy could eat all my sprouts and then she might be happy to be here. Because last time we spoke she said that she's a vegetarian now. And they like sprouts, don't they, Daddy?'

'Yes, vegetarians like sprouts and all sorts of vegetables.' Ethan reached out and ran a hand over Tilly's hair. Around the table, his family had fallen quiet and he knew they were feeling bad for Tilly too.

'Will Mummy be lonely at Christmas?' Tilly asked. 'My teacher said people without families often get lonely... especially at Christmas.'

'Mummy will be all right.' Ethan gulped. There was such a fine line between being completely honest with Tilly and sparing her some details that would simply hurt her. Like that fact that Melanie would never want to spend the holidays in Cornwall and would rather die than sit around a family table eating a turkey dinner with all the trimmings, even before she turned vegetarian. It just wasn't who Melanie was or how she liked to be perceived.

'What about all the other lonely people?' Tilly put her fork down and looked around the table. Her eyes were wide and earnest. 'We're okay because we have family, so we are very lucky, but some people won't be. Some people will be very lonely at Christmas and they probably wish they had somewhere to go.'

Ethan's throat ached and he couldn't think of a reply. Tilly was right. He'd been lonely over Christmas and would have loved to have had some company – another adult to pull a cracker with, to talk to as they ate and to sit with afterwards.

'I have an idea.' Ethan took a deep breath and met Audrey's warm gaze. 'About Christmas Day.'

Audrey put her knife and fork down and steepled her fingers in front of her, showing her willingness to listen.

'I don't want to overstep the mark, what with me being a new arrival and all that, but how about if we don't have Christmas dinner here?'

'I think I know where you're going with this.' Audrey smiled.

'What do you mean, Mum?' Harper asked.

'Just listen for a moment, Harper. Carry on, Ethan.' Audrey nodded.

'How about if we have it at the tea shop?' Ethan held his breath.

'But why?' Gary shrugged. 'We always have dinner here at home around the table.'

'So do most people with families,' Ethan said, 'but some people don't have that and would benefit from a place that opened its doors on Christmas Day.'

A silence fell around the table as everyone digested the idea.

'Ethan and Tilly have made a very good point.' Audrey nodded. 'Why stick to just us when we could share Christmas with others? Surely more people would mean more festive joy? Let's open the doors of the tea shop to all the lonely people of Penhallow Sands.'

Goosebumps rose on Ethan's arms. How he had wished for someone by his side at times, sharing the same hopes and fears he'd known. He'd worried about what Tilly could be missing out on over the years and spent many lonely nights in front of the TV after she'd gone to bed. He'd eaten many meals with Tilly but many times alone if she was in school or if she was at a friend's. There had been countless times when he'd have appreciated some company, some compassion, some friendship.

'I think it's a wonderful idea, but only if you all agree.' Ethan looked around the table at his relatives. 'We can cook up a feast and share it with anyone who would be spending Christmas Day alone.'

His mind flashed to Fran. Who did she spend Christmas Day with if her parents were away and there was no man in her life? He still wasn't sure about that one, of course, but he'd hate to think of her being alone, eating a meal for one. Now that she was expecting, she needed someone to look out for her more than ever. He found that he wanted to look out for her, to make her feel that she had people to turn to. Not that she seemed at all vulnerable or needy but everyone should have some people to rely on.

'Let's do it then.' Audrey raised her wine glass. 'To sharing the festive cheer!'

Around the table, Ethan's family nodded their approval. Thankfully they all seemed just as keen to share Christmas with others. Ethan clinked his glass against Tilly's and something inside him gave a small leap. It wasn't a feeling he was used to, but it was nice nonetheless. He thought it might actually be excitement, but he'd settle for hope. Hope was a good feeling.

At last, after years of feeling that there wasn't much for him to do – other than to be the best dad he could be, and that was nothing to sniff at – he now had another purpose. He could share in making the lives of others better, even if only for one day of the year, and what better day to improve things for those in need than Christmas Day?

They could create a delicious dinner and offer it free to the lonely people of the village, and in doing so, create a better festive experience for everyone who came.

Wasn't that what Christmas was all about, anyway?

–

The next morning, after Ethan had dropped Tilly at school, he went to the small grocers in the village and picked up a box of chocolates and a bunch of colourful tulips. Over dinner with his family last night, the discussion had moved on from Christmas plans for the tea shop to how Ethan was settling in. There had been discussion of locals and Fran had been one of those mentioned. As Audrey had spoken about Fran's kindness to animals and people and about how she always had a cheery disposition, whatever she was going through personally – even when her best friend, Holly, had disappeared for months – Ethan had felt a dark cloud descend over him. He hadn't been very nice to Fran yesterday about her dogs and it wasn't her fault or the fault of her four-legged companions. She had no idea what had happened to him, so how could she have understood his discomfort around creatures of the canine variety?

Therefore, he had decided to take her some flowers and chocolates to apologise and so that he could explain to her exactly why he'd behaved as he had the previous day. She had been nothing other than nice to him and she certainly didn't deserve to feel bad just because Ethan had a phobia of dogs. It was something he'd always wished he could overcome, something he'd always pushed away, but sometimes it was the right time to face your fears and to move on. This seemed like one of those times.

He drove up to Fran's cottage and parked outside, relieved to see that her car was there. If he'd had to come back, he might have lost his nerve. He liked Fran but he wasn't used to trying to deal with women and their moods and had no idea if she would be at all receptive to his apology. From what he'd seen of her though, she was warm and friendly, so he was cautiously optimistic.

He knocked on the door and flinched at the sound of barking from inside. It seemed to echo around the cottage as if it were reverberating off the walls and when the door opened, it would burst out and knock him off his feet. He braced himself, preparing to see the dogs – and not run away – when she opened the door. However, as the door swung open, he wasn't expecting to see Fran looking quite so delectable.

His breath caught in his throat, because she looked utterly gorgeous. She was wearing denim dungarees over a tight navy vest top, her small feet were bare, exposing bright pink toenails, and she had a red and navy scarf tied around her hair. Her red-framed glasses were different than the ones he'd seen her wearing so far and they matched the natural red of her kissable lips. Her face was free of makeup but she had a lovely glow to her cheeks and her indigo eyes were like deep lagoons that he could have plunged right into.

'Ethan! Hello.' She frowned. 'Did I give you another wrong box?'

'No… no. Not at all.' He held out the flowers and chocolates. 'I just wanted to apologise for yesterday.'

'Whatever for?'

'I thought I might have been a bit rude or uh… blunt about the dogs.'

Her expression softened. 'Not at all. Honestly, I wasn't offended.'

Relief flooded through him and he realised exactly how worried he'd been that he might have upset her.

'Well, these are for you anyway.'

'Thank you, although you shouldn't have.'

She took the chocolates and flowers and sniffed the blooms. As she did so, her eyes closed and a spark of desire shot through Ethan, nearly unbalancing him. His heart raced and as he exhaled, his breath sounded shaky to his own ears, and he wondered if Fran had picked up on it too, but she appeared to be oblivious to the effect she was having upon him.

'Excuse the state of me but I was in my workshop.'

'You look incredible.' He started, realising what he'd said.

'Incredible?' She rubbed at her cheek with the back of her hand. 'I'm probably covered in clay and dog hair.'

He peered at her. 'There is a tiny bit of clay there.' He gently rubbed at her cheek below her glasses, then raised his eyes to meet hers. The way she was looking at him made his racing heart skip a beat and something else, something primitive, stirred inside him. He cleared his throat, trying to reset his body, to return his vital signs to normal.

'Would you like to come in and have a coffee?' she asked.

'I don't want to disturb you when you're working.'

'I was going to take a break anyway. I can lock the dogs in the lounge if they're making you nervous.'

He straightened his shoulders and puffed out his chest. 'It's fine. I need to get over this stupid fear anyway.'

'It's a fear?'

'I'll tell you about it over coffee.' He sighed. 'It's all a bit embarrassing, to be honest.'

She nodded. 'Come on in then.'

In the kitchen, Ethan sat at the wooden table and looked around while Fran boiled the kettle. Thick dark beams lined the white ceiling, hinting at the age of the cottage, there was an old yellow Aga against the back wall, an apron-fronted sink and the cabinets had green wooden doors – some were missing handles. It was a warm, lived-in family kitchen and the aroma of spices and woodsmoke hung in the air. It suited Fran and he realised that it was the type of home he'd expected to find her living in. She didn't seem the type to reside in a swanky new apartment with shiny surfaces and chrome gadgets, or to live somewhere spotlessly minimalist. Fran was an artist, a collector, and her home reflected her personality. Ethan liked it instantly and felt himself relax as the heat from the Aga filled the room. He could happily sit here all day, even with the dogs eyeing him from their beds, which were placed wherever there was space in the kitchen. They didn't look as though they were going to pounce on him or as if they resented his presence; in fact, now that they'd settled, they seemed indifferent to him. He'd take indifference over growling any day.

'Milk and sugar?' Fran asked.

'Just milk, please.'

Fran brought two mugs to the table and set them down.

A low grumbling from under the table made them both peer beneath it to see the little white dog that had growled at Ethan yesterday. Fran reached out a hand and the dog shuffled over to her and licked her fingers.

'Come here, boy.'

She lifted the small white dog onto her lap and he sat there staring across the table at Ethan. His shoulders tightened, but he vowed to remain calm. This was Fran's home, the other dogs weren't bothered by him being there, and this tiny dog couldn't do any harm, could it?

'I don't think he likes me.' It was worth checking what Fran thought.

'He doesn't know you to dislike you.' Fran rubbed the dog's ears. 'I think he must have had an unpleasant experience with a man at some point because he seems fine with women.'

'Poor boy. Will you keep him?'

The dog tilted its head and sniffed at the air.

'He's settling in and my dogs have made him welcome, but I don't know yet. It depends if I can find someone who'll adopt him. I'm always happy to take dogs in but I have so many passing through here that if I adopted every single one, I wouldn't have any room left.'

'Tilly would probably like to meet him.'

'Does she like dogs?'

'She loves animals of all sorts. She's asked for rabbits, cats, dogs, you name it.'

'I have cats here too but they tend to spend most of their time in the bedrooms or chasing mice and other small furries in the outbuildings. Sometimes they sneak upstairs to lie on the beds, but not every day. They're far more independent than dogs.'

Ethan nodded. 'I haven't given in about getting a pet up to this point because we didn't have anyone to help in Bath and the extra responsibility seemed daunting, but perhaps now we're here, she can have a pet of some kind.'

'Like a dog?' Fran raised her eyebrows.

Ethan shuddered. 'Uh… not sure about that. It's a big step, that one.'

'What happened to you to make you fear dogs so much?'

'Simple story, really, although telling it always makes me flinch. I was about seven and I was playing in the park with some school friends. Two dogs were off their leads, playing in the adjacent field. One of them got a bit overexcited and ran into the park. For some reason, it decided that I looked like fun and it bit me.' He felt warmth spread into his face. 'Right on the bottom.'

'No!' Her eyes widened behind her glasses.

'It did. I was wearing rather small shorts – well I was only young – and it took a chunk out of my left bum cheek.' The area smarted now as if in response to the memory. He'd heard that people who lost limbs could still feel them itching or aching and sometimes he was convinced he was suffering from the same thing with his bum cheek.

'So you have a part of your bottom missing?' Fran wasn't laughing but he could see the amusement battling concern in her eyes. He hoped she wasn't going to ask for proof because it wasn't an area he was keen to expose, especially in a room filled with dogs.

'It's nothing really, just a faint white scar now, but at the time I was so small that it looked far worse. And there was rather a lot of blood.'

'Your poor thing. That must have been terrifying.' Fran shook her head. 'No wonder you're scared of dogs.'

'It wasn't a great childhood experience and made me very wary of them.'

'Well, of course it would. No one wants to lose a chunk of their bottom to a dog bite.'

'The owner was horrified and explained that the dog was still basically a pup but my parents were furious, especially my mum. She would have had the dog put down but the owner promised to take it to training classes and to never let it off lead in public places again, so she relented.'

'What about you, though?'

'I couldn't sit down properly for a while but I guess it could have been worse.'

Fran nodded. 'It could have been far worse. It was lucky it wasn't your face or neck.'

'And that is why I'm nervous around dogs. In my experience, they're unpredictable. It makes me worry for Tilly because she's so keen to pet any animal she encounters and even though I've warned her that not all dogs are friendly, she still approaches them. Sometimes my heart is in my mouth when we go out.'

'Yes, she does need to be a bit more careful because some dogs are nervous around children, although I can't imagine Tilly invading a dog's space in a way that would make it nervous enough to react aggressively. Dogs can be unpredictable, but when you're around them a lot you get to know them and to understand their body language. I would never leave a small child alone with a dog, but as long as they're trained and feel secure in their environment, they can be loyal and protective companions.'

The dog on her lap turned its head and licked her chin.

'This little one will make a lovely pet once he's calmed down and accepted that not everyone is out to hurt or abandon him. It's about trust and mutual respect.'

'A bit like people, then.' Ethan stumbled over his words, knowing he'd revealed more than he intended. 'What I mean is... that when we get hurt, it can take us time to heal and to accept that not everyone is out to get us or abandon us.'

'Exactly.' Fran nodded. 'Trust has to be earned.'

'Thanks for the coffee.' Ethan drained his mug then set it on the table.

'Any time.'

'I guess I should get back. Cakes to bake and all that.'

'If you don't have to rush off right this minute... would you like to see my studio?'

Ethan met Fran's pretty eyes. 'I'd love to see it. Thank you.'

He hadn't wanted to leave but also didn't want to impose if Fran had things she needed to do. This was the perfect excuse to stay a bit longer at her invitation.

'Come on then.'

Fran stood up and gently set the small dog on the floor, then led the way through the kitchen and through a door into a small extension.

—

Fran had been surprised to see Ethan on her doorstep that morning but also pleased. After he'd seemed afraid of the dogs, when he'd come to get the box of mugs for the tea shop, she'd been disappointed, but today he'd made an effort to explain why he was afraid of them and no wonder! If she'd been bitten by a dog as a child, and lost part of her bottom, she'd probably have felt the same.

She led him into her studio then closed the door behind her. The studio was warm from the log burner in the corner and brightly lit from the strip lights overhead. She needed to have good lighting in here so she could see exactly what she was doing. On summer days, there was plenty of natural light flooding in through the big windows, but on dark winter days and in the evenings when she had a project she needed to finish, she was glad of the electric lighting.

Ethan wandered around, peering at the work on the shelves ready to be boxed up and at the works in progress. The painting she was working on for Holly and Rich was on her easel, covered by a dust sheet.

'What's under here?' he asked, fingering the corner of the sheet.

'It's a gift for Holly and Rich. They're getting married after Christmas so I'm painting them a landscape of Greenacres.'

'Are you one of those artists who doesn't like people looking at their work until it's finished?' he asked.

Fran nodded. 'Sorry.'

'Hey, don't apologise. I respect that. I'm the same when I'm baking a wedding cake. I guess it's superstition really, but it's a bit like the idea that the bride and groom shouldn't see each other before the wedding in case it leads to bad luck. I always worry that something will go wrong and I'll have to start from scratch and it's a lot of work.'

'You make wedding cakes?'

'Sometimes.' He shrugged. 'They're not my speciality but I do make them from time to time. At the moment, even though it's a bit late in the day and they won't have time to mature as well as I'd like, I need to focus on making more Christmas cakes, especially if we're going to go ahead with our open doors for dinner on Christmas Day.'

'What do you mean?'

'Last night, over dinner, we were talking about what we could do at the tea shop over the festive season and we agreed that we'd like to open the doors on Christmas Day to anyone who might be otherwise lonely. We'll offer a free dinner and company and a chance for people to be with others instead of being alone.'

A flush spread across Fran's décolletage. What a thoughtful man.

'Ethan, that's wonderful!'

He nodded. 'I think so too.'

'Lots of people don't have anyone and to know that there's somewhere they could go on Christmas Day for company and delicious food will be such a lift for them.'

'What do you do on the big day?'

'Sometimes I'm here alone with the dogs, sometimes I go to Greenacres and sometimes my parents are home. They won't be here this year though.'

'So… will you be going to Greenacres?'

She met his beautiful green eyes. 'I have been invited but I also don't like to impose. Holly and her family are lovely but this year they have so much on with their baby, Luke, and her granny Glenda has been a bit under the weather and they have the wedding right after Christmas and—'

'Then come to Rosewood!'

They both froze. Ethan's eyes widened. Fran's heart thudded in her chest.

'Shall I? I could help with everything. I'd see to the dogs in the morning then drive over for a few hours before coming home afterwards.'

He nodded. 'Yes, come. There'll be plenty to do and it would be lovely to have you there.'

'Okay... I will.'

Fran was warmed right through by the offer and by the prospect of spending Christmas Day doing something worthwhile instead of just stuffing her face with turkey and consuming her bodyweight in chocolate or feeling that she was imposing on Holly's family. It wasn't that they ever made her feel unwelcome or as if she was imposing, but Holly had Rich and Luke and another baby on the way. The last thing she needed was more pressure and another mouth to feed, and although Fran would have helped with the cooking and washing up and so on, now she had an alternative and Holly wouldn't feel bad if Fran didn't go to Greenacres. Plus, she would get to spend Christmas Day with Ethan and Tilly, as well as Audrey and her family – all people she really liked and enjoyed being around. It sounded perfect.

'So this is your potter's wheel, eh?'

Ethan had straddled the stool attached to the table with the wheel on it. His long legs were bent at the knees and Fran couldn't help noticing how muscular his thighs were in his jeans, hinting at the fact that he exercised regularly. She wondered how firm they would be if she touched them, if she ran her hands over them and up to...

She shook herself from the fantasy. What was happening to her?

'Would you like to have a go?' Fran forced the image of Ethan's naked thighs from her mind.

'I've never tried this before, but isn't it really difficult?'

'It takes some getting used to but it can be a lot of fun once you've mastered the skillset.'

'Go on then, but I'll probably be rubbish.'

'I bet you'll be a natural.' Was it hot in the studio today? She ran the back of her hand over her forehead.

'I'll give it my best shot.' He grinned and his face lit up.

Fran handed him a lump of clay. 'Right... the first thing you need to do is to prepare the clay, which means that you need to get all the air out of it.'

'Why's that?'

'It can cause the clay to crack during firing, which will ruin whatever you've made.'

'Okay, so how do I get the air out?'

'You knead it like bread dough. You should be good at that.'

'I am good at making bread.' He nodded.

Ethan started to knead the clay and Fran watched, mesmerised, as his strong hands worked it, turning it easily and expertly, twisting it to compress it so that the tiny air bubbles popped. She could have watched him work like that all day, and realised that she'd like to watch him making bread dough one day too. The bonus with that might be that she'd get to eat it afterwards and she did love freshly baked bread.

'Is it ready now?' he asked, holding it up for her inspection.

'It looks good. Now we need to put the bat on the wheel to provide a surface for the clay.'

Fran selected one from her range and attached it to the wheel.

'What am I making?' he asked, a smile playing on his lips.

'How about a bowl? You could give it to Audrey for Christmas.'

'Brilliant idea.'

'Place the clay on the centre of the bat and start the wheel.'

Ethan did as he was told.

'Now apply water to the clay and push it up and down to ensure there's no wobble.'

'No... what?'

'It means make sure that it's centred so you don't lose control of the clay.'

'Okay...'

Fran stepped closer to Ethan. She was almost touching him and she could feel the heat emanating from his large frame. She watched carefully as he tried to run his hands up and down the clay. This was always tricky for beginners and she bit her lip as he struggled to keep control of the slippery wet lump.

'You need to open the clay up.'

'How?' He glanced at her, panic in his eyes.

'Hold on.'

She leant over and placed her hands on the clay too, helping him to steady it, then guiding his other hand to the middle and pushing his thumb down into the centre. She was so close to him she could smell his sandalwood cologne and the clean fresh scent of his skin. She could feel his warmth against the side of her body and every so often, as she moved, his blonde hair tickled her cheek.

She turned her head and found him gazing up at her and her eyes wantonly roamed his face, his mouth, his broad shoulders, the way that his Adam's apple bobbed. On the plate, the clay collapsed and fluttered to one side, forgotten, but Ethan and Fran's hands remained joined, sticky with wet clay, their fingers sliding together.

Before she could stop herself, Fran had turned and wrapped her arms around Ethan's neck and they were nose to nose, forehead to forehead and mouth to mouth. They kissed gently, exploring each other tentatively, and as the kiss deepened, Fran moaned with desire. She had never experienced such a connection with a man before and she wanted more...

When Ethan pulled away gently, Fran almost cried with disappointment.

The kiss had been so sweet, his lips full and sensual under hers. Everything inside her had felt alive, on fire, illuminated, and her chest heaved with yearning and longing as something deep inside her unfolded, loosened, opened.

Ethan held her there, perched on his one knee as he gasped, his cheeks red, his pupils dilated, his brows meeting in a frown of confusion.

'Ethan... I'm sorry. I don't know how that happened. I don't make a habit of bringing men in here to seduce them at my pottery wheel.' Her voice was husky, betraying her lust.

He shook his head. 'I didn't think that you did, it's just that... it was amazing... but... we can't do this.'

'No...' Fran frowned. 'Why not?' She wanted to pull him closer and to kiss him again, to wrap her legs around him and surrender to the sensations and the yearning flooding through her body. Need was overtaking reason and she wanted to submit to it like never before.

'I... I have Tilly and... you're... pregnant. And isn't there a father on the scene too?'

It was as if someone had dropped a bucket of icy water over Fran's head. *Of course!* The fictional pregnancy. A partner she hadn't yet thought about. What was she going to do about that?

Bloody hell!

Fran stood up on shaky legs and took a few deep breaths. She couldn't believe the effect Ethan had upon her. So that was what desire felt like. She'd been with men before and enjoyed their company and the physical side of things but it had never felt like that. Ethan was just... *Wow!* And they had only shared a kiss, so she couldn't imagine what making love to him would feel like.

But now she would never find out because he thought she was pregnant and possibly had a partner on the scene. She wanted to tell him that there was no man around, no father to her fictional baby, but if she started that conversation she would have to tell even more lies, so perhaps it was better just to leave the dust to settle. And, of course, Ethan had to put his daughter first, which was admirable.

'Would you like another coffee?' she asked, keen to try to act as if what had just happened, hadn't happened at all. She wiggled her fingers, suddenly aware of how sticky they were and how it wouldn't be easy to leave this moment behind; it would cling to them like cold, wet clay if they didn't make the effort to move on. Their skin would be stained with grey traces of clay; their hearts would be grey too, devoid of any colour after the beauty of this moment when everything had seemed so bright and clear. She didn't want that, didn't want to lose Ethan completely, so they had to put this behind them and become good friends as she hoped they could be.

'A cool drink would be great, thanks.' He smiled, but there was tension in the way he held himself and wariness in his eyes and it saddened her.

'Sure. I'll go and get us something.' She washed her hands in the sink in the studio, picking the clay from her nails and the creases of her knuckles, then went through to the kitchen, leaving Ethan behind so he could wash his hands and take a few moments to recover.

As she filled two glasses with water, Fran was chilled right through. She really liked Ethan but he'd made it clear that nothing could ever happen between them. It seemed so unfair, but then their situation was hardly ideal. Of course he had to think of his daughter and then there was the pregnancy that Fran hated deceiving him about, but what else could she do? Fran had made a promise to Holly and she had to keep it, even if that promise involved keeping a secret that was part of the reason why she couldn't get close to the first man she had liked this much in her whole life.

Chapter 9

After school finished on Friday, Ethan picked Tilly up and took her home to Rosewood. She changed into jeans, a jumper and boots then ate the snack that he prepared for her. They had closed the tea shop at two so they could get everything ready for the annual tree-decorating event. It was something that Ethan recalled from his childhood and he had good memories of joining in, with his mum and dad looking on, feeling happy and secure at the way his mum's love and approval filled her eyes. Audrey told him that it was a big event now and that lots of villagers came to participate.

He'd been baking all day: mince pies, gingerbread stars, iced elves and evergreen trees, and putting the finishing touches on the ten Christmas cakes. He'd made some savoury snacks including cheese straws, mini three cheese pizzas and turkey, sage and cranberry puff pastry parcels. The kitchen at the tea rooms had smelt incredibly festive and it had made him look forward to Christmas Day in a way that he hadn't done in a long time.

It had been a strange week, as after his trip to see Fran to deliver his apology, he'd been even more confused than before. He'd been having fun trying out his hand at pottery, aware that something was electrifying the air between them, but trying to act as if he hadn't noticed because he didn't intend on acting upon it. Then Fran had tried to help him with the clay, and things had gone wrong. Or was it right? It had felt pretty damned right when they touched and when they kissed but it couldn't possibly be right because he had Tilly to consider and Fran had a baby on the way and possibly a partner – although she still hadn't confirmed or denied the latter. But it didn't matter one way or the other, because Ethan was in no place to get involved with someone. So why had his heart pounded as they'd kissed and why had he dreamt about her every time he'd closed his eyes to sleep since it had happened? In his dreams she was wearing those dungarees with her cute headscarf, and had clay on her hands, her arms and her cheeks. They'd embraced and kissed, then he'd removed those dungarees and the things he'd imagined happening when he'd actually been in her studio had unfolded. He woke from the dreams frustrated and sad, because they couldn't become reality, and it seemed that his unconscious mind was craving the beautiful artist and trying to tempt him with more thoughts about her. He had to admit that he found Fran completely enchanting and he had no idea how to deal with the feelings she evoked inside him. He didn't want to feel them, and yet, he did. He didn't want to surrender to them, and yet, he did. It was all so bewildering and yet so... exciting.

'Daddy?' Tilly interrupted his thoughts.

'Yes, my angel?'

'Should I wear my bobble hat this evening?'

'I think so, Tilly. It's very cold out already and it's probably a good idea to take your gloves too.'

'Okay, Daddy, will do!'

Tilly ran off upstairs to find her gloves and Ethan washed her plate and glass then set them on the draining board. The cottage his aunt had given them to live in at Rosewood already felt quite homely and Tilly had settled in well there. It was nice to have family so close, to know that if he ever needed anyone, he could have help at a moment's notice. Of course, after so long being independent and self-reliant, it was also a bit strange, but in a good way. He didn't feel quite so alone any more and there was comfort in knowing that if anything should happen to him, then Tilly would have people around her who cared. He wanted to be around for Tilly for a very long time but losing his own mum meant he was always aware of how fragile life could be. Knowing he had family near had eased the pressure on his shoulders and he hoped it would enable him to enjoy things more, without worrying all the time that something could go wrong.

Unfortunately, this evening, before they headed out for the festivities, Melanie was due to Skype Tilly. She didn't do it often enough in his opinion, but he was sometimes glad that it didn't happen more regularly, as it occasionally unsettled Tilly and sent her into the *I want my mummy* vortex. Of course, it wasn't really Melanie that Tilly wanted because Melanie had never been the mother that Tilly needed or deserved. But then Melanie had never wanted to be a mother and when she'd discovered that she was pregnant, she had considered terminating the pregnancy, but it had been Ethan's persuasion that had led her to see it through. Looking back, he could see that her heart had never been in motherhood and he couldn't blame her for that; it was just how she felt. Though how she could bear to be away from Tilly was beyond him.

He went through to the hallway and checked his reflection in the full-length mirror. He didn't really care what his ex-wife thought of his appearance but he also didn't like the thought of her looking down her nose at him, so he always made sure that he was as presentable as possible before her video calls. It was about his pride and goodness knew how little of that he'd had left when Melanie had walked away from him, but he was trying to cling to what self-esteem remained.

Tilly trotted down the stairs and into the hallway.

'Got them, Daddy!'

'Good girl. Are you ready to speak to your mum?'

Tilly hugged Glitterbug to her chest. She must have got the toy off her bed when she was upstairs. 'Do I have to?'

'What do you mean, Tilly?' He crouched down in front of her. 'You like to chat to your mum, don't you?'

Tilly stared hard at the floor, unblinking, in a way that worried Ethan. It looked as if she were trying to control her emotions and surely six was a bit young to be suppressing tears?

'Sometimes I do but today I want to go and do the decorating with Aunty Audrey and Harper and Scarlett. I like being with them because they're nice and fun and kind and they don't make me feel silly like I said the wrong thing.'

'And we will go to decorate the tree, but you're meant to speak to Mum first and tell her about your week.' He sucked in a breath. 'And you never say the wrong things so you don't need to feel silly, ever. Okay?'

Tilly pouted at him and he had to bite his tongue. He completely understood why she didn't want to speak to Melanie. Two weeks ago, when Tilly had waited for Melanie to Skype, she'd called an hour late and only stayed online for five minutes – during which time she corrected Tilly's grammar and vocabulary at least six times – as she'd had an evening meeting to get to. It just wasn't good enough and he was concerned about the message that it was sending to Tilly – that she wasn't as important as work. But in spite of this type of behaviour from Melanie in the past, Tilly had always been keen to speak to her mum, so something must have changed.

'Tilly, is there any other reason why you don't want to speak to Mum?'

She sighed and tucked Glitterbug under her chin. 'I don't like to say, Daddy.' Tilly pushed her face into Glitterbug's head.

'You can tell me anything, Tilly. I love you and I'm not going to judge you for your feelings. Remember how we talked about feelings and how they aren't things we can help but we can try to deal with them? I want to try to help you understand your feelings if I can.'

Tilly sighed and looked up at him. 'Aunty Audrey is much nicer than Mummy. Aunty Audrey always hugs her daughters and tells them she loves them and makes them dinner and cakes and laughs at their jokes, even when they're not funny. Mummy's never here to make my dinner or to hug me and when I told her a knock-knock joke she didn't laugh at all. Not one teeny bit and that… it made me sad, Daddy. And she makes me feel like I've said things wrong and I don't want to feel sad today. Can I speak to her tomorrow instead?'

Ethan gently took hold of Tilly's shoulders and kissed her forehead. 'Tilly, it's entirely up to you, and I do understand why you feel that way, but if you don't speak to her today, I'm not sure when she'll call next.'

He watched as his young daughter thought about what he'd said. It was so hard to see her running the idea through her mind, deciding whether her mother was worth speaking to or not, and he realised that Tilly probably understood more than he gave her credit for. In her six years she had worked out that her mother was unreliable and selfish, even if Tilly didn't exactly understand the concepts themselves. She'd seen how Audrey was as a mother and compared it to Melanie's behaviour and was drawing her own conclusions.

'Her calls are always fast, aren't they?' Tilly met his gaze, her pretty brown eyes serious as they studied him.

'Usually, yes.'

'Okay then… I will speak to her but only for a short time. It can be a fast call and I won't say much and then she can't make me feel silly.'

'Okay.'

He nodded, gave her a quick hug, then went to turn the laptop on. He wished he could take all of Tilly's worries and sadness away and give her the mum she deserved, but all he could do was try to help her to deal with the situation and her emotions and help her to work through them.

The video call came in ten minutes late and by the time Melanie appeared on the screen of his laptop, Ethan was already annoyed with her. He wanted to give her a piece of his mind but would never do that in front of Tilly.

'Hello, Cornwall!' Melanie sang as she waved both hands, her long pointy nails with their fancy manicure catching the light. There even appeared to be diamantes sparkling on some of them, which to Ethan seemed to be highly impractical. What if they caught on something or fell into a bowl of soup or cereal? The length of her nails made him shiver, as he couldn't imagine how she could do anything with nails like that, but then that was her problem and not for him to worry about.

Tilly glanced at Ethan then back at the screen. Something passed over her face but Ethan wasn't sure if it was impatience or exasperation at Melanie's over-the-top greeting.

'Hello, Mummy.'

Melanie leant closer to the camera. 'Well look at you, Tillyo. You have grown so much, my little pumpkin.'

Melanie called her daughter Tillyo when she was trying to sound affectionate.

'I'm not a pumpkin, Mummy, but I have grown and I need new school shoes.'

'Do you now?' Melanie frowned. 'Are you all right for those, Ethan, or do you need me to transfer something across—'

'It's fine!' Ethan cut in. 'I'll get her feet measured next week. Her shoes aren't that small anyway but one of her new friends has a pair with a doll in the heels and Tilly wants a pair of those.'

'I do!' Tilly nodded at the laptop. 'They are so pretty and you can get ones with flashing lights in the heels and a doll or a fairy and... and....' Tilly stopped talking and pressed her lips together as if remembering that she wasn't going to say much.

'Then you must have them, baby girl.' Melanie nodded.

Ethan cringed. This was what Melanie did. She failed at parenting in general then made a video call and seemed like the most doting, loving mum a girl could want. For all of five minutes. He hated what it did to Tilly in terms of messing with her heart and her head and he hoped that as she got older, she'd see it objectively for what it was and not be hurt by it. She was already starting to see through the act but didn't always understand it. Ethan wanted Tilly to see that Melanie's behaviour was a reflection of herself and no one else, especially not Tilly.

'Thank you, Mummy.' Tilly sat Glitterbug on the edge of the table.

'Is that Glitterbug I can see?' Melanie asked.

'Yes.'

'Hello, GB!' Melanie laughed, tossing her silky brown hair over her shoulders then running her long nails through it before scooping it back over one shoulder. It was a gesture that Ethan had once thought of as sexy; it had, in the past, made his heart beat faster, but now he knew it was just her way of buying time to think about what to say next. Funny how knowing someone meant that you saw through their body language and their art of deception.

'Mummy... are you coming home for Christmas?' Tilly asked.

'What?' Melanie's perfectly shaped brows shot up her forehead and she blinked rapidly.

'Well, my friend Frankie said that her mum is in the army and she will be home for Christmas. She's so excited and I thought that seeing as how you're not even a soldier, so you don't have to protect anyone with a tank and a gun, then you could come home and see me and Daddy.' Tilly stared at the screen, her mouth set in a thin line, and Ethan realised that she was testing Melanie.

Melanie licked her lips and her eyes flickered to Ethan. 'Did your daddy suggest this?'

Tilly shook her head and Ethan followed suit. He wasn't taking the blame for this one.

'Not at all,' Tilly said, sounding sixty rather than six. 'I just thought I'd ask seeing as how Frankie's mum can manage it.'

Ethan felt a chuckle rising from his gut and he coughed to try to dislodge it. Melanie had turned puce and was clearly not amused at Tilly's reasoning.

'No, Tilly, Mummy is very busy here in Dubai and I will not be coming to Pendallow Sandbay for Christmas.'

'For goodness sake, Mummy, get the name right.' Tilly tutted. 'It's *Penhallow Sands.*'

Melanie glared at them from the laptop screen. 'Whatever! Stupid seaside names. Anyway… I have a dinner this evening with—'

'It's fine, Mummy.' Tilly cut her off and raised a hand to the screen. 'Daddy and I have important plans this evening and we can't possibly spare you any more time, so enjoy your shampoon reception and we'll enjoy our evening.'

With that, Tilly blew a kiss at the screen, got up and left the kitchen with Glitterbug under her arm. Ethan watched her go, amazed at what had just happened. The calls usually ended with Tilly tearful and desperate for one more minute from her mother, but instead his six-year-old daughter had got sassy and put Melanie firmly in her place. Melanie glared at him now, bug-eyed with shock. When her smile slipped and her anger rose, the beautiful façade that she so carefully erected crumbled and she didn't look so beautiful any more. He'd read something once about inner ugliness finding its way out and showing on the face and he wondered if that would happen to Melanie, or if she'd repent about what she'd done to her daughter at some point in time, and how she would look then. External beauty faded anyway, and that was why Ethan had always appreciated what he could see in someone's eyes. Inner beauty shone through and made a person more appealing. Perhaps that was one way to interpret the saying 'beauty is in the eye of the beholder'.

'Was that your fault?' she croaked finally.

'I have no idea where that came from, Melanie, but let's be honest, you kind of deserved it.'

Melanie's eyes widened, then she adjusted the low neckline of the black dress she was wearing and leant forwards, clearly wanting to flash Ethan a glimpse of her enhanced cleavage. In the past it would have floored him, left him yearning for days gone by and wondering *what if*… Now, not so much. In fact, not at all. His daughter was starting to see Melanie for what she was and he found that it had helped with his own perception of her. But something else had also changed inside him. He might have only known Fran for a short time, but she had integrity and a calm air about her that he'd never seen in Melanie. His ex-wife was always too groomed, too keen to radiate confidence and coolness, too concerned with appearances and how she could use them to control other people. Fran wore dungarees and headscarves and got covered in clay and dog hair. She wore glasses rather than having her eyes lasered as Melanie had, and she ate cake and ice cream sundaes and laughed at her own jokes. She was kind and warm and funny and made Ethan feel comfortable, not undermined. There might not be any chance of anything happening between him and Fran, but in just a few weeks, he'd seen the opposite of Melanie and it had given him a much-needed boost. There was life after this woman and it was a life worth living.

'You think I deserved that?' Melanie scowled at him, the attractive mask now fully gone.

'I'm not going to argue with you, Melanie, but you should take some time to think about it. Tilly's getting older, she's at a new school and she's surrounded by people who care about her. She's learning all the time, changing and growing and her eyes are opening to the world and people's behaviour. She's a bright child and she amazes me every day with how much she already knows and with her thirst for knowledge.' He coughed then, realising that the sassiness had probably come, in part, from watching and being around Scarlett.

'Well… whatever. She knows that I love her.' Melanie applied some lipstick, using the screen as her mirror.

'Does she? Are you sure about that? Actions speak louder than words, Melanie.' Ethan paused to swallow his irritation. He didn't want an argument with Melanie and he didn't want to ruin her evening. He just wanted her to try to show her daughter some love and attention before it was too late and she lost her completely. 'Let me know when you want to call next. Try not to leave it too long. Things can change quickly for a six-year-old.'

Melanie nodded then ended the call and Ethan was left staring at his laptop, which featured a montage of photos of Tilly from when she was a tiny baby right up to her first day at Penhallow Sands Primary. She really was growing up very quickly and Melanie was missing so much. It was a shame that she hadn't been around for the past two years, but then it had given him far more precious time with his daughter than he might have had if they'd shared custody. Not that it was something Melanie had ever wanted or would be likely to ever want, but even so, he just wished she'd take more of an interest in Tilly.

He shut the laptop down then closed the lid and stood up. As he turned, he spotted Tilly in the doorway in her coat, hat and gloves.

'Come on then, slow coach!' She grinned at him. 'We're going to have a fun evening.'

'Yes we are,' he replied as he took her proffered hand.

'We have lots of fun times, Daddy, so don't be sad. Mummy is a very silly billy to miss out on this. In fact, she's vermitable... vertible... uh... a *veritable* fool, but it's her loss.'

'Tilly?'

'Yes?'

'Where did you hear that expression?'

'I've been listening to grown-ups talking. Frankie said you hear lots of interesting things if you listen and I'm trying to grow my voa... cabumary.'

'Your voa... cabumary?'

'Yes, because my teacher also said that the more words you have, the better you will be able to speak and write.'

'I see. So is a good voacabumary the same as a good vocabulary?'

Tilly gave a chuckle that tinkled like bells on a sleigh, lifting Ethan's heart high. 'Daddy, you are so silly sometimes. You don't know all the words, remember?'

He laughed. 'Of course I don't. I'll just grab my hat and coat and we can get going.'

'Daddy?'

'Yes?'

'I also think that if I have more words then Mummy can never make me feel silly for using wrong ones.'

He reached out and stroked her cheek and smiled at her. 'You're amazing, Tilly, and you never need worry about things like that. Just be yourself.'

Tilly nodded and he turned and padded up the stairs, smiling with pride at how wonderful his little girl was even as his chest ached because he hated to know that anything caused her pain or sadness. But Tilly was clearly stronger than he sometimes gave her credit for and being here at Rosewood was having a positive effect upon them both.

He found that he was really looking forward to the evening that lay ahead and it felt good. Happiness had evaded him for quite some time, but now it seemed as if it might be within reach and it was all thanks to him accepting the job at the tea shop at Rosewood.

Chapter 10

Fran climbed out of the warmth of her car and hurried towards the tea shop at Rosewood, shivering as the freezing air enveloped her. It was already dusk but the lights in the car park and the thousands of fairy lights that were draped around the lamp posts and the front of the tea shop illuminated her way. They swayed in the breeze, casting their light across the ground like tiny golden flames and making Fran think of tales about fairies and sprites.

The car park was filling up quickly and Fran could see that it was going to be a busy evening, which was a good thing as it meant more business for the tea shop and hopefully more of the locals getting together to celebrate the festive season. Penhallow Sands was a supportive community and she loved living here, especially during the Christmas period when there weren't so many tourists around and the locals had more time to socialise.

Fran pushed open the door of the tea shop and went inside. The warmth embraced her like a hug and the smells of cinnamon and baking greeted her like old friends. After saying hello to some familiar faces, she went up to the counter and found Audrey and Harper serving hot chocolates and mulled wine.

'Hello, Fran, how are you feeling?' Audrey winked at her and Fran knew that she was referring to her fake pregnancy.

'Not too bad thanks.'

'What would you like?' Harper asked, her long blonde hair partially hidden by a thick purple bobble hat.

'I'll take a mulled wine, please.'

'One won't hurt you, I'm sure,' Audrey said. 'It's not too strong as there's a lot of fruit juice and water in it too, and I used to have the odd drink when I was pregnant. Or was it when I was breastfeeding? Gosh, the years fly by and the memories often merge together. Anyway, I know there are guidelines about these things nowadays, but you know what you want to do and no one should tell you otherwise.' Audrey blushed and a tiny muscle in her jaw twitched as if she felt she'd put her foot in it with Fran. 'You do what's right for you, Fran.' Audrey smiled and Fran smiled in return, not wanting her friend to feel awkward.

'Is Holly coming tonight?' Harper asked.

'I don't think so. She hasn't been feeling great what with the p...' Fran bit her lip. 'What with the baby, you know... Luke and her grandmother being a bit off colour and Holly's tired with all the wedding planning and that.' She avoided eye contact and feigned interest in a jar of candy canes on the counter.

'Poor Glenda. I hope she feels better soon.' Audrey handed Fran a steaming mug. 'There you go, love, that will warm you up.'

'Thanks.' Fran went to pay for her drink but Audrey shook her head.

'No you don't, love. It's all free for you this evening. You do enough for us.'

'You pay me for the work I do.' Fran held out the money again.

'And it's beautiful work, so I don't want a penny from you. Just make sure you eat and stay warm because it's freezing out there and... sit down when you need to. There's plenty of food available, so help yourself. Ethan has baked up a storm today!'

'It does smell incredible in here.' Fran's mouth watered.

'Well get stuck in!' Audrey pointed at the tables, which were positively groaning with food, so Fran headed over to them and loaded up a plate. She found herself a seat and made herself comfortable so she could enjoy the food and keep an eye on who came in. She intended on having a good evening and a plate of delicious treats along with a mug of spiced wine was a good place to start.

–

In the yard outside the tea shop, everyone gathered in the chilly evening air. People were holding mugs of steaming mulled wine and hot chocolate and some held plates of food that they'd brought from the tea shop. A small choir stood to one side of the tree singing a variety of Christmas carols and pop songs, filling the yard with festive joy.

Ethan held tightly onto Tilly's hand, nervous about losing her in the crowd, and they went to the table that had been set up with boxes of tree decorations.

'Pick the ones you want.' Ethan gestured at the boxes.

She browsed for a while before deciding, then selected a fat red Santa Claus, a jolly snowman complete with a hat and scarf and a sparkly gold reindeer with a red nose.

'Aren't they pretty, Daddy?' Tilly held them up in turn. 'Can we get some like this for our tree?'

'They're very pretty and yes, we certainly can.'

Audrey clapped her hands and a hush fell over the yard.

'Good evening, everyone, and thanks for joining us! We're delighted to have so many of you here this year for our annual tree decorating. As you will be aware, there are plenty of decorations on the table over there for the children to choose from. We'd like them to line up and take it in turns to place their chosen decorations on the tree. Then it will be the turn of the adults, as you can reach the higher branches. Finally, the lights that my wonderful husband, Gary, has already wound around the tree along with the star at the top will be lit, and that will mean that Christmas at Rosewood tea shop will officially begin!'

A cheer spread through the crowd and Ethan smiled down at Tilly as she gasped with excitement. This was a truly fabulous way to start the festive season. He was enjoying it immensely, so for a young child it must be truly magical.

'Please help yourselves to food from the buffet indoors and don't forget that my daughters, Harper and Scarlett, will be serving mulled wine and hot chocolates all evening, so stay warm with our delicious beverages. There's plenty for everyone. And while I'm here... I would like to say an official welcome to my nephew, Ethan Clarke, and his daughter, Tilly. They recently moved here from Bath and I hope with all my heart that they will fall in love with Penhallow Sands and choose to stay here. Ethan is a talented chef and over the next few weeks you will have the chance to sample plenty of his cooking, so please come to Rosewood to see us regularly.' She smiled at the crowd. 'One more thing... we have decided that this year we will open the doors of the tea shop to anyone who would otherwise be spending Christmas Day alone. So if that means you or someone you know, then come and join us for a free lunch this year and also, please spread the word. Christmas is a special time for many, but it can be difficult if you don't have people around you, so we want to share our day with anyone who doesn't have someone nearby.'

Cheers spread across the yard and people clapped and whistled their approval. Pride spread through Ethan; he was a part of this and he would be there to support this wonderful initiative over the festive season. Offering food and company was one of the simplest things a person could do, and also one of the most effective in boosting someone else's mood. In his opinion, people needed to take better care of each other and Christmas was a good time to start showing some kindness and generosity.

'Okay, children, let's get this tree looking good, shall we?' Audrey said, then the children started to line up.

The choir began to sing *We Wish You a Merry Christmas* and Ethan squeezed Tilly's hand. 'Go on then. Or do you want me to come with you?'

'Don't be silly, Daddy, it's the children's turn first. You'll look funny standing there with all of us. Anyway, I can see Frankie!'

Tilly ran over to her friend and they bounced up and down as they queued, chatting excitedly with the antic-ipation of six-year-old children. He had a sudden vision of what his daughter would be like as an adult and it filled him with pride and love. He hoped he'd be around to watch her grow up and one day even to see her with children of her own if that was the path she chose to follow. A pang followed his elation as he remembered that his mother had missed out on meeting her granddaughter. Nothing was guaranteed; today was to be treasured.

'Hello, Ethan.'

He turned to find Fran at his side. He did a double take because she was so wrapped up in her hat and scarf that he almost didn't recognise her and it was only her voice that enabled him to identify her.

'Hi, Fran.'

'How are you today?'

'I'm okay, thanks.' He nodded slowly. 'You?'

'Yeah, can't complain.'

'Good.' He exhaled and his breath puffed out like smoke and disappeared into the evening air.

'The food is incredible. Did you make it all?'

'The food?'

'Inside.'

'Oh… yes I did. Glad you like it. I'm trying out some new festive recipes and really enjoy experimenting with flavours and amounts of herbs and seasoning. It's all about getting the balance right in order to create something mouth-watering.'

'You've done well!' She nodded. 'And the spiced wine is delicious. The combination of fruit juice and spices is perfect.'

'Sorry?'

'The mulled wine.' She held up her mug.

'You're drinking wine?'

'Yes…'

He shook his head. 'Fran… I know it's not my place to say anything, but surely that's not good for the baby.'

'What?' She tilted her head as if she were struggling to hear him.

'Well… I know there are different views about safe limits of alcohol during pregnancy and all that, but isn't it better not to take any chances at all?'

Fran peered up at him, her glasses reflecting the fairy lights above them, her hat and scarf creating a frame around her pretty face. The tip of her nose was red and her breath was visible in the cold air.

'Ethan… thank you for your concern but I really don't need it. I'm only having one mulled wine and I'm making it last. You do seem like a nice man but you don't have the right to go around telling women what to do with their bodies.'

He winced. 'No! No, sorry, Fran… I… uh… I didn't mean to interfere, it's just that…' He rubbed a hand over his eyes. 'I'm really sorry. It's none of my business. I just don't know if anyone is looking out for you and sometimes, a lot of the time, in fact, I feel bad because of how my ex behaved when she was pregnant and how she's behaved since. She… uh… she did drink when she was pregnant and I'm fairly certain she was having the odd cigarette too, probably her way of rebelling because she didn't really want the baby. And since then… well… she's not exactly been Mum of the Year to Tilly. But… uh… that doesn't give me the right to go around advising all mums–to–be or those with children. You are right about that. Absolutely right.'

Fran nodded but she didn't reply.

'Do you accept my apology?'

'Sure. Don't worry about it. I'm fine.' She flashed a tight smile then looked into her mug. 'See you later.'

As she walked away, Ethan's heart sank into his boots. What was wrong with him? He had no right to push his views onto anyone else and normally, he never did. But there was something about Fran that made him care about her welfare and that of her baby. He still didn't know if there was a man in her life and although it was none of his business either, he found that he wanted to look out for her. She seemed so strong and independent and was clearly capable of taking care of herself, but that didn't mean that it wouldn't be nice for her to have someone to lean on from time to time. Even if Ethan couldn't offer her anything else, and despite their embrace over the clay Fran must know that he could still offer her friendship. He would like to be her friend. He wanted her in this new life that he was building. Christmas was coming and he wanted to see her enjoy the celebrations.

He scanned the yard, looking for her, but she had disappeared, then Tilly caught his attention as she called to him from the tree.

'Look, Daddy! What do you think?'

He smiled and nodded his approval at where she'd placed the decorations she'd selected and she beamed back. He'd almost missed helping her decorate the tree because he'd been thinking about himself and Fran and about what he wanted. It wasn't right; he couldn't be distracted from being a good dad to Tilly.

Ethan had to focus on his daughter now and stop thinking about Fran; he couldn't allow his mind to keep wandering and to indulge in daydreams about her.

He just wished that life had worked out differently so they could have been something more, but he had his priorities and they were what mattered the most.

Fran had hurried away from Ethan and into the tea shop. It was quiet inside with just a few elderly people discussing the Christmas dinner the tea shop was going to offer and one of Audrey's daughters serving behind the counter.

Fran considered asking for another mulled wine but couldn't face the possibility that someone else would comment on her drinking during pregnancy. Besides which, she also had to drive home and wasn't sure how strong the spiced beverage was. Instead, she grabbed a paper plate and got some more food then went to sit down.

As she chewed a cheese straw, savouring the strong cheddar and buttery pastry, she thought about what had just happened. Ethan had been expressing his concern for her unborn child. It had sent her hurtling through a range of emotions: pleasure at his concern, confusion at his interference and anger, first at him for thinking he could tell her how to live her life, then at herself for deceiving him in the first place. There was no baby, not in her belly at least, and she hated how this lie was continuing. It made her want to hide away at home until the new year when Holly would announce her pregnancy to the world and Fran would be free of the fake pregnancy that was causing her so much stress. And most of that stress was centred around Ethan because she found that it was his opinion that was bothering her most. She didn't want him thinking she was pregnant and she certainly didn't want to lie to him any more. That was why she'd walked away rather than discussing the drinking of mulled wine during pregnancy with him. She'd felt terrible leaving him there after he'd apologised but staying would have meant continuing the conversation and she just couldn't face it. It was far too uncomfortable, far too painful and lying went against everything that she'd always thought she was.

Perhaps it was better that she avoided Ethan over the next few weeks so she didn't have to lie to him again. That thought wasn't pleasant, as she really liked him, but neither was the idea of continuing the deception and getting deeper and deeper into the lie while she got closer to the truth being revealed. Whatever would Ethan think about her then? Would he understand her motivations for pretending to be pregnant or would he be outraged at how deceitful she had been? Would he even care either way?

The whole situation was exhausting, so she'd head on home, take a bubble bath and get an early night. Hopefully things would seem clearer in the morning, although until she was free of the fake pregnancy, she couldn't imagine how anything could possibly seem better.

When she headed back out to the yard, she paused in the doorway. Just around the corner from the tea shop were two figures – a tall one and a very short one. As the tall one turned slightly to gaze at the Christmas tree, she could see that it was Ethan. If she left now, she'd have to pass him and Tilly to get to her car, so she'd wait in the cover of the doorway and hope that they moved on.

'Daddy?' Tilly's sweet voice filled the night air.

'Yes, my angel?'

'I love you.'

'I love you too.'

'I've had fun this evening.'

'Me too.'

Tilly raised her arms and Ethan lifted her and settled her on his arm. It made Fran's heart melt to see how close they were, a real father–daughter team.

'I was thinking about earlier and Mummy and… well… I like it with just us two.'

'Like we've been since Mummy went to Dubai?'

'Yes, Daddy.'

'I know, Tilly, and I'm sorry that Mummy isn't around for you.'

Tilly shook her head. 'I don't mind, Daddy. It's just you and me and Aunty Audrey and her family now and that's how I want it to be. I'm really happy here.'

'I'm happy that you're happy.' Ethan kissed Tilly's forehead.

'Just us, Daddy.'

'Time to get you home.'

'One more hot chocolate?' Tilly asked and Fran held her breath. If they came this way, she'd have no choice but to reveal her presence and to try to explain that she'd been there all along.

'You can have another one tomorrow, Tilly. I think two is plenty for one evening.'

'It was worth a try.' Tilly giggled.

'Let's get back to the cottage and you can have a glass of milk as an alternative.'

'Thanks, Daddy!'

Fran stepped out of the shadows of the doorway as Ethan carried Tilly across the yard to their cottage. He obviously loved his daughter and she him. They were a team of two and if Ethan were to become involved with someone like Fran, then that woman would – inadvertently – be taking some of his time and attention away from his daughter. Fran wouldn't want to do that to the little girl as it sounded like she'd already been through enough with her absent mother.

Fran would never want to get between Ethan and Tilly in any way, shape or form. It was becoming clearer by the day that any romance between Fran and Ethan just wasn't meant to be.

Chapter 11

A few days later, Fran and Holly walked into the bridal shop where Holly had come for a dress fitting. Fran hadn't seen the dress yet, as when they'd initially gone dress shopping, Holly hadn't been able to make up her mind, so she'd gone back the next day alone to decide upon her favourite. However, Holly had then seen a different dress in a different shop, so Fran had no idea what to expect. Fran's stomach was filled with butterflies because she knew this would be an emotional experience. She'd loved Holly her whole life and they'd shared such a lot, so the idea of seeing her best friend in her wedding gown was overwhelming. She had stuffed plenty of tissues into her bag and was taking lots of deep, steadying breaths, but tears were already hovering behind her eyelids, threatening to fall.

A tiny old-fashioned bell on the shop door tinkled as it closed behind them and Fran looked around. The shop in Newquay was old and smelt of lavender and thyme and something else, a slightly musty aroma that hung in the air and presumably came from the heavy garments and dress bags. It wasn't unpleasant but it made Fran feel as though she'd stepped back in time and that outside, at any moment, there could be an air raid warning or a Victorian barouche could pass drawn by two large blinkered horses.

A shiver ran down her spine and she shook herself, amused at her thoughts triggered by the smell of the place.

The shop was empty, and Fran wasn't surprised because it was tucked away on a side street. When she had asked how Holly had found it, her friend had told her that she'd seen a leaflet at the dry cleaners a few weeks before she'd gone looking for a dress, and something had drawn her there when she'd been trying to decide on what type of dress she wanted for her big day.

'It's very quiet, isn't it?' Fran asked.

Holly nodded. 'It was like this last time. That's a good thing, though, because it means they have a wider selection of dresses available. Some of them are quite retro.'

'How retro?'

'Vintage sixties and seventies.'

'Wow!' That impressed Fran, as she loved fashion from other decades. She wouldn't have been at all surprised to find a regency frock on the rails, complete with demi train and short French sleeves edged with lace. 'Do they have originals?'

'Oh yes. I tried lots on when I came here the first time. I couldn't stop.' Holly giggled, her pretty face lighting up with her smile. 'Ooh!' She grimaced. 'Here it comes... another wave of nausea.'

'Cracker time?'

'Please.'

Fran opened her handbag and pulled out the small plastic bag containing salted crackers that she'd brought along just in case. Holly's morning sickness was getting worse and only crackers and ginger ale seemed to help.

As Holly munched on a cracker, her attention focused on overcoming the queasiness, Fran wandered around the shop looking at the gowns on display. There were ivory ones, peach ones and bright white ones. Some had sequins on the bodices and hems, some had long sleeves and some were backless. Some had short skirts and some had fishtails. Fran found herself yearning to try some of them on just to see how they felt against her skin, but that would be a bit weird seeing as how she wasn't getting married.

'Ladies, my apologies!'

A small old woman with short white hair, a tanned face, deep lines around her eyes and mouth and silver rimmed half-moon glasses approached them. In her powder-blue two-piece suit, she looked as though she was off to a wedding herself, and all she needed was a fascinator or a hat to finish off her outfit.

'Demelza!' Holly finished her cracker then opened her arms and the two women embraced.

'So good to see you, poppet.' Demelza peered up at Holly and Fran realised that the woman must be no more than four foot two inches. She was tiny! 'And who is this?' Demelza gestured at Fran.

'This is my best friend, Fran, and I'm hoping that you can find her a dress too.'

'What?' Fran frowned. 'But I'm not getting married.'

'But you are going to be my maid of honour, aren't you?'

Fran opened her mouth to speak but nothing came out. Instead, her vision blurred. Holly had spoken to her about this a while ago, but then they'd been interrupted, and time had gone on and Fran hadn't wanted to raise it again. After all, not everyone needed to have bridesmaids and follow traditions and all that, and Holly was getting married at Greenacres, so it wouldn't be a big fancy wedding ceremony. It was why they'd decided to get married at the vineyard, because they wanted to keep things as informal and relaxed as possible. And, of course, it kept their costs down, which was an important consideration for everyone these days, especially those with young children to raise. Fran was happy to be going as a guest. Plus, not buying bridesmaids dresses would surely save Holly and Rich a lot of money.

'Holly... I can wear something that I already have if you definitely want me to do this. Save your money for other things. I'm sure I have a few smart frocks at the back of my wardrobe.'

'No, Fran. I know you have some pretty dresses, but I want you at my side in a new dress bought especially for the occasion. I've been thinking about it and you're so important to me that I need to have you as my maid of honour.'

'But the wedding's less than four weeks away.'

'I know, and I meant to sort this out sooner but I've been feeling so poorly and I've been sidetracked by... other things.'

'Aren't you well?' Demelza asked, concern etched on her wrinkled face.

'I'm okay.' Holly smiled. 'Just...'

'You are with child?'

Holly nodded.

Demelza held out a hand to Holly's middle. 'May I?'

Holly glanced at Fran then back at Demelza. 'Okay.'

The elderly lady placed her hand flat on Holly's stomach and her eyes widened.

'It's very early days,' Holly explained. 'But I have been feeling dreadful and I swear I'm already gaining weight, even though the nausea means I'm eating less.'

Demelza shook her head. 'Holly, my poppet, you have a special pregnancy.'

'I do?' Holly frowned. 'How so? Am I carrying a genius or someone who's going to stop global warming and put an end to world hunger? Wouldn't that be amazing, Fran, if Rich and I had a child who helped to save the world?'

Fran smiled and nodded. 'Amazing.'

'It is not that.' Demelza shook her head. 'Well, your child might save the planet someday, but that wasn't what I meant. I can't see that far ahead, but what I can tell you is that... There is more than one baby in there.'

'What?' Holly's hand flew to her chest then she emitted an uncertain laugh. 'There can't be.'

'It's good news, though.' Demelza smiled. 'Two beautiful babies to fill your world with love.'

'But I already have Luke.'

'And he will have two lovely little sisters to care for.'

Holly held out a hand to Fran. 'Cracker, please. Quickly.'

Fran handed Holly the plastic bag and Holly pulled out a cracker and stuffed it into her mouth. She chewed it then grabbed another one, closing her eyes as she digested the carbs and the news.

Fran took a deep breath and let the idea of Holly having two babies settle in the air. It wasn't how they'd thought the dress fitting would go, obviously, but it certainly was interesting news. If it was correct, that was, because how could this strange old woman possibly know something that hadn't even been confirmed by a medical professional yet?

An hour later, thoughts of twin pregnancies had slipped from her mind and Fran felt like a princess as she twirled in front of the long mirror, her body clad in silver silk. The silver chiffon sleeves of the dress sat just above her elbows, the silk bodice was gathered under her bust and the skirt fell to her ankles where it seemed to glide against her skin. Combined with the silver headband set with tiny pearls and diamantes and a pair of silver wedge heels, the outfit was perfect. All it needed now was a matching pair of earrings and possibly a different pair of glasses. Demelza hadn't needed to measure her or ask her size, she'd just disappeared into the back of the shop and returned with this perfectly lovely dress.

'Are you ready?' Holly asked from the adjacent changing room.

'I am. Are you?'

'Yes. On three?'

'One. Two. Three!'

They pushed the curtains aside and stepped out into the communal changing area and gasped in sync.

'You look amazing!' Fran squealed as she gazed at Holly.

'So do you!' Holly clapped her hands. 'I knew that dress would be perfect for you when Demelza brought it out to show us.'

Demelza smiled at them both, her hands clasped in front of her, and she nodded gently.

Fran gazed at Holly's dress, a silver silk Grace Kelly-inspired affair with a corset-style bodice, lace shoulders and lace sleeves. It was gathered at the waist then it clung to her hips and fell to her feet. There was a lace overskirt that was the same length as the dress but it was left open at the front. Holly's blonde hair had been loosely tied back and on her head was a delicate tiara and a silver veil that drifted delicately down to her shoulders.

'Holly, it's just perfect.'

'I know.' Holly smiled. 'When I came in here, Demelza said she had the perfect dress just waiting for me and when I tried it on… I knew it was the one. Then I told her about you and she said she had a wonderful dress to match this one and… oh… it's just wonderful on you. Thank you, Demelza! You are such a star.'

Demelza chuckled, shaking her white head. 'I just know what suits beautiful young ladies and you two are an absolute vision. You will have a wonderful wedding and a happy marriage, Holly – this is just the beginning. And you will too, Fran.'

'What?' Fran stepped backwards. 'Me?'

'Oh yes, poppet. It's in your future. I see it as clearly as I see you standing here before me. He's very handsome, isn't he?'

The hairs on Fran's arms stood on end and she swallowed hard. This was silly, superstitious talk and she'd take no notice of it, although she couldn't deny that her interest had been piqued.

'Who's she going to marry?' Holly asked and Fran shot her a warning glance.

'Someone she already knows. Not well, not yet, but she likes him and he likes her. They have some obstacles to deal with first but nothing that can't be overcome.' Demelza tapped the side of her nose. 'And I'm seeing something else… is it clay? Or bread dough? He's working

it with big hands with lovely long fingers and… yes.'
Demelza grinned at Fran.

Fran made a mental note to tell Holly later that what
Demelza had said could be applied to anyone and it really
was silly. But the clay/bread dough comment was a bit
close to home. She hoped Demelza hadn't really been able
to see anything, especially not what had happened when
she'd been with Ethan and they'd both been covered in
clay. Of course she hadn't though, the shopkeeper clearly
picked up on information about people and was good at
reading them, and Holly had probably let it slip that Fran
was a ceramist last time she was here and… Her head
ached from trying to reason it away, so she pushed all
thoughts of how or why from her mind and focussed on
the lovely dresses instead.

'Ooh!' Holly grinned. 'That's so exciting! Who do you
think it could be, Fran?'

'I have no idea.' Fran rolled her eyes at Holly, trying
to indicate that she didn't want to discuss her imaginary
future husband further. Instead, she moved the conversation in Holly's direction. 'Why don't you tell us more
about Holly's twins, Demelza?'

Holly's eyes bulged and she held out a hand. Fran
handed her the cracker bag and Holly pulled out a cracker
and nibbled at it.

'I can't tell you more than I can see, but yes, Holly, you
have two little princesses in your belly and they will arrive
late spring, possibly early summer.'

Again, Fran stayed quiet but thought that it was quite
a broad guess.

'Look at my stomach.' Holly looked down and Fran
watched as she ran a hand over the gentle curve. 'It's much

bigger than it was with Luke and if my dates are correct, I'm almost nine weeks along, which is still very early to have a bump. Of course, I could be wrong about my dates and it could just be that I'm a bit bloated because of the nausea, but I won't know until my scan. What if it is twins and that's why I'm bigger? What will Rich think?'

Fran smiled then shrugged but she tried to inject a warning to Holly to be cautious about believing this prediction into her gaze. 'Why not wait and see what happens?'

She didn't want Holly to run away with this idea, then find out that it was the mumblings of a very nice, but somewhat eccentric old shopkeeper, so for now it was probably better not to feed the idea any further.

'Do you know, Demelza, Fran is such a good friend that she's been keeping my secret about the pregnancy and pretending it's her who's pregnant?'

'How so?' Demelza asked.

Fran waited while Holly filled the old lady in.

'What a good friend you are, Fran,' Demelza said. 'Holly is lucky to have you.'

'Oh, I'm lucky to have her too.' Fran smiled at Holly. 'I can't deny that it's creating some challenges, pretending to be pregnant, but it's not for much longer so I can live with it.'

'Do you mean challenges with other people who think that you're expecting?' Holly asked.

'Yes. Ethan Clarke for one.' The name tripped off her lips before she could stop it, as if it had been waiting there all morning.

'That's the one!' Demelza clicked her fingers as if Fran had just mentioned a name she'd forgotten.

'He thinks I'm pregnant and I've had all sorts of issues arise because of it. He insisted on carrying the boxes I delivered to the tea shop at Rosewood, reprimanded me for drinking mulled wine at the Christmas tree decorating and stopped kissing me because he said it was wrong.' Fran started as she realised she'd just told them about kissing him.

'You kissed him?' Holly's eyebrows were almost touching the ceiling.

Fran stared hard at the carpeted floor and her scalp tingled uncomfortably. 'I might have.'

'When? How?'

'That's when the clay came into it.' Demelza laughed.

The tingling spread from Fran's scalp to her armpits, but she nodded. 'Oh... we had a bit of a moment at the potter's wheel and ended up kissing but he pulled away and said it was wrong. Not just because I'm, apparently, pregnant, but because of his little girl and because he doesn't know if I have a partner.'

'Fran, you must tell him the truth!' Holly had her hands on her hips now and her eyes were filled with determination. 'You can't let this lie continue if it's going to ruin something you could have with that gorgeous man.'

'No, it's fine.' Fran shook her head. 'I'm not going to force myself upon a man who's not interested. Anyway, he just confuses me. I have no idea where I am with him and I find my own feelings about him completely baffling.'

Plus he's already rejected me once and I simply couldn't bear it if it happened again...

'You love him.' Demelza nodded sagely.

'I do not!' Fran heard the horror in her tone. 'I don't even know him very well.'

And even if I want to get to know him better, I can't possibly get in the way of what he has with Tilly. It's just not fair on the little girl to turn her world upside down.

'Doesn't matter. It's love. I can feel it in my water.'

'Perhaps that's the three cups of Earl Grey you've had since we arrived.' Fran raised an eyebrow at Demelza.

'Ha ha! You'll see, young lady, then you'll be back for a wedding dress and you'll tell Demelza she was right.'

Now the old dear was speaking about herself in the third person, so it was probably time to go. Fran only hoped she wouldn't get the dress orders muddled up, as she really liked the dress Demelza had selected for her. It was a perfect fit, which was lucky as it meant that she wouldn't need to have it altered and therefore, she wouldn't need to come back to this shop where she felt oddly exposed, as if Demelza really could see into her heart. What Fran might want deep down, and what she knew she couldn't have at a more rational level of consciousness, were very different things, and she didn't need anyone – not even a kindly old lady – poking around in her emotions. Fran already knew that she had to accept things were how they were and could not change. Tilly's feelings and Fran's fear of rejection were as solid as blocks of concrete around her ankles and they would stop her from getting carried away with fantasies about Ethan Clarke and what they could have had if the circumstances and timing had been different.

'Anyway…' Fran sighed, letting go of her less-pleasant thoughts. 'You look wonderful, Holly, and Rich is going to adore you in that dress.'

'Will it stretch if I get much bigger, Demelza?'

'How many weeks until the wedding?'

'Three and a half.'

'It will be fine. The silk is loose around your belly anyway and if it gets a bit tight, you can order a bigger bouquet to hide it, or just enjoy being with child – or should I say children – and letting the world know.'

'Sorted!' Holly said.

'Well, let's get changed so we can go and buy some cake.' Fran gently removed the headband from her hair. 'All this emotion has made me ravenous.'

'Me too,' Holly said. 'And apparently, I'm eating for three now.'

Fran sent out a silent prayer to the universe to ask that Holly not allow herself to become too excited about the idea of having twins. Just in case it wasn't true. It was a lovely idea, but surely it was better to wait for the scan to find out? Just like Fran would have to wait to find out if there was a husband in her future, a husband like Ethan, because that one seemed even more unlikely than the chance of Holly having a multiple pregnancy. She certainly wouldn't be holding her breath! Although... the more time she spent around Demelza, the more she was starting to believe that she had some weird psychic quality. It was true that the Internet was a source of information that Demelza could well have utilised, and Fran could see how knowing things about your clients would help to sell dresses and get them to recommend you to others, but something was telling her that there might be more to Demelza's predictions that that.

A tiny part of her wanted it to be true and it flickered like a candle flame in a draught, so fragile it could be extinguished at any moment, unless it was protected and nurtured. Could she allow herself to do that?

Whatever the truth behind it all was, Fran did like Ethan and Holly did seem surprisingly excited at the idea of having twins, so whether Demelza was right or wrong about these things, she certainly knew how to make other women smile.

Chapter 12

Hairway to Heaven was one of Fran's favourite places. From the moment she stepped inside the salon owned by the warm and friendly couple Jamal and Bradley, to the moment she left, she was able to relax, unwind and let go. Today was no different.

'Good morning, Fran!' Jamal walked towards her and kissed both her cheeks. 'How are you?'

'I'm good thanks.'

He smiled, flashing his perfectly straight white teeth. His spiky dreadlocks were pulled back with a wide navy headband and his beard was neatly trimmed. With his beautiful bone structure and black skin he attracted admiring glances from women and men alike, but he always made it clear that he had eyes for one man only and that was his husband, Bradley Jones-Wilson. The couple were inseparable.

'Take a seat, Fran, and we'll be with you shortly.'

He gestured at the sofa in the bay window, so Fran sat down and picked up a magazine, but she didn't open it. Instead, she gazed out of the window and across the street at the beach beyond the road. Fluffy white clouds raced across the bright sky, reflected on the surface of the dark blue water below. White breakers curled and foamed then lapped at the wet sand of the shore and Fran shivered, realising how cold the water would be. The dark grey cliffs at either end of the curved beach hugged the shore protectively, and gulls launched themselves from ledges and swooped and dived into the water then emerged with full beaks. Fran could sit here and gaze at the view all day and wondered how Jamal and Bradley ever got any work done.

'Tea? Coffee?' Jamal asked, breaking into her musings.

'Coffee would be lovely, thanks.'

'Decaff, I take it?' Jamal winked.

'Oh… uh… not really. I could do with the caffeine this morning, thanks.'

'Well…' Jamal clasped his hands in front of him. 'I guess one is all right.'

As he walked away, Fran frowned. What was it with people telling her what she could and couldn't drink? Then she caught sight of the title of the magazine she'd picked up – *Your Pregnancy Month by Month* – and she groaned inwardly. Of course, Jamal had seen her with the pregnancy test and with everything else that had probably spread around the village about her, he was probably convinced that she was pregnant too. She tossed the magazine onto the corner table and slumped on the sofa. How could one white lie get so out of hand? She was suddenly tempted to run out of the shop and straight into the cold blue water to escape the pressure. The image of her diving into the water, fully clothed, while people looked on made her giggle; it would surely set tongues wagging more than her fake pregnancy had. Perhaps she should do it to divert attention from the pregnancy. But then, it was so warm and cosy in the salon, whereas outside it was freezing and the sea would be too. She'd stay here and take her chances; hypothermia was not something she'd ever wanted to experience.

Jamal returned with a coffee that he set down on the table. 'I added one sugar because I thought you might need it.'

'Right. Thanks.' She pulled her lips into a smile.

'Bradley is just finishing up a blow-dry then he'll wash your hair.'

'Okay, wonderful.'

Fran reached for her coffee and sipped it slowly. It was warm and sweet and it smelt delicious; Jamal obviously used good-quality coffee. She gazed around the shop, eyeing the posters on the walls featuring perfect models with even more perfect hair and pouts that would make her look ridiculous if she tried to imitate them. Then there were shelves lined with the latest products to maintain colour, or to keep hair sleek and glossy or tangle and frizz free. Weren't they basically the same things? Or did they all work differently? How did you know what to buy to create the right effect, because surely if you used them all simultaneously, your hair would end up as a greasy mess? She shrugged, glad that her hair was so low-maintenance.

The air in the salon was laced with the scent of a combination of hair products, from perming solution to dye and bleach, to mousse and hairspray. It was a comforting aroma that made Fran think of being pampered and spoiled, of time that was just for her. Jamal and Bradley had been very successful since they'd set up their small business and they even had an area for beauty treatments now, which was run by a newcomer to Penhallow Sands called Lucy Challicombe. Her little boy attended the village school and Lucy worked at the salon, but also at the library, and seemed to be as enthusiastic about beauty as she was about books.

On the far wall behind the counter were some framed photographs of competitions that Jamal had entered, and the most recent ones were from this summer when Catherine Bromley and Mark Coleman – a romance writer and Catherine's partner – had modelled for Jamal. They had worn elaborate outfits and been perfect models and the whole competition had brought even more tourists to Penhallow Sands, which was always a positive for the location as many of the locals relied on the tourist industry for their incomes.

'Fran?' Bradley appeared in the archway that led to the sinks. Bradley's slim torso was shown to perfection in one of the shop's T-shirts featuring the logo of a staircase with a woman at the top, her long hair cascading down to the ground. 'Are you ready to be washed?' He ran a hand over his shiny bald head that looked whiter than ever because his well-shaped eyebrows had recently been dyed jet black.

She nodded enthusiastically. Bradley did the best head massages she'd ever had and she knew that a lot of customers went to Hairway just to have Bradley wash their hair. Jamal often joked about the noises that some of the customers made while Bradley washed their hair and Fran always tried to press her lips together to avoid moaning and groaning with pleasure. She could understand why some of the men and women who came to the salon would relax to the point where they couldn't keep quiet, though; Bradley had magic hands.

She finished her coffee then followed Bradley to the sinks, sat in the chair then removed her glasses.

'Let me just wrap this towel around your shoulders.' Bradley fastened it at the front with a butterfly clip then gently eased Fran backwards so her neck rested on the lip of the sink. 'How's the water?'

'Perfect, thank you.'

Fran closed her eyes and drifted as Bradley ran warm water over her scalp while his fingers smoothed it around her head and behind her ears. When he added some shampoo, the smell of apples and cinnamon washed over her, and as his fingers got to work, Fran felt her mouth drop open – in spite of her attempts to keep it closed – and her shoulders loosen. Who cared about fake pregnancies and possible husbands and handsome chefs when Bradley was around?

'Fran?'

'Uh?' She blinked and peered around. She was still reclining at the sink, her body limp, her mouth open.

'Are you all right?' Bradley was frowning at her.

'Oh… did I fall asleep?'

He nodded.

'Sorry.' She giggled then wiped a hand across her cheek, realising that she'd actually dribbled a bit too. 'Your magic fingers are to blame.'

'I don't know how to change that.' Bradley held his hands up and shook his head at them. 'It's just a talent, I guess.'

'It certainly is. I didn't snore, did I?'

'No, darling, thankfully you spared us that.' Bradley chuckled.

Bradley undid the clip that was holding the towel around her shoulders then gently squeezed the towel over her hair. 'There you go. Head back through to the front and take a seat.'

Fran put her glasses back on then got up and walked on slightly unsteady legs into the brighter area out front. She felt as though she'd been asleep for hours and could easily head straight to bed to sleep some more. She sat in front of a mirror that reflected the street outside and felt glad that she hadn't decided to run out of the shop earlier and race into the sea, as she'd have missed out on Bradley's magic touch.

A woman who was sitting on the sofa in the window got up and passed Fran on her way to the sinks, and Fran smiled at her as their eyes met in the mirror. The lucky woman was off to have her scalp massaged.

'Righty ho.' Jamal put down the phone and came around the counter. 'Let's see what we can do with your hair then, shall we? Are we cutting much off?'

Fran ran a hand over her crop. 'Not a lot. Just a trim, please.'

'A pre-Christmas trim?' Jamal ran his big hands through her hair, checking the length.

'Yes, please.'

'It's grown quite a lot, Fran.'

'I know. It always grows quickly. I think it's all the ice cream I eat.'

'Could be! Plenty of Cornish dairy. You know what though, Fran?' Jamal tilted his head. 'You really are glowing.'

'Glowing?'

He nodded then leant closer to her. 'Is it the pregnancy?'

'Making me glow?' She frowned at her reflection.

'Yes. That's what they say, isn't it? That it can give you a special glow. I can even see it in your eyes... it's like they're illuminated from within.'

Fran met his warm brown gaze in the mirror and something inside her cracked. Her vision blurred and her bottom lip trembled.

'Hey, Fran, what is it? What did I say?'

She shook her head and covered her eyes.

'Fran, I'm so sorry.' Jamal gently squeezed her shoulders.

'It's... okay. It's... not you.'

'Then what? Oh no... you haven't lost the baby have you?'

Fran lowered her hands and met his eyes. 'Jamal... there is no baby.' Her whisper was so quiet she wondered if she'd actually uttered it but Jamal's eyes widened.

'*Was* there a baby?'

'No.'

'Oh, Fran, I'm so sorry. Did I get it wrong?'

She nodded. 'Not your fault though. I was buying the test for someone else.'

'Oh... okay.' He smacked his forehead. 'I really am sorry, Fran. That didn't even occur to me. I guess I shouldn't ask who it was for?'

'Please don't.' A tear trickled down her cheek and plopped onto Jamal's hand. 'I don't want to tell any more lies.'

'Who have you lied to?'

'Everyone who's got the wrong end of the stick.'

'I'm sure no one will blame you for this, as it seems like you were covering for someone. Am I right?' He raised his eyebrows.

'Yes.'

'And that is completely admirable and I'm sure you have your reasons.'

He wrapped his arms around her shoulders and hugged her, his cheek next to hers, their eyes locked in the mirror.

'Don't you blame yourself at all, honey. You listen to Jamal.' He kissed her cheek. 'Now, let's make you feel as beautiful on the outside as you are on the inside.'

'Thank you.' She sniffed and wiped her cheeks with the tissue Jamal handed her.

Twenty minutes later, just as Jamal was putting the finishing touches to Fran's hair, the door opened. Fran looked up to see Ethan and Tilly.

'Hello.' Jamal greeted them. 'What can I do for you?'

'Hi, I'd like to book Tilly in for a haircut, please.'

'Of course. Come with me and we can find a suitable appointment.' Jamal led Ethan to the counter and Tilly wandered over to Fran.

'Hi Fran.'

'Hello, sweetheart.'

'I've been to the dentist.'

'Have you? I wondered why you weren't in school when you came in.'

'It's a new dentist so I had to see her today and she gave me sticker for being a good girl.' Tilly pointed at the round pink sticker on her school shirt, which showed a hippopotamus grinning broadly.

'That's a lovely sticker. Did you have any teeth out?' Fran asked.

Tilly shook her head. 'I'm brushing them very well, the dentist said, but some of them are a bit loose so they will fall out soon.'

'My goodness!' Fran feigned shock. 'Are you nervous?'

'No because Daddy says the tooth fairy will come and I can have money then I can save up and buy a... a... a dog!'

'You want a dog?'

Tilly nodded. 'Daddy said no when we lived in Bath but now he said *we'll see.*' Tilly deepened her voice as if imitating her father, then she shrugged. 'It's what Scarlett calls progress.'

'It is indeed.' Fran smiled. She could see how Tilly might be able to convince her father to do anything she wanted. 'Are you going back to school now?'

'Yes, in a bit. Daddy said to pop in and book a haircut on the way.' Tilly stepped closer to Fran and peered at her hair. 'Have you had your hair cut?'

'I have.'

'It's short.'

'I like it short.'

'So do I.' Tilly twirled some strands of her long blonde hair around her finger. 'But I like mine long.'

'It's very pretty.' Fran smiled. 'It suits you long.'

'But when I'm grown up I might have it short like yours. It's probably easier to wash.'

'It saves me a fortune on shampoo.' Fran laughed.

'Daddy uses shower gel on his.'

'Does he?'

'He likes to be fast in the shower so he uses the same gel to wash his hair and body. He said it's a man thing.'

'Right.' Fran tried to shake the image of Ethan showering from her mind.

'Fran, I'm going to be a star in the Christmas play.'

'A star! Wow, that's wonderful, Tilly.'

The little girl chewed at her bottom lip then reached out and touched Fran's hair. 'Fran... will you come to my play?'

'Tilly, stop touching Fran's hair. She's just had it styled and doesn't want your little fingers all over it.' Ethan walked over to them and took Tilly's other hand.

'Sorry, Fran,' Tilly whispered.

'It's fine, honestly.'

'Daddy, I asked Fran to come to see my play.'

'Oh...' Ethan's eyebrows rose slowly.

'Will you come?' Tilly asked.

'Uh...' Fran look up at Ethan. 'I...'

'She'd clearly like you to be there.' Ethan smiled.

'Well, in that case, I'd love to come. I can't wait to see you as a star.'

'Yay!' Tilly bounced on the spot. 'I'll say my lines nice and loud and I won't forget them at all and then you can all be proud and clap and have a merry Christmas.'

'She's been practising since Monday when they sent the lines home with the children,' Ethan explained.

'I'm already excited,' Fran said to Tilly. 'I will really look forward to it.'

'Right, we'd better get you back to school, Tilly.' Ethan led his daughter to the door. 'See you at the weekend, Jamal. And Fran... I'll get your number from Audrey and text you details of the play.'

'Wonderful.' Fran nodded, trying to appear calm, but her belly was filled with excitement.

As the door closed behind Ethan and Tilly, Jamal returned to Fran. 'So...' He raised his eyebrows.

'So?' She shrugged.

'Ethan, eh?'

'What do you mean?' Heat flooded her face.

'I can see why you might fall for him. He's a very good-looking man and a single father too.'

'Jamal, I have no idea what you're talking about.'

'He's lovely!' Jamal started to spray something into Fran's hair as he tweaked the ends with his thumb and forefinger. 'You two would make a good couple.'

Fran shook her head. Jamal was just being kind and had no idea what he was talking about. The situation was far more complicated than he realised.

She couldn't help thinking…

If only it wasn't…

—

Ethan had dropped Tilly back at school and although he needed to get back to the tea shop, he hadn't given Audrey a definite time, so he decided to take a quick stroll along the beach. He walked back down the hill and along the front then padded down the stone steps to the sand. The breeze that met him was chilly so he pulled his coat collar up and tucked his hands into his pockets. He should have brought a hat but hadn't known he'd come for a walk.

The tide was going out and the vast expanse of wet sand stretched out before him, dark gold broken up by blobs of green seaweed, pieces of driftwood and shells. He headed right, in the direction of the cliffs, knowing that he could return then along the sand and get in a decent walk.

Above him, seagulls cried, black and white forms against the gunmetal grey sky. Somewhere above the fast-moving clouds, a plane engine hummed and he could make out the crash of the waves as they hit the shore. The air was filled with the tang of brine and the deep, salty depths of the sea. It was refreshing, invigorating, and it lifted him, reaffirming how great it was to live so close to the beach. Under his feet, shells crunched and the sand sucked at his shoes, flicking droplets of water up into the air as he walked.

As he neared the cliffs, he paused and peered up at the houses that sat there on a fancy development. The properties must have cost a fortune because the land wouldn't have been cheap with such a prime position overlooking the sea and the beach. It was something he'd probably never have, a home like that, but it was something to aspire to. He wanted to have dreams again, dreams that involved more than getting through each day. He yearned, sometimes, in the quiet of the early hours, to find what he was looking for, to feel complete. Growing up, he'd had dreams, but then his mum had become ill, suffering on and off with cancer that was treated then returned, never releasing its hold on her body, until her flesh finally gave up its fight. All he'd wanted for such a long time was for her to recover completely, for her to have more time. He'd become lost in sitting with her, holding her hand and trying to hold on to the moment because he knew that if he looked ahead, then she might well be gone and his whole world would change irrevocably.

He felt the familiar stinging of his eyes and nose, so he turned and stared hard at the water, watching as it ebbed and flowed, sucking at the sand then foaming over it again. He breathed deeply until his vision had cleared, not wanting to let go right now, fearing the abyss that his grief could bring even after eight years had passed. When his mum had lost her battle, he'd faltered for months, struggled to keep going, but he'd also tried to support his dad. Then Melanie had come along and he'd focused on her, made her the centre of his world, put her high on a pedestal as he tried to fill the gaping hole of grief by loving another woman. Of course, in retrospect, he'd been trying to put a round peg into a square hole. He'd lost his mum and no one would ever replace her, plus it wasn't fair to expect Melanie to heal him. He needed to grieve his loss and to feel the pain and to deal with it. Instead, he'd given himself a whole new set of problems. Except, of course, for Tilly. His daughter was the best thing that had ever happened to him and he would always be grateful to Melanie for giving him Tilly.

He turned and started to walk back in the direction he'd come, feeling the sand dragging at his heels and the wind ruffling his hair, making his eyes water. He wished his mum could be here to walk along the sand, to breathe in the sea air and, most importantly, to see her beautiful granddaughter. She would be so proud of Tilly and would be very excited about the school play. In the past, she'd spoken to him about having grandchildren one day and about how she'd look forward to things like the school run and school plays. She'd had no idea that she'd be taken so young, that all her hopes and dreams would be whisked away by the cruelty of cancer. The illness had been debilitating, painful and a dirty, dark thief; it had stolen the biggest gift of all from his mum – it had taken her time, her future and her dreams and made them impossible to realise.

He gulped his grief down then pulled the image of Tilly into his mind. Focusing on her and the joy she brought always helped him to stay positive. Only today, Tilly had surprised him by inviting Fran to see her play.

He hadn't expected to see Fran in Hairway to Heaven, and was very pleased that he had. He found himself thinking about her a lot. When Tilly had told her about the play, he'd initially felt a bit concerned that Fran wouldn't be at all interested, but she'd seemed delighted. It would be nice to have someone else there to see Tilly perform, although Audrey, Scarlett and Harper had asked him to try to get extra tickets, so if that worked out, then Tilly would have quite a crowd there to cheer her on.

His chest expanded and he recognised the emotion burgeoning inside him: gratitude. He was grateful for the people in his life, for his family, but also, especially, for Fran. When she was around, the world seemed more colourful, more hopeful. When he thought about her, saw her and spent time with her, he felt… better about everything. As if there was hope for something else in his life.

But what that something else could be was yet to be determined.

Chapter 13

Ethan parked his car outside the shop at Greenacres then got out and looked around. The vineyard certainly was impressive. Audrey had asked him to go and collect the wine order for the dinner at the tea shop on Christmas Day. She'd emailed her order over to Greenacres so that Holly could get it ready and Ethan was glad because although he liked wine, he didn't know a great deal about it and would have struggled to pick out a large order for other people to drink.

He walked across to the shop and pushed the door open. Inside, it was warm and smelt of spice and paper. The reasons for both became clear when he spotted Holly at the counter wrapping something, then noted the oil burner on a shelf behind the counter. She must be burning a festive oil to create an appropriate mood in the shop. There was a holly wreath pinned to the counter and mistletoe and festive greenery draped on some of the shelves.

Holly looked up and waved at him, gestured at the customer standing in front of the counter then held up a hand to indicate that she'd be five minutes, so he nodded. He was glad to have the chance to have a look around and to try to familiarise himself with some of the wines before collecting the order.

The shelves were well stocked with bottles of wine but there were also shelves of pottery goblets and bowls, candle holders and small festive figures like snowmen and Santas. He wondered if they were all Fran's work and suddenly he was hit by a flashback of that kiss over the pottery wheel. What an embrace that had been! Ethan hadn't been with many women in his life and Melanie had been his only major relationship, but even so, kissing Fran had been a completely different experience. She had reached something inside him that had made desire rise like flames. He could only imagine what it might have actually felt like to make love to her, because if a kiss could be so powerful, then surely even more physical contact would be incredible?

He turned and wandered over to the other side of the shop and gazed at the paintings on the wall. Some had 'SOLD' stickers on but three were still for sale. They had Fran's signature at the bottom and it made his heart ache. She had created these wonderful works of art, perfectly capturing the village of Penhallow Sands through different seasons. The wintery one caught his eye, with the red light of the setting sun out over the water and the drifts of snow over the houses and pavements of the pretty village like it had just been sprinkled with icing sugar. He could make out the fronts of a few of the shops and see the steps he had descended to get to the sand. The sea was a dark expanse, appearing cold and fathomless, and he shivered as he imagined how it would feel to dip so much as a toe into its depths in the winter months.

Next to the Penhallow Sands paintings were some of Greenacres. Two were of the house and winery together, and one was of the house but from a different angle. It was set back in what appeared to be a lower field of the vineyard so the perspective looked up at the house and winery, capturing the vines rich and heavy with fruit and the vibrant green of the surrounding land. The piece was exquisite and if hadn't had a 'SOLD' sticker on it, Ethan would have bought it immediately. Fran had such an eye for detail and she was able to transfer that to a canvas as if she'd taken a photograph and printed it. In the same way that she brought vibrancy to a room or location, her art did the same. His admiration for her just kept growing and again, something inside him wavered, as if he was experiencing an internal debate over whether or not his heart was ready to give love another chance.

He shook his head. It couldn't happen. Just because Fran was attractive, sweet, funny and talented didn't mean that Ethan was about to throw himself at her feet. He could not allow himself to make Tilly vulnerable and it surely wouldn't be fair on pregnant Fran either when her emotions were probably already up in the air – she had enough on her plate as it was without a new relationship and the changes it could bring.

'Hello, Ethan.' Holly waved at him as the customer left the shop. 'Have you come to collect the wine for Rosewood?'

'I have, although Audrey showed me the email she sent you and I'm not sure I'll get it all in my car.' He laughed.

'It is a really decent order.' Holly smiled. 'Rich has packed it ready so I'll help you carry it.'

'I can do that if you just show me where it is once I've paid.' Ethan got the credit card Audrey had given him from his pocket and handed it to Holly.

'There's a discount on this because Audrey and Gary are regular customers and because it's a bulk buy,' Holly said as she rang the sale through the till. 'I saw you admiring Fran's work.'

'Yes, she's very talented.' He nodded. 'It's a shame that the one of the vineyard isn't for sale or I'd have bought it.'

'The perspective of that one is from down by the old oak tree in one of our fields. It's beautiful, isn't it?'

'Stunning.'

'I'm sure that Fran would consider painting another for you if you wanted to commission one. She'll probably be able to do it in the new year.' Holly smiled at him, her blonde bob framing her pretty face, her green eyes kind and friendly.

'I wouldn't want to give her extra work to do... what with her expecting and all.' Ethan frowned. He hated the thought of Fran being overworked.

'Oh... she'll be fine.' Holly waved a hand.

'Not if she overdoes it.' Ethan shook his head. 'She needs to take care of herself.'

Holly dropped her gaze to the counter and colour crept into her cheeks. She tucked her hands into her jean pockets and shifted her weight from one foot to the other.

'She is okay, isn't she?' he asked, concern filling him. 'As her best friend, you'd know, wouldn't you?'

'Yes, she's okay.' Holly nodded. 'She's not unwell if that's what you mean.'

'Well, I hope that her partner is looking after her properly.'

'Her partner?' Holly frowned. 'Oh, Fran doesn't have a partner!' Holly's eyes widened in horror. 'What I mean is that... uh...'

186

'You mean to tell me that some idiot got her pregnant and now he's not even on the scene?' Outrage filled Ethan and his whole body tensed. 'What kind of man does that?'

'No, it's not like that.' Holly shook her head. 'Not at all. See… Fran's very independent and she… uh… she…'

'It's okay.' Ethan sighed, trying to unclench his jaw. 'It's not really any of my business. I just… I don't like to think of someone as sweet and kind as Fran struggling with a baby alone. It's not easy, you know.'

'Yes, I do know.' Holly nodded.

'You do?'

'I wasn't here when I found out I was expecting Luke. Rich and I had broken up and I left Penhallow Sands. It was a difficult time and doing it alone was scary.'

'That must have been very hard for you.'

'It was very lonely. But… I came home for my grand-father's funeral, thinking I'd leave again afterwards, only it never happened. It was so wonderful having my family around me again and then Rich and I were able to talk and find a way through our problems and now we're closer than ever.'

'That's a happy ending. Good for you and for your baby.'

'Yes.'

'I found the same moving here. After being a single father for so long it's incredible to have Audrey, Gary and the girls around us, and I know that Tilly loves it too. There's security in having people who love you nearby and it's something I'll never take for granted, as I know what it's like to be alone.'

'I'm sorry that you were alone.'

'It's certainly not your fault.'

'No.' She smiled. 'But all's well that ends well, right?'

'I certainly hope so.'

'Would you like a hand then?'

'No, honestly, you just show me where the wine is and I'll take it out to the car. You have another customer anyway.' Ethan gestured at the elderly man gazing through the shop window.

'So I do.' Holly opened a door to her right and propped it open. 'Your boxes are just in there.'

'Great, thanks.'

'Ethan...'

'Yes?'

'Fran was meant to have spoken to you about... some things. She does need to talk to you and she will do, but knowing Fran, it will be in her own time. I won't say any more because I don't feel it's my place to interfere, but please, when she's ready to talk... listen and try not to judge.'

'Uh... okay. Of course. I'll try.' He nodded, really confused about what Holly meant and quite worried, but wanting to be agreeable and approachable. This was Fran's best friend and she would know what was going on with Fran and her situation.

Ethan picked up the first of four boxes and carried it out to the car. It was heavy but the bottles inside were tightly packed, so he wouldn't need to worry about them clinking together as he drove home.

But when he'd loaded up all of the boxes, started the engine and left Greenacres behind, it wasn't wine that was worrying him, it was the thought that Fran didn't have a partner to lean on; her family were away in Italy and within months she was going to have a baby to care for while juggling her work and her animals. Even if he couldn't be there for her in some of the ways he would like, he could be there for her as a friend.

–

'You told him what?' Fran stared at Holly, her heart racing. 'But I was deliberately vague about whether or not I had a partner because of the whole fake pregnancy issue.'

Holly sighed and sank onto a kitchen chair. She grabbed the open packet of biscuits on the table and stuffed one into her mouth. 'It slipped out. Perhaps it's baby brain or something?' Holly shrugged. 'Anyway, at least now he knows you're single.'

'And what difference is that going to make to anything?'

'Well… you might be in with a chance.'

'A chance of what, Holly?'

'Of love.'

Fran shook her head and reached for the biscuits. 'The poor man thinks I'm pregnant and now, thanks to you, he thinks the father didn't consider me worth sticking around for. He also has a child of his own and she is his priority. At the very most all I'm going to get is sympathy, but he also now thinks I want to talk to him about something, although it sounds like you left that quite mysterious too with your comments about *in her own time.*'

'Fran… trust me on this. I know you're Miss Independent and Miss Strong, and that you've had a few dalliances with the opposite sex – more than I have certainly – but I also know that you've never been in love before.'

'What do you mean "before"? That suggests that I might be in love now.'

'Ethan really likes you and I know that you like him. The concern in his voice when he spoke about you earlier was evident and I actually believe it's more than just concern. You should have a frank conversation with him and be completely honest with him.'

Fran took a sip of her tea then shook her head again. 'Stop meddling, Holly, and focus on your wedding planning. That's why I'm here this evening: to help with that, not to be persuaded into hoping for something with Ethan or to be convinced that I might be in love with him. Some of us are just not meant to settle down. I have my own home, my dogs, cats, bearded dragons and my freedom. Why would I want any other complications? Why would I want to do anything to jeopardise my peace of mind and to… to risk being hurt or rejected? You and Rich are happy but I've seen what love does to other people and it's not always pretty. So thank you very much, but I'll stay single. And that's all I have to say on the matter.'

'You might not be rejected.'

'Holly, I already have been and it wasn't pretty. When we kissed over the pottery wheel… it was him who pulled away, not me—'

'Oh, Fran, I'm so sorry.'

'Don't be because even if he had wanted me, it wouldn't make any difference. His little girl needs him and the security of having him all to herself. It's just the way it is.'

'But Fran, it doesn't have to be like that. You could bring so much to her life and to his and—'

Fran shook her head. 'Please don't, Hols. Leave it there, now. Please.'

She met Holly's gaze and her friend nodded reluctantly. Holly just wanted her to be happy and Fran knew how that felt, but sometimes she also had to let things go.

Holly munched her way through another biscuit and nodded, so Fran finished her tea then reached for the notepad that was on the table.

'Right then...' Fran tapped the pen on the paper. 'The next item on the agenda is... the wedding cake, seeing as how Lucinda has hurt her wrist by slipping on some ice and can't make it as promised.'

'I was thinking... before you just told me what you did... that perhaps you could speak to Ethan about that for me. He might be able to whip something up.' Holly shrugged nonchalantly, her eyes wide with innocence, but Fran scowled at her.

'I know what you're playing at, Holly Dryden, and it's not going to work. I thought you understood me just now when I explained things.'

'Fran... I have no idea what you mean. This is purely about my wedding cake.' Holly poked out her tongue and Fran started to laugh.

'You are incorrigible! Do you know that?'

'Who? Me?'

Fran shook her head. 'Okay I'll ask him tomorrow.'

'Thank you.'

'Thank me if he says yes.'

–

The next morning, Fran drove up to Rosewood as she had promised Holly she would. Throughout the drive there, she debated turning around and heading for Newquay to see if she could find an understanding baker who would put together a wedding cake at very short notice, but then she'd remind herself that she was only going to ask Ethan and that the worst he could say would be no.

Outside the tea shop, she gazed at the Christmas tree. The lights weren't on because it was only ten o'clock, but the wonderful variety of colourful decorations sparkled as they caught the light and the star at the top of the tree was like a symbol of hope shining down on the yard. She wondered which decorations Tilly had chosen and if Ethan had done so too when the adults' turn came. It was a lovely tradition and one that could be very special for families and it was something to look forward to every year.

She took a deep breath. She could do this for Holly. Of course she could!

Inside the tea shop, it was warm and cosy. A few tables were occupied with people enjoying brunch or an early break, and the familiar aromas of baking and coffee filled the air. Christmas songs drifted from the speakers in the corners of the tea room and Fran felt the frisson of excitement that always came with the festive season. It was a throwback to when she was a child, but it was still very pleasant when it burst into life again, reminding her of what a special time Christmas could be.

She went to the counter and Audrey smiled warmly.

'Hello, Fran. It's cold out today, isn't it?'

'Very. I seem to spend my days wrapped up, indoors and out.'

'Can I get you a warm drink?'

'I'm actually here to see Ethan, but I would love a latte, please.'

'Of course. Anything to eat?'

'No thanks.'

'Mince pie?'

'Oh go on then, you've twisted my arm.' Fran laughed. 'I can't resist mince pies, they are an all-time favourite.'

'Take a seat and I'll call Ethan and get your drink and treat.'

'Thank you.'

Fran pulled off her gloves and hat then sat at a small round table for two near the counter. As she shrugged out of her coat, her stomach flipped. She was nervous about seeing Ethan and about asking him to do this for Holly. Why, she didn't know, because she'd seen him before and asking him to make a wedding cake wasn't exactly beyond his remit – and he could always say no – but even so, she had some serious butterfly action in her belly.

Fran pulled her smartphone from her bag and checked the screen. No new messages; nothing to distract herself with. She opened the photos and scrolled through the ones she'd taken of Luke yesterday. He was such a beautiful child and so happy. How he would adapt with a sibling coming along – maybe even two if Demelza was right – she had no idea, but with his loving parents, grandfather and great grandmother, as well as his grandparents on Rich's side, she felt sure that he'd be fine. He was still very young and would be close in age to the baby, or babies, so they might even end up being good friends. Fran hoped so because having siblings must be nice. When she was younger, she'd longed for a sister or a brother, but as she'd grown up she'd realised that being an only child meant that she got all of her parents' time and attention, like when her dad taught her to drive and when her mum would sit and help her with her homework for hours on end, or when they'd both pack up a picnic and take her on hikes around the beautiful Cornish coastline. She'd had a joyful bucolic childhood and had been lucky enough to feel secure and content in her parents' love. Of course, these days they lived away, but they weren't far and Fran knew that she could speak to them whenever she wanted to.

Just then, the tinny tone of a video call rang out from her phone and she almost dropped it with surprise. She quickly pressed accept to cut off the noise and her mum's familiar face appeared.

'Frannie!' Her mum waved at her.

'Mum? I wasn't expecting a call this morning.'

'I know, sweetheart, and—'

'Oh God, is everything all right? Dad? Nonna?' Fran tensed.

'We're all fine, Frannie. It's just that I... I heard something and I wanted to ask you about it before it worried me. You know how I build things up if I don't get them out in the open and... well... I found out last night and it's been going round and round in my poor head.' Her mum's dark blue eyes peered out of the screen.

'Okay...' Fran didn't like the sound of that. Her mum could be a terrible worrier and for her to video call early in the morning, rather than at their customary time of after six in the evening, showed how concerned she must be.

'Frannie, how are you feeling?' Her mum's dark brows met above her nose in a frown.

'I'm good, thanks.'

'Do you want me to come home?'

'Hi, Fran.' Ethan sat opposite her. 'Oh, sorry, you're on the phone!' He pressed a finger to his lips.

Fran flashed him a smile. 'Hi, Ethan.'

'Fran?' Her mum's voice rang out from her phone.

'Yes, Mum?'

'Who's that?'

'It's Ethan Clarke. He's the new chef at Rosewood Tea Shop.'

'Is he the father?'

'What?' Fran stared at her mum then slowly moved her gaze up to Ethan.

He was staring right back and had obviously heard what her mother had said.

'I asked if he's the father. Frannie, we know you're pregnant. Why didn't you tell us? We're delighted, obviously, but it's such a surprise.'

'No... uh, Mum. It's not like that. See...' Fran could feel Ethan's gaze fixed on her face and heat crawled up her neck and around her ears, making them hot and itchy. She should have spoken to her parents about the fake pregnancy before now but she'd been delaying, hoping they wouldn't hear about it, aware that even though they'd understand why she was doing it for Holly, they'd be concerned about the effect it could have upon her if it spread around the village.

'But you are pregnant?'

Fran sighed inwardly. How was she going to get away with this? If she told the truth, Ethan would know she'd been lying and Holly would be exposed, meaning it would all have been for nothing. But if she lied, then she'd be lying to her mum.

'Look, Mum, it's complicated and I'm at the tea shop right now, so I'll call you back as soon as I get home. I don't really want to discuss this in public.'

'Of course, Frannie.' Her mum nodded. 'Call me as soon as you get home. Immediately! Promise?'

'I promise. Speak to you later—'

'Before you cut me off, just turn your phone around, so I can see Ethan, will you?' Her mum pointed left as if she knew where Ethan was sitting from her position in Italy.

Fran grimaced at Ethan but he smiled.

'Okay, Mum. Gwyneth, meet Ethan. Ethan, my mum.'

'Hello, Mrs Gandolfini.' He smiled and it lit up his handsome face.

'Hello, Ethan, darling, and welcome to the family.'

'*Muuuum!*' Fran grimaced, feeling like she was a teenager and her mum had just embarrassed her in front of her school friends.

Ethan's eyes widened but he didn't say anything. Fran turned the phone back around.

'Mum, I have to go. Speak later.' She ended the call quickly before her mother said anything else that would mortify them all.

She tucked her phone in her bag then placed her hands on the table, fingers splayed, as if to ground herself.

'I am so sorry about that.'

He shrugged. 'It's fine. We're family now apparently, so anything goes, right?'

'Thanks for not shooting her down.'

'Why would I? It seems like she's worried about you and so she should be. Fran… yesterday I found out that the father of your baby isn't around. I'm so sorry. I can't believe someone would do that to you.'

Fran shook her head. 'No… it's not like that. Please don't worry.'

'Will your parents be upset when they find out?'

'Ethan, I'm thirty-one years old. It's not like I'm sixteen, jobless and homeless. I'll be fine.'

He nodded but there was concern in his gorgeous eyes.

'Anyway… I came here to ask you a favour.'

'To pretend to be your baby's dad?'

'No! Of course not.'

'What then?' His eyes crinkled at the corners as he smiled at her.

'I…' Would he have done that for her if she'd asked it of him? Was he that generous? She pushed the thought away; it wouldn't matter anyway because she wasn't really pregnant. 'I wanted to ask if you would consider helping me out with something. See… Holly is getting married on New Year's Eve but Rich's mum was meant to be making the wedding cake, and I know it's short notice but Lucinda slipped a few days ago and hurt her wrist so she can't do the cake now and…' She stopped talking because Ethan was nodding and smiling.

'Of course I'll make it. I'd be happy to. With such short notice though, sponge would be better than fruit cake, as it won't have the time to mature. Unless we use one of the Christmas cakes or…'

'Sponge will be fine. Anything will be fine, actually. As long as they just have a cake.'

'I can do that for you. Get Holly to text me some images of what she likes and I'll have a think.'

'You are wonderful!' Fran reached across the table and grabbed his hands.

'Uh… thanks.' He smiled shyly, his cheeks flushing.

'You really are, Ethan. How many men would be so accommodating? In just ten minutes you've offered… well, asked if I want you to pretend to be my baby's father to stop my mum worrying and now you've agreed to bake my best friend's wedding cake. You are one of the nicest men I've ever met.'

A tiny line appeared between his brows and his smile dropped.

'Ethan? What is it?'

He shook his head.

'I've upset you?'

'Not you. Just… what you said about being nice. It hasn't always worked in my favour.'

'Well, from now on it should do.' She squeezed his hands. 'You are truly nice in the best possible way.'

'Thank you.'

They stayed that way for a while, until Fran realised that Audrey was gazing at them from behind the counter, grinning at their clasped hands, so she released Ethan and made a show of eating her mince pie. Ethan pulled out his phone and started searching for some images of cakes, showing them to Fran and making her laugh at the more ostentatious ones. When she finished her coffee, he got her another and one for himself, and they sat together, using the excuse of looking at cake ideas to spend the rest of the hour together.

It was one of the loveliest hours that Fran could remember ever spending at the tea shop.

Chapter 14

Ethan took his seat in the school hall and looked around. So far, he was alone, but he needed to keep four seats, so he spread his coat, hat, scarf and gloves out on the chairs either side of him. The play was due to begin at ten thirty and he'd been waiting outside the school gates from nine thirty, worried that he might not get seats together. He'd purchased three tickets (the amount allotted to each pupil) as soon as they'd gone on sale then waited to see if there would be spares. There were, and he'd snapped up another two. It was surprisingly stressful wondering if he'd get enough tickets to please everyone and quite different to wishing that he had someone else, even just one more person, to come and see Tilly's plays with him. He definitely preferred this to coming alone and was looking forward to having company.

The hall filled up slowly; mums and dads, grand-mothers and grandfathers, aunties and uncles, guardians and carers were all filing in and removing hats, gloves and coats. Aromas of mints, perfume and cologne, and cigarettes smoked hastily before entering the school grounds filled the air and mingled with the school scent of chips and paint.

Ethan kept glancing at the doorway behind him, until finally, he saw Audrey, Harper and Scarlett bustling in, their cheeks and noses pink from the cold, their eyes scanning the room. He waved and they came and took their seats. All he needed now was for Fran to arrive then he could relax and enjoy the show.

—

Fran ran a hand over her hair, trying to flatten it after her hat had created static, as she hurried into the hallway. The last thing she'd wanted to do was to be late but the new dog had experienced a toilet emergency just as she'd been about to leave and she'd spent precious time cleaning it up then waiting to check that it wouldn't happen again. Most likely, he'd been nibbling at rabbit droppings in her garden or, as he seemed wont to do, licking bird poo off the bench. It wasn't his fault, but it did make her squirm whenever she caught him doing it. She hoped that with time and care he would grow out of those habits, but there was no way to be sure because she had no idea what he'd been through before he'd come to her.

She looked around the hall for Ethan and was relieved when he waved her over.

'Sorry I'm a bit late,' she whispered as she sat next to him. The chairs were very close together and she found her leg pressing against Ethan's almost immediately. She tried to inch over on the seat but the shape of it meant that she couldn't manage to balance on one bum cheek, so she gave in and let her leg rest against his. He was warm and solid next to her and it was a relief after the cold outside.

In jeans and a blue and white checked shirt with the top button undone, Ethan looked gorgeous. His hair was shiny and his skin clear except for the stubble that he always seemed to have, as if it grew within hours of him shaving. Fran had an urge to run her hand over it just to feel it tickling her palm. She knew from their kiss that it would tickle her face and a tingle spread through her at the memory.

It wasn't fair that he was so nice and so darned attractive. How was she supposed to keep her mind from straying to thoughts of kissing him and holding him close? As it was, she could gaze at him all day long and never get bored. His rejection had stung but she knew why he had put a stop to their intimacy and the fact that he continued to be so kind to her made her hope that it was indeed because of Tilly and the fake pregnancy and not because of any other reason.

'No worries. Just glad you're here. Tilly really wanted you to come.'

He smiled at her and she could have plunged into the green pools of his eyes and stayed there.

Suddenly warm, she shrugged out of her coat and tucked it behind her then ran a hand over her hair again, wondering if it was still sticking up. Glancing at Ethan, she saw that he was grinning.

'Static.' He reached out and gently smoothed her hair down. As his fingers reached her ear, they sank lower and brushed against her neck and she gasped at the bolt of desire that shot through her. Ethan's lips parted and he seemed to be as shocked as she was by the impact of their physical connection, as if during the time since their kiss, their attraction had continued to grow, and the air between them seemed filled with the anticipation of things to come. Ethan released a shuddering breath then folded his hands together in his lap and stared straight ahead. Fran glanced around, wondering if anyone had seen what had just transpired, but parents and grandparents, aunties and uncles were all reading their programmes and their phones, excitedly chatting about their little ones' starring roles.

Fran took a few slow breaths and focused on the details of the hall, from the large Christmas tree in the corner with its twinkling lights and colourful baubles to the tinsel draped around the stage and the high windows. Colourful paper and foil streamers hung from the ceiling and carols drifted through the air from speakers above the stage, creating the perfect background to the conversational hum.

Then Ms Jowanet Tremayne walked, or rather marched, along the centre aisle and climbed the steps to the stage. The hall fell silent as if she'd rung a bell or raised her voice. She commanded respect and she knew it, but there was no arrogance about her, merely acceptance of her position in the community.

'Good morning to you all!' Jowanet smiled broadly at the crowd. In her heels, the tall woman was positively statuesque, and Fran realised that she must seem like a giant to the youngest children. She had a severely cut white bob, small square glasses and beady hazel eyes and she was wearing a grey two-piece suit over a white blouse, her sturdy calves encased in thick flesh-coloured tights. Fran didn't think she'd ever seen the head teacher wearing anything else, certainly nothing more casual. 'It is a delight to be able to welcome you to our annual Christmas performance. This year, we have a play written by the children themselves. It's called The Lonely Star, and having seen the dress rehearsal, I can tell you that it is a magical, festive delight. Please refrain from using your cameras during the performance for safeguarding reasons, but afterwards there will be the opportunity to have photographs with your children in front of the stage. And now… enjoy this wonderful play that will carry us all into the Christmas holidays!'

There was a round of applause and some cheers, then Jowanet padded down the steps and took a seat at the front. The hall fell silent again and a spotlight appeared on the stage. Fran sneaked a look at Ethan and her heart squeezed, because she could see a tiny muscle in his jaw moving, as if he were struggling to deal with the emotion of the situation. She moved her hand over her leg so it rested next to his, and without looking at her, he moved his hand over so that their fingers touched.

Fran swallowed hard. These feelings and emotions were so new to her and she had no idea how to react to any of them. All she knew was that when she was with Ethan, she felt good, and when she wasn't, she missed him. She knew that she couldn't be with him, but it didn't stop her wanting to be close to him. And right now, their little fingers were entwined; they were connected, and she suspected that their connection ran a lot deeper than a physical one.

–

'That was just about the most emotional hour I've ever had,' Fran said as she dabbed at her eyes with a tissue. Her throat was tight and her eyes burned with unshed tears that she'd tried to hold back to avoid full on sobbing in the hall.

Next to her, Ethan was smiling, but his eyes glistened and on the other side of him, Audrey was openly crying.

'I'm so proud of her.' Ethan sniffed. 'She was so confident.'

'She was wonderful. You've done such a good job of raising her.' Fran squeezed his arm.

'It hasn't been easy at times but it's always been a pleasure. She's an amazing little girl.'

'I'm... so... glad... you... came home.' Audrey clung to Ethan's arm and cried on his shoulder. Mascara ran down her cheeks and her foundation was streaked but it was clear that Audrey didn't care; she'd enjoyed the play too much to be concerned about her appearance.

'Hey, Audrey, it's okay. I'm glad we came to Penhallow Sands too.'

Audrey blew her nose then composed herself. 'It reminded me so much of when my two girls were little and I know that if your mum was here, Ethan, she'd be proud too.'

Ethan seemed to freeze and his Adam's apple bobbed furiously. Fran slid her hand through his arm and held tight. He was silent for a few moments, as if he'd gone somewhere in his mind to escape, then he seemed to return to the room as he took a shaky breath. Fran wasn't used to dealing with men and their emotions, but she knew from things her mum had said about her dad and things Holly had told her about Rich that some men struggled to express their grief, their pain and feelings of vulnerability. Culture often taught little boys to swallow their fears and to put on a front and that could run into adulthood too. She could see that in Ethan now, see how he battled his emotions, and she wanted to hug him and tell him that everything was okay, that it would be all right from now on. She wanted, she realised, to comfort and support him; her feelings for him were deepening, spiralling out of her control in spite of her attempts to reason with her heart.

'Mum would be very proud. I wish she was here to see things like this. It's such a shame.'

He glanced at Fran and she offered what she hoped was a reassuring smile. 'I'm sure that in some way, she knows.'

'I hope so.' He nodded. 'It's comforting to think that she might be able to see Tilly doing so well.'

'Ladies and gentlemen!' Ms Tremayne was back on the stage. 'If I can just have your attention for a moment?'

The crowd had already fallen silent.

'The children will return to the hall for photographs, then they will need to go back to their classes with their teachers. When they have gathered their belongings, they will be released to you ready for the Christmas holidays. And on that wonderful note, the staff and I would like to wish you all a very merry Christmas and a happy and healthy new year.'

With that, the Christmas carols began again, filling the hall with festive cheer, and parents lined up to have photographs done with their children.

Ethan stood up. 'Better get in the queue or we'll be last.'

'Okay. See you in a bit.' Fran smiled.

'Come with me?' he asked.

Fran blinked. 'Sorry?'

'I said come with me.'

'Oh… you don't want me in your photos. Unless you'd like me to take them for you, so you can all be in them?' Fran offered.

'Come with me and let's see, shall we?' He held out his hand. Fran took it, then he led her to the front of the hall. His hand was warm, his grip around her fingers firm, and she felt happy and secure, cared about by a man in a way she never had been before.

Audrey and her daughters joined them and soon the children trooped back out from behind the stage, still in their costumes of stars, the sun, the moon, some clouds, some squirrels, badgers, foxes, rabbits and mice. They ran to their families and hugs, kisses and praise were showered upon them. It was lovely to watch and Fran had a lump lodged in her throat the entire time. She hadn't been a part of this world before, not having children and not expecting to ever be a mum, so being here like this was a real privilege. Ethan had opened up his world and invited her in and it was a very special gift to give. She would always appreciate his kindness and his warmth, and would treasure the memory of today, whatever happened after it was over.

'Daddy!' Tilly ran towards them and flung herself at Ethan and he scooped her up in his arms and hugged her tight.

'My little star!' he exclaimed as he held her out and smiled at her. 'You were wonderful!'

'You were,' Audrey and her daughters agreed.

Tilly turned to Fran. 'Was I?'

'Absolutely amazing. You sparkled on that stage like a diamond.'

'Were you proud of me?'

'I was so proud,' Ethan said.

'Were you proud of me, Fran?' Tilly asked.

'Extremely.' Fran took Tilly's proffered hand. 'I've never seen a more talented, beautiful star in all my life.'

Tilly beamed at her and Fran thought her heart would break. This was too much emotion and happiness for one day, surely?

–

Ethan posed for some photographs with Tilly then he encouraged his family to join in. When they'd all had some taken, he held out a hand to Fran.

'Come on then, this side of the camera.'

'No, it's all right. You won't want me in your pictures.'

'Yes we do!' Tilly grabbed Fran's hand. 'Come on, quick, before someone else needs the stage. My teacher said we weren't to be long on here because lots of people need photos then everyone needs to get home for Christmas. *People have plans, children, so be quick!*' Tilly rolled her eyes and giggled at her own imitation of what Ethan assumed must be her teacher.

Audrey took Ethan's phone from Fran and held it up ready to snap away.

'Come here, Fran.' Tilly led Fran to the rear of the stage, then they stood in front of the backdrop of a beach at night. The sky was navy blue, the sea a black carpet spread out behind them, the moonlight a silver ribbon curling over the water's surface. Tilly took Fran's hand in hers then Ethan took her other hand and Fran stood between them, her cheeks flushed, her eyes bright behind her glasses. 'Now smile at Aunty Audrey!'

Fran smiled and allowed Tilly to direct her poses, and soon, Tilly, Ethan and Fran were giggling as they poked out their tongues and framed their faces with their hands and Ethan pretended to throw Tilly through the air so she could be a shooting star. It felt so natural including Fran in his family unit, as if she'd always been there. She fitted in like the missing piece and he was so comfortable around her. He'd never felt like this with Melanie, always felt as if he was on guard, waiting for her to criticise him or to find fault with something, anything that he'd done, so she could start a row then storm off. It had been like walking on eggshells the entire time and Ethan had begun to realise recently, with the way that Melanie behaved towards Tilly during their Skype calls, that it would have been the same for Tilly had her mother stayed. But with Fran, there was no pressure to be anything other than himself, and Tilly was relaxed and happy around her too, and it was refreshing, enlightening and just... wonderful.

'Right, I think we have enough photos and we'd better give someone else a turn.' He nodded at the queue.

'Okay, Daddy!' Tilly skipped to his side. 'I have to go back to class now to collect my things, then we can go home.'

'And start Christmas?' he asked.

'Yaaaaay!' Tilly clapped her hands before running off the stage.

'Ethan, the girls and I are going to head back to Rose-wood now.'

'I'll be up as soon as I can.' He descended the steps from the stage. 'I'll just wait for Tilly then we'll head home.'

Audrey stepped closer and said quietly, 'There's no rush, love. You just take your time. Perhaps go for a coffee with Fran.'

'Oh...' Ethan glanced behind him at Fran, who was chatting to someone she knew in the queue.

'Go on, love, let your hair down. Today's a special day. The tea shop will always be there but today is a moment in time that you'll never get back, so enjoy it.' Audrey gently touched his cheek and he nodded. 'Come on then girls, let's get back to your father. He's probably emptied the fridge by now looking for his morning snack.'

'See you later.' Ethan waved as they walked away.

'I should be going too.' Fran had joined him.

'What, now?' Disappointment swept over him.

'I still have some things to sort before Christmas and a few orders to drop off to people.'

'Oh… okay.'

'I could do it later, though.' Fran smiled. 'If you fancy grabbing a coffee or something first.'

'That would be great.'

She smiled up at him and he stuffed his hands in his pockets, worried that if he didn't, he would pull her to his chest and hug her tight.

—

As they walked out of the school and into the yard, Tilly squealed.

'It's snow—ing!'

'So it is.' Fran looked around them. 'The forecast gave us a forty per cent chance of snow but I didn't think it was quite cold enough.'

'It's freezing, Fran!' Tilly laughed. 'Daddy said if I didn't take my hat and gloves today my fingers might fall off with fostbike.'

'Fostbike, eh?' Fran raised her eyebrows at Ethan.

'Fostbike is a terrible thing.' He nodded. 'But I think you mean frostbite, Tilly.'

'How can frost bite?' she asked.

'It doesn't actually bite,' Ethan explained. 'But it can—'

'Oh never mind, Daddy. Tell me later. Let's go and walk on the beach in the snow.'

Tilly skipped ahead and waited outside the school gate, her head tilted backwards and her mouth open to catch some snowflakes.

'She'd absolutely adorable.' Fran tightened her scarf around her neck and pulled her hat lower over her ears.

'She's a good girl.'

'A credit to you.'

His smile made her heart flutter.

'Is she excited about Christmas?'

'What do you think?' He laughed. 'I still need to pick up a few things though. Trouble is, as she's getting older, it gets harder to pick out things she'd like. You know… trinkets and stocking fillers and that. As a man, it can be complicated shopping for girls.'

'I could always come shopping with you… if you like.' Fran held her breath. Was that appropriate or had she overstepped the mark?

'You'd come with me? To help me?'

'Of course.'

'I haven't had help with shopping for Tilly for ages. Even when Melanie was around, she'd do most of her shopping online and have it gift wrapped too. I like to wander around the shops and markets and pick things out. It adds to the festive experience. Although, having said that, I do get apprehensive now that Tilly won't like what I've bought and it would be wonderful to have a second opinion, especially a female perspective.'

'Then tell me when you'd like to go and we can go together.'

'Fabulous.'

They walked out of the gate and down the hill towards the beach. Tilly had found some of her friends and they walked together, chatting away about Christmas and TV and about their teachers. The snow was falling heavily but not sticking as the ground was quite damp and Fran felt a bit disappointed, as it would have been lovely for Ethan and Tilly to see how pretty Penhallow Sands was in the winter.

Suddenly, Fran skidded and yelped, then flailed her arms as she lost her balance. Two strong hands caught her under her arms and helped her to stand firm again. Her heart raced and her breath came in short, fast gasps.

'It's okay, Fran. I've got you.'

Ethan held her against his chest and she held on to his jacket, waiting until her heart had slowed again. His delicious scent washed over her and she breathed him in, wanting to capture his sandalwood cologne and the scent beneath that was all his own, and hold on to them so she could smell him anytime she liked.

'I'm so nervous about falling,' she said as she peered up at him. 'The idea of breaking a wrist or my arm terrifies me because I need them to make a living. Thanks for saving me.'

'Of course I'd save you. I saw you lose your balance so I reacted. There must have been a patch of ice where that pipe is leaking.' He pointed behind Fran at the retaining wall of a house where a pipe had leaked water over the pavement.

'I didn't see it.'

'Black ice most likely.' He rubbed his toe over it. 'Yup. Dangerous stuff. Are you all right?'

She nodded. 'A bit shaky but I'm okay.'

'You need to get some sugar into you for the shock.'

'It's okay, I'm not straight out of the Victorian era.' She laughed. 'I don't need smelling salts either.'

When Ethan didn't laugh, she stepped back and looked at him. He was frowning.

'I'm sorry.' She touched his hand, although as they were both wearing gloves, it seemed a bit of a wasted gesture. 'I was just joking. I didn't meant to sound ungrateful.'

'It's okay, Fran, I'm just... sometimes I can be a bit sensitive. Stupid, I know, and probably what some people would class as unmanly, but it's just because of what I've been through. Although, having said that, my mum always did call me a sensitive soul.'

'That's nothing to be ashamed of.' She touched his arm now. 'In fact it's admirable.'

'You think so?' He peered at her from under the rim of his black wool hat.

'I do.'

He smiled and relief flooded through her. She'd hate to upset him or hurt his feelings when all he'd done was be so kind to her.

'Take my arm, Fran, because we don't want you slipping again.'

Her heart soared as she slid her hand through the crook of his elbow and moved closer to his side.

'Especially in your condition,' he added, causing the smile to slide from her face.

Down on the beach, Ethan watched as Tilly twirled on the spot, catching snowflakes in her mouth. The clouds were thick above them, the winter sun a dot of white light straining to pierce their density. Everything seemed muffled, from the shouts of children on the beach to the cars on the road to the cawing of the crows on the cold rail that separated the beach from the pavement.

Next to him, Fran walked in silence, and he wondered what she was thinking. After seeing Tilly's play, was Fran wondering what her own child would be like? If she would sit alone to watch his or her school plays or if she'd have a partner? Ethan knew what it was like to be alone and he didn't want that for Fran. Having someone to share such experiences with made them even better, just as having someone to speak to about memories did too.

'I wonder if Holly will have a white wedding.' Fran removed her glasses and wiped them with a tissue then put them back on.

'Would she like that?' he asked.

'As long as her guests could get there to help celebrate.'

'How's she feeling?'

'Very excited but also a bit tired. It's a lot of planning and she's also running Greenacres, along with her dad and Rich.'

'It must be cool to have your own vineyard.'

'I think so, and it's all Holly's ever known.'

'So she lives there with Rich, Luke, her dad and grand-mother?'

Fran nodded.

'Where's her mum?'

Fran stopped walking and turned to him. 'She passed away when Holly was younger.'

Ethan sighed. 'That's sad.'

'You know what it feels like.'

He nodded. 'But I was twenty-seven.'

'That's still young to lose a parent.'

'It was really hard. Mum was... she was just brilliant.'

'You miss her.'

'Every day. She always knew what to say to make me feel better and she was such a positive person, even when she had cancer and knew she wasn't going to make it. She just stayed so brave, trying to help me and Dad along, trying to ensure that our last memories of her would be happy. She tried to leave us with a positive message to keep us going, but as time has passed, it sometimes seems harder and harder to hold on to what she was, to what she did and to who she was. Does that make sense?'

'It does and I think it's nature's way of protecting us. If our grief always stayed as acute as when we first lost someone, we'd never be able to go on, would we?'

'No, not at all. I mean... my grief is still painful, but it ebbs and flows. Some days, I can hear Mum's laughter as clearly as my own, then others, I feel like she's been gone for a lifetime and that she's getting further and further away from me and that one day... I'll forget her face.'

'You'll never forget her, Ethan, but you will adjust. It's what we do. You've already adjusted to deal with your loss but that doesn't mean that you'll ever stop loving her. She'll always be in your heart.'

'She will and it sounds better when you say all that. You're very reassuring, Fran.'

She smiled. 'I haven't lost a parent but I was with Holly as she went through it, so I did a lot of reading to try to help her with her grief and I learnt quite a lot about the grieving process. You've done really well to cope as you have.'

'You're very kind.'

'And as for your mum and what you've told me about her... she sounds wonderful.'

'She was.'

Fran reached for his hand and he held on tight. Her kindness was soothing in the same way that his mother's had been. She was warm, friendly and non-judgemental and he felt safe with her. He had never expected to feel that around a woman again. Perhaps it was because he'd reassured himself that he wasn't in a place to fall in love, so his heart was in some way protected, or perhaps it was because something inside him knew that Fran would never do anything to hurt anyone, not even him.

'Let's walk for a bit longer so Tilly can enjoy the snow, then go and get some hot chocolates, shall we?' she asked. 'That way, we can warm up and enjoy a sugar hit before you head home.'

'Sounds like a very good plan.' Ethan nodded.

And as they followed his daughter, their hands stayed joined, and Ethan allowed himself to start to believe that he wasn't completely alone any more.

Chapter 15

Fran and Ethan had arranged to meet in Newquay to do some Christmas shopping. Audrey was looking after Tilly for him, so he'd be free to purchase her presents – with Fran's help, of course.

Since the school play, Fran had been floating along, experiencing unfamiliar, but wonderful, emotions and looking forward to seeing Ethan again. When they'd walked on the beach in the snow, Ethan had started to open up to her about his mum and she had felt privileged that he wanted to speak to her about the woman he'd loved so much. Fran could see how losing his mum had left a gaping hole in his life. She might not see her parents every day but she knew they were there if she needed them and losing either of them was something she couldn't bear to think about. She wanted to be there for Ethan and to support him as much as she could do. He was a good man and he deserved to have friends and family around him and Tilly.

Fran drove slowly around looking for a space, then parked her car in the overflow Christmas parking near the sports centre. The snowfall the other day hadn't come to anything much, but small mounds of snow remained, soiled now from cars and bikes, a sad reminder of how pretty it could be when everything had a cold white covering.

She pulled her coat tighter across her chest and made her way to the Christmas market in town. Ethan had suggested that they meet by the enormous Christmas tree that stood at the entrance to the market, so when Fran arrived there, she looked around for him.

'Fran!' He waved at her and her pulse quickened at the sight of him. He was just so handsome that he literally took her breath away. She swallowed, hurried over to him and he hugged her then kissed her cheek. His now familiar scent made her ache, in a physical and emotional way, to hold on to him. She forced herself to let go, but even though she stepped back, her heart held on.

'Hi.' She gave him a mischievous grin. 'I hope your credit card is ready for this.'

'What, you mean it's going to take a battering?'

'I do indeed.'

He grimaced. 'Yikes! Good job I set some money aside for Christmas.'

'Very wise.'

'Would you like to grab a drink or something to eat or shall we do some shopping then stop for some refreshment?'

'I like how you always think of food. You're a man after my own heart.'

'I think it's important to keep my blood sugar and hydration levels even, as well as yours, seeing as how you're currently creating a new person as well as fuelling yourself.'

Fran dropped her eyes to the ground and swallowed her protest. She couldn't tell him, she just couldn't, but she didn't know how much longer she could keep up the pretence either. It was just horrid. Holly had told her to be honest with Ethan but it didn't feel like the right time to air it all. Besides which, she was afraid of telling Ethan in case he saw her differently, which surely he would do when she confessed that she'd been lying to him? It was such a mess.

'Hey, why the sad face?' he asked, reaching out and gently raising her chin. 'Come on, it's almost Christmas and we're going to have some fun.'

'I'm okay.' She nodded, conscious of his hand touching her chin. He slid it up to her cheek and ran his thumb over her skin, causing the hairs on her arms to rise and other parts of her body to awaken.

'As long as you're sure. I want us to have an enjoyable day.'

He removed his hand from her cheek and held it out to her and she entwined her fingers with his.

'Let's see what the stallholders have to offer then, shall we?'

They headed under the festive banner and into the market.

All around them, people browsed the different stalls, and as Fran and Ethan walked, they pointed at the variety of available wares, from wooden toys to jewellery to sweets and clothing made from sustainable sources. There were stalls with gadgets, some with elaborately carved wooden clocks and some with beautifully covered classic books. Then there were the food stalls, from cinnamon sugar-coated nuts to crepes to fat shiny bratwurst to mulled cider and wine. The aromas spiced the air, making Fran's stomach rumble even though she'd had poached eggs on toast just over an hour earlier.

'Everything smells so good,' Ethan said, making a show of sniffing the air. 'We should definitely get something to eat while we're here.'

'I agree. Ooh! Does Tilly like things for her hair?' Fran asked, pointing at a stall to their right.

'She does. Unfortunately, I'm not the best at creating different styles but she does have Scarlett now to help with that and has run over to Audrey and Gary's several mornings to get her hair done because… *Daddy can't get plaits right.*' He rolled his eyes. 'I'm useless at some things.'

'Not at all. Hairstyles take certain skills. I've kept mine short most of my life because… well… it's just easier.'

'It suits you.' He fingered the rim of her bobble hat. 'Although I can't see it today, but I do like your hair.'

'Thank you.'

'No need to thank me. I'm just telling you what I see.'

'Let's check out the headbands and bobbles then.' Fran led him towards the stall and they browsed the range of hair accessories.

Ten minutes later, Ethan had purchased two headbands – one red and one purple – and some bobbles in a variety of colours, as well as two scrunchies – one green and one red to match the headband. Fran had managed to persuade him to try the one headband on, which had sent the young female stallholder into fits of giggles. Ethan had pretended that he was buying the headbands for himself and he'd been quite convincing.

They strolled to the next stall, which sold stationery, wooden toys and carvings.

'Would she like a toy dog?' Fran picked up a tiny British Bulldog and moved its legs back and forth. 'I'm not sure that it does much but it's cute.'

'Stocking filler?' Ethan took the dog from her.

'And they've got a greyhound.' Fran pointed at the shelf. 'She could have one of each.'

'Good plan. When she next asks for a dog, I can tell her she already has two.'

Fran laughed and shook her head. 'I'm not sure that she's going to fall for that, but it's worth a try.'

While Ethan paid, Fran looked at the stationery range and selected some pencils and a pencil case that all had dogs on them. She added a pencil sharpener and a pack of erasers, then a drawing pad with a dog on the cover.

'For you?' Ethan asked as he joined her.

'No, for Tilly. I thought that if she has some time over the holidays, I could do some drawing with her.'

Ethan smiled. 'She'd love that. She's not a bad little artist but sometimes the proportions are a bit out and it creates some hilarity for those being sketched. The portraits she's done of Audrey and Gary have caused Scarlett to laugh so much, she said that she thought she was going to burst. And the ones she does of me always have really long legs and a tiny body, as if I'm some kind of arachnid, then there's usually a floppy fringe on top.'

Fran giggled. 'I could teach her some basic techniques and she can use the toys you just bought as models to try to get the proportions sorted, although I think getting proportions wrong is quite normal in children's sketches.'

Fran paid then waited as the stallholder wrapped the stationery in tissue paper and put them into a paper bag.

'Where next?' Ethan asked.

'How about some jewellery?' Fran pointed at a stall selling silver jewellery. 'Are her ears pierced?'

Ethan shook his head. 'She has asked but I've made some excuses so far. I can't face sitting there while someone puts holes in my daughter's ears.'

'I can always take her to get them done if you don't want to.'

'I might have to take you up on that. I know it's just one of those things that people get done, but even the thought of it makes my palms clammy.'

At the stall, they found a delicate silver chain with a small locket set with a moonstone and Ethan purchased it for Tilly along with a stretchy bracelet featuring a matching charm.

'I don't know about you, Fran, but I am starting to get a bit peckish.' He took her hand again. 'How about a crepe?'

'You've twisted my arm.'

They headed for the stall where pancake-flavoured steam escaped into the chilly air and ordered two chocolate-orange crepes with vanilla ice cream, then they sat at one of the picnic benches in front of the stall and tucked into the delicious treats.

–

The crepe was delicious and even better was eating it sitting opposite Fran. She ate with gusto and he was glad that she wasn't being plagued by morning sickness or dizziness like Melanie had been. He was also pretty happy with how they'd done so far with the Christmas shopping and couldn't wait to see Tilly's face when she opened her gifts. Obviously, he had a lot more to get, but having some help with choosing things for her was brilliant. He had never liked doing all of this alone, but had always got on with it. This year, however, he was really enjoying the whole process. He needed to pick up some gifts for Audrey, Gary and the girls too, so he'd try to do that today and get Fran's help and advice while she was with him.

'All done?' he asked as Fran licked her lips.

'That was so good.'

'Want another?'

She pursed her lips. 'I could eat another one but I think I'd like to do some more shopping, then we could try something else. There's plenty of choice here and I did fancy those cinnamon sugar-coated nuts.'

'Well let's do some more shopping then we can pick some up.'

They binned their plates and serviettes then walked out into the thoroughfare again. As carols filled the chilly air with the promise of Christmas just around the corner, Ethan held out his arm and Fran tucked hers though it. He hadn't realised how much he missed having company just for simple things like shopping. Having someone to hold his hand, laugh at his jokes and respond positively to him was uplifting and something he didn't want to lose. He couldn't help wishing that things had been slightly different – if Fran hadn't been pregnant, if he hadn't been so worried about bringing someone else into Tilly's life, then there might have been a chance for something more to develop between him and Fran. They had the spark of attraction, they got on really well and Tilly liked her. But how could he bring a new woman into his and Tilly's lives along with a new baby? It would be too much at once and he didn't know if he could handle it, let alone his daughter.

Nope. Tilly had to be his priority and anything else he might be feeling would have to be put to one side. For the time being at least. Fran had a big year ahead of her and he didn't want to add any complications for her either. It seemed that she'd had one man mess her around, the idiot who'd got her pregnant then disappeared, and Ethan couldn't stand the idea of letting her down himself. He would always have to put Tilly first, and if something happened between him and Fran and he had to choose between her and Tilly, his daughter would be his priority, even if it meant failing Fran in some way.

However, he definitely wanted to be there for Fran and to support her as much as he could. They passed a stall of baby clothes and he had an idea.

'Tell you what, Fran, let's head for the shops then come back here later.'

'Why?' She smiled up at him.

'I have an idea. Come on.'

They made their way back to the market entrance and as they passed the big Christmas tree, Ethan could barely keep the grin from his face. He just hoped Fran would like his idea too.

–

Fran giggled as Ethan led her through the crowds on the high street, guiding her past the Salvation Army as they played Christmas favourites, then around a man on a mobility scooter and past a twin pram. He kept checking that she was okay, that she wasn't too tired and that she didn't need a drink or a sit down. He was so attentive and it was wonderful; no man had ever shown her so much respect or consideration before.

Finally, he stopped in front of a shop and placed his hands on her shoulders.

'Look, Fran, I know it's early days for you, and you need to have your antenatal appointments and all that, but I thought it might be nice if we had a look around in here. Just to get you thinking about what you need to get and what you'd like. You have an exciting and exhausting time ahead of you, but I'd really like to be there to support you in any way that I can and I think this is a good place to start.'

She frowned at him, not sure what he was getting at, but his enthusiasm was infectious.

He turned her gently so she could see the shop he'd brought her to and her heart plummeted to her boots.

'Oh…' She took a deep breath. 'We don't need to do this yet.'

'Come on.' He pulled her towards the shop. 'It'll be fun. You don't have to buy anything… probably shouldn't yet anyway, but it's nice to have a look at what you can buy when you're ready.'

Fran's mouth was bone dry and she could barely swallow as they entered the shop. The smell of baby products hit her immediately, sweet and fruity, reminding her of apricots and vanilla. She tried not to look at anyone or anything, but as they walked around the shop, prams, high chairs, bottles and maternity clothes all loomed like spectres at the corners of her vision, taunting her because she was a fake and a fraud. Everywhere she looked, she saw women in various stages of pregnancy, rubbing their bumps protectively, placing supporting hands on their spines, and others with tiny babies that they wheeled around in fancy prams or carried strapped to their chests in papooses. It was like a nightmare where she was being reminded about the horrid lie she was perpetuating, and being forced to walk around the shop with this charming man was her punishment. She was a liar and when Ethan found out he was going to hate her.

'Ethan!' She gasped, pulling her scarf away from her throat. 'Ethan, I...'

'Sorry.' His eyes widened. 'Too much too soon. I'm such an idiot. Are you superstitious? I know some people are and they won't even tell anyone they're expecting until after the twelve-week scan. Fran, I'm so sorry. I should have asked but I got carried away with the idea that this would be... well... sweet and kind and thoughtful.' He smacked his forehead. 'Please forgive me.'

'No, Ethan, it's not that.'

Fran stared around her at the teddy bears that mocked her with their *It's a Boy!* or *It's a Girl!* banners, at the racks of dummies and beakers, at the rows of bouncy chairs and feeding cushions, and panic gripped her. A cold sweat broke out on her back and in spite of her coat, scarf and hat, she was chilled to the bone.

'What is it then?' He touched her arm gently and she snatched it back.

She hated what she was doing to this man, to this kind, sensitive man who had become her friend and who she now knew she adored. How had she fallen for him in such a short space of time? Holly had always told her that when you met the one, you'd fall hard and fast and it seemed that Fran's best friend was right. Fran had feelings for Ethan that stretched beyond friendship, that had made something inside her shift and loosen and filled her heart and mind with his image, his scent and his whole being. She adored him and yet… here she was, lying to him every single day.

He deserved far better.

'Fran, please, you're scaring me.'

She opened her mouth to tell him the truth, to clear the air, to spill the beans. If she were pregnant then her baby wouldn't even be as big as a bean now, or would it? How pregnant did Ethan think she was? How pregnant was she pretending to be? She'd hated lying so much that she hadn't even allowed herself to consider the finer details of the deception.

'I'm so sorry, Ethan. Please… I'm so sorry. I…' She tried to tell him but the shop seemed to fill up in an instant. To her right, to her left, behind her, people pushed and jostled, squeezed past them, and the air seemed to be sucked from the room. Her hat and scarf prickled her skin and suddenly, she was hot all over. The sweat trickling down her spine was warm now and her armpits burned and itched as if she'd sprayed deodorant too close to her skin.

Fran tried to suck in a breath, scanned the shop for somewhere quiet she could take Ethan to tell him what she'd lied about, but there was nowhere. The walls and ceiling closed in on her and she wanted to scream.

She had to get out.

She needed fresh air.

She couldn't do this right now.

She was the worst person in the whole world…

'Why are you sorry?' Hurt and confusion stretched across his face and she knew she'd never seen anyone looking so bewildered in her life. Without meaning to, she had hurt him, and it would only get worse when he knew the truth.

She shook her head. 'Sorry!'

Then she turned and pushed her way through the shoppers, ignoring the exclamations and the annoyed stares as she shoved people out of the way, and she didn't stop until she was out on the street, her hat in her hand, the cold December air soothing her burning cheeks and sweaty scalp, cooling her aching throat and raw lungs.

She glanced back at the shop but Ethan had been swallowed up by the crowds. It was as if he had never existed, as if she had imagined him and their time together, and she felt that was her punishment, exactly what she deserved. There was no turning back now, so she hurried away from the high street, shame crawling all over her like stinging ants, tears running down her cheeks and sadness swelling in her chest.

Ethan didn't deserve any of this and she was devastated to be the cause of his hurt and confusion. It had to be up there with the worst days of her life. She knew that as long as she lived she would never be able to clear the image of Ethan's hurt and confusion from her mind.

Chapter 16

Ethan picked up his mug of tea and sipped it, then winced. It was cold. How long had he been sitting on the sofa staring into space? He'd been unable to face returning to the Christmas market after Fran had run off, so he'd gone back to his car and sat there for half an hour with his mobile in his hand. He'd been really worried about Fran and had tried to call her five times but she hadn't answered and at some point it seemed that her phone had been switched off. Finally, he'd started the car and driven back to Rosewood, but when he'd gone to collect Tilly, she'd begged him to let her stay with Scarlett as she was going to give her a makeover. Ethan had been glad to leave his daughter there, not wanting her to pick up on his low mood, and when Audrey had said that she'd give Tilly her dinner and bring her home later on, he could have kissed her. Instead, he'd thanked her and whispered that he had some gift wrapping to do.

And now, as the afternoon had worn on, he felt terrible. Taking Fran to the baby shop had been a huge mistake and incredibly naïve of him. He should have thought about it more, even asked Fran if she'd like to go there, but no, he'd allowed himself to get carried away with the idea that she'd like to look at maternity clothes and baby things. What an idiot! He'd upset Fran and she'd been so distressed that she'd had to leave the shop.

But he'd also been hurt. He'd put his trust in her and let his guard down and look where it had got him. His gesture had been mistimed by a few months perhaps, but rather than talk it through, Fran had run away and now Ethan had no idea where he stood with her. What if Tilly had been with them and Fran had stormed off? How would his little girl have felt? Everything would have been so much worse if Tilly had witnessed the scene that had unfolded.

He put his mug down on the table and buried his face in his hands. There was so much about this situation that was wrong. He shouldn't have allowed himself to like Fran so much and he'd also mistakenly believed that she felt the same. He knew they couldn't get romantically involved but had hoped for friendship, had even started to wonder how things could progress between them given time. And look what had happened.

Confusion and doubt hung above him like dark clouds and he wished he could draw the curtains and climb the stairs to bed. The idea of trying to get through the evening ahead seemed unachievable, but he knew from past experience that he would survive. He had been through worse. He just had to go through the motions and try not to dwell on his worries.

He got up and took the mug through to the kitchen then emptied it down the sink. At least if he made another cuppa it would give him something to do, something normal and that had saved him many a time in the past.

He switched the kettle on then leant against the kitchen unit, gazing out of the window at the small garden behind the cottage. The sky was dark, even though it wasn't late, and a few snowflakes drifted down but they melted as soon as they touched the grass. Some things in this world came to nothing, and that was something Ethan was trying to come to terms with.

Just like delicate snowflakes, Ethan's hopes for his friendship with Fran melted away. Some things were too difficult to hold on to.

–

Fran stood outside Ethan's front door, her heart pounding and her mind racing. She'd driven home from Newquay earlier with a heavy heart and when she'd got home she'd cried her eyes out. She felt awful for running off and leaving Ethan but she'd panicked and it had seemed like the only option at the time. Now, though, she realised that it had been completely the wrong thing to do. Ethan must have been distraught wondering where she'd gone. The battery on her phone had died but when she'd charged it, she saw that she had several missed calls from Ethan and it dawned on her exactly how worried he must have been.

So now she had come to apologise and to try to explain. Holly had told her to tell Ethan the truth about the pregnancy and now she felt that it was either that or lose him completely. She could only hope that he would understand and accept her apology.

She took a deep breath and knocked on the door, then stood back and waited. Being here at Rosewood like this was strange because usually she'd be going to the tea shop or to see Audrey about an order. Ethan's cottage was set back behind the tea shop, so it was quite private, but even so, she wondered if someone might see her and wonder what she was doing here.

Calling on a friend!

The voice in her head came from out of nowhere but it made her smile. It was true... she was calling on a friend. But in the next instant she stopped grinning at the thought that he was a friend who might hate her now and with good reason.

The door swung inwards and Ethan stood in front of her. His face was pale, his hair was a mess and he looked exhausted.

'Oh!' He frowned and pushed his hands back through his hair. 'Sorry, I wasn't expecting to see you, Fran.'

'I should have called.' She sighed. 'But I worried that if I did you'd tell me not to come and I really needed to come and see you and to... Ethan, I need to apologise and to explain why I behaved as I did.'

His face changed before her eyes as he clearly tried to process what she'd just said.

'You don't owe me anything, Fran, it's fine. Honestly. I was a bit surprised when you ran off but I feel like an idiot for taking you to a baby shop in the first place. It was too much too soon and I understand.'

'No. You don't.' Her tone was abrupt and she shook her head. 'What I mean is that... it's complicated.'

'Okay.'

'Can I come in? Please? I'd prefer to discuss this privately.'

'Yes, of course. Sorry.'

He stepped back and she entered the hallway. The cottage smelt of toast and coffee and something else – it was like a magnification of Ethan's scent, a combination of his soap, fabric conditioner and cologne. It was comforting and uplifting and it made her yearn for a hug. What if she never got to hug him again, to feel his strong arms holding her, his breath tickling her cheek? The thought made her crumble inside. How would she cope without his kindness, his friendship and just knowing that he was there, not far away? She'd known him for just weeks but those weeks had been intense, packed with emotions she'd never felt before, and the thought of losing everything that she felt for him was unbearable.

'Come on through to the lounge.'

Ethan closed the door then led the way.

'Can I get you anything?' he asked. 'A tea, coffee or water?'

'No, thank you.' She looked around. 'Where's Tilly?'

'She's with Audrey. She'll be home later.'

'Right.'

That was good; it meant they had time to talk.

Fran perched on the edge of the sofa and Ethan sat on the chair opposite.

'I've never had a conversation like this,' she said as she rubbed her palms on her knees. 'It's so difficult.'

'What do you mean?' he asked.

'Well... a relationship conversation. Not that we have a relationship as such, but we have a friendship and... and...' She tapped her knees. 'See what I mean? I'm so afraid of saying the wrong thing, then my mouth runs away with me and it's like... blah blah blah... shut up, Fran!'

Ethan watched her, his expression neutral, and she wished she knew what he was thinking. Was that hatred in his eyes already, or pity or apathy?

'Fran... I really am sorry. It was insensitive of me to take you to a baby shop. I thought about it afterwards and I should know better. Some people are really superstitious and worry that they'll get excited then something will go wrong with the pregnancy and… and—'

'I'm not pregnant!'

His mouth fell open.

'What?' He frowned, then his eyes widened. 'I am so, so sorry. When did it… happen?'

'Why are you sorry? When did what happen?'

'Have you… did you…' He covered his mouth and shook his head. 'You've lost the baby?'

'No. It's not that, Ethan.' Fran ground her teeth together. This was getting worse. 'I never was pregnant.'

He tilted his head to one side then the other, then he stood up and shook his head before sitting down again.

'I don't understand.'

'Ethan… It was all a big misunderstanding.'

'But the positive pregnancy test at the tea shop.'

'It wasn't mine.'

'Then why did you… who did you… what was it doing…' His eyes flickered around the room as he tried to digest the information.

'Look… it was never meant to go this far—'

'What was it? Some kind of horrible, sick joke?' He stared at her, his eyes filled with horror.

'Of course not!'

'Then what the hell, Fran?'

'It was Holly's test.'

'Holly?'

'Yes, she's pregnant. She did the test at the tea shop and I was the only person who knew at the time. Rich knows now, but no one else. See… she's getting married soon and her grandmother has been unwell and she didn't want

everyone to know and for it to overshadow the wedding…
and so on… so I agreed to let people think it was me.'

'But…' He rubbed his eyes. 'That doesn't make any sense. I can understand that Holly and Rich might want to keep it quiet until after the wedding, but for you to pretend that you were pregnant and to deceive so many people…'

'Looking back on it now, no, it doesn't make sense and it has gone way too far, but I never thought we'd get on so well or that you would be so sweet and caring or that… that I'd like you as much as I do.'

'When were you going to tell me the truth?'

'As soon as I could.'

'I feel so stupid. I fell for it all. I believed in you, Fran. I believed in us.'

'I am so sorry, Ethan. You're not stupid at all. Why wouldn't you have believed me? I wanted to tell you before but I also felt the need to protect Holly. If I'd told you and you'd told someone else, then it would have got round the village and Holly would have had even more on her plate than she already does. If she'd lost the baby then her granny would have had to deal with that and she's already so fragile… I care about Holly and her family; I've known them all my life. It just seemed easier to let people think it was me then to clear it up after the wedding.'

'Right.'

Ethan leant on his knees, his eyes fixed on a spot on the floor.

'Ethan?'

He didn't reply.

'Do you hate me now?'

'You're definitely not pregnant?'

'No, I'm not.'

'And you never were.'

'No.'

'Right.' He nodded but didn't raise his eyes.

'Can't you even look at me now?' She could hear the pain in her own voice.

'I just… I need some time to process this. I thought I'd upset you, Fran, that I'd done something awful in taking you to the baby shop and that… that I was in the wrong. I felt bloody dreadful. And all the time, you were lying to me.'

'Not just to you. It was stupid, I know, so very stupid, but I did it with good intentions.'

He looked up now and his green eyes were cold and hard, as if a shutter had come down or he'd flicked a switch. They weren't the eyes she knew and adored. The eyes she had wanted to lose herself in. The eyes of the man she was beginning to love.

'I… I need some time, Fran. This is all rather… confusing.'

'Of course.' Her throat burned and her eyes stung as she pushed herself up to her feet. 'I was torn, Ethan. I've known Holly my whole life. She's my best friend. You have become a good friend to me and I…' *I have other feelings for you.* 'I…' She couldn't get the words out; they threatened to choke her with their significance and their impact. Even if she uttered them now, would it make any difference? She couldn't see how and the fear of what the rejection would do to her if she did tell him and he turned her away made her tremble. 'I'll go.'

She left the room, and in the hallway she sucked in deep breaths, trying to regain her composure before leaving the cottage. The pain in her chest was horrendous; she'd never hurt like this before. Was this heartbreak then? Had she lost Ethan's friendship, respect and any chance of anything more because she'd been protecting another friend? She hadn't wanted to deceive him but it seemed that she'd really hurt him by doing so.

A knock at the door made her jump and she gasped as the door opened and Tilly walked in with Audrey. Fran quickly wiped her face and dragged a smile to her lips. She felt that she must look like a ventriloquist's dummy, the smile on her face frozen and fake. As fake as her pregnancy had been.

'Oh, hello, Fran!' Audrey beamed at her. 'I wasn't expecting to see you here. I have a key, obviously, but I usually knock first. In future, I'll make sure to knock and wait.' She winked.

'Hello, Audrey. No, please don't do that on my account. I… uh… was dropping something off for Ethan. He put it in my bag by mistake when we were at the Christmas market this morning.'

'I see.' Audrey nodded, her eyes wide. She clearly thought there was more to this than Fran was letting on.

'There's my girl!' Ethan had appeared in the lounge doorway and he scooped Tilly up into a hug, burying his face in her hair.

'Daddy! Why are you hugging me so tight? Did you miss me so much?' Tilly giggled as she patted Ethan's shoulder.

'I'll… uh… be going now.' Fran stepped out of the open door. 'See you soon.'

She gave a brief wave and Tilly and Audrey waved back, but even though he had raised his head, Ethan kept his eyes on his daughter.

Fran hurried along the path out of the gate to her car, biting her lip until she tasted blood to stop the tears from falling. She had messed up big time and she had no one to blame but herself. It was time to go home to her animals where she wouldn't hurt anyone or upset anyone and where she felt safe. She clearly wasn't any good at this relationship business and that was why she'd remained largely single for thirty-one years. It was how she intended to stay.

It seemed that even if she had wished otherwise, it wouldn't change a thing.

–

Ethan kissed Tilly's forehead then padded out of her room. She'd fallen asleep as he was reading her a second story. Audrey and Scarlett must have tired her out and he was grateful because he needed some time to think.

All evening, he'd tried to push Fran from his thoughts but it wasn't easy. Her sad indigo eyes and trembling hands kept popping into his mind and tugging at his heart, and her explanation was like a merry-go-round in his brain. She hadn't wanted to lie, hadn't intended on deceiving him. She'd been protecting her friend, the woman she'd known and cared about since childhood. It all made sense when he thought about it rationally and yet... The fact that she'd deceived him stung.

Ethan knew why. He had his own issues and the feelings he was developing for Fran made him vulnerable. He didn't like being vulnerable and the thought of being hurt scared him, but even more, the thought that Tilly could be hurt terrified him. Fran had reasons for what she'd done but Ethan didn't know if he could get past the fact that she hadn't been open and honest with him. He wouldn't hold it against her, but whether he could open his heart to her now – even as a friend – was something he didn't know.

Also… the fact that she wasn't pregnant changed things completely. Ethan had wanted to be there for her, to help and support her in any way he could, but she wasn't pregnant and there was no absent father. The Fran he had known didn't exist; she had deceived him and he would need to get to know her all over again. She wasn't about to begin a journey as a single mother; in fact, she was as free as anyone could be. He wasn't sure how he felt about that because it was a whole different situation to the one that they'd been in before. Fran wasn't having a child, so surely their situation was less complicated? And that was actually quite scary. One of the major reasons why Ethan believed he couldn't become involved with Fran had disappeared in the blink of an eye and now…

What now?

He really didn't know.

Ethan still had Tilly to think about. He no longer knew if Fran could be trusted. He wanted to believe what she'd said about protecting Holly and not wanting to deceive him. But believing her meant opening himself up to the possibility of loss or pain, as well as placing Tilly in a very risky position. Tilly's mother had let her down. Would Fran let her down too?

He had no idea what to do.

So perhaps it was better to do nothing and just let things work themselves out in whatever way was best. His mother would have said, *What will be will be…* and more than ever before, Ethan wanted to try to trust that she was right.

Chapter 17

Sundays could be delightfully relaxing affairs when the only person you had to please was yourself, but this particular Sunday was one of the worst Fran had ever experienced. After the disastrous way yesterday's shopping trip had ended, she'd fallen into a fitful sleep filled with nightmares about searching for Ethan and Tilly and being unable to find them. Every time she'd woken, she'd longed to find a warm solid presence next to her in bed so she could snuggle close and feel less alone, but, of course, she was alone.

She had finally dragged herself out of bed at five a.m. and trudged down the stairs to make coffee and to watch the sunrise through her kitchen window. The dogs had fussed around her, sniffing at her hands and feet and trying to comfort her, and she'd hugged them all in turn and thanked them for their love. But try as she might, she couldn't get Ethan from her mind, couldn't stop wondering what he was thinking today and if he hated her as he had every right to do.

The gifts she had bought for Tilly were on the kitchen table and it hurt to look at them, but it also gave her an idea. She wanted to give Tilly the stationery for Christmas, but on its own, it didn't look like much. Ethan had said that Tilly had always wanted a dog, and although

Fran couldn't actually give her a real dog, she could give her something quite close to it.

'Come here, boy.' She held out a hand to the small white Westie and he plodded over and sniffed it then gave her palm a lick.

'How do you fancy posing for me?'

He gazed up at her, his eyes filled with trust and love and she scooped him up and hugged him to her chest.

'You are a lovely boy and you deserve all the kindness a person can give. You're safe here now and I promise that you'll never be scared or lonely again.'

For a moment, Fran wondered if she was echoing her own feelings, possibly even projecting them onto the dog, but then, he'd been through such a lot and even if she couldn't cure her own heartbreak, she could help him to overcome his.

Ten minutes later, she'd settled him in a basket in front of the Aga and she sat in front of him, cross-legged on the floor with an A3 sketch pad in front of her. She worked quickly, her hand holding the pencil almost independently of her body, so used to drawing that it flew across the page sketching the dog's outline.

Soon, the lines on the page started to take shape and the image of the dog in his basket became clear. She could see his small black nose, his fluffy ears and his brown button eyes, open to keep an eye on her and to ensure that she remained close. It was all that this little dog wanted; to be loved and cared for and to love and care for his owner in return. Such simple needs and ones that Fran wanted to fulfil for him.

As she made smaller, lighter strokes with the pencil to add depth to his fur, a snuffling at the back of her neck made her giggle and she turned to find Crosby, her large golden lab, right behind her.

'What are you up to, Crosby?'

The dog's tail wagged in wide arcs and Fran giggled, feeling her sadness lift for a moment.

'Sit next me then, Crosby, and let's see if we can get this portrait of our little boy right, shall we?'

Crosby sat next to Fran on the tiles and she continued to draw, knowing that although she felt an emptiness, a space in her life where Ethan had been, she would always have the love and devotion of her furry family members. They understood her in ways that it seemed many people never would.

She had thought that perhaps Ethan was the exception, but she'd destroyed the chance of finding out if she was right by hurting him. A tear plopped onto the paper and she sniffed then wiped the tear away. She wanted this portrait to be created with love and happiness, not tears and pain, so it was time to pull herself together and accept that although she had done wrong, she could not control how things would work out from this point on. All she could do was be kind and caring and show love and understanding, just as her dogs always seemed to do.

—

'So what's the occasion?' Fran asked the following day as she stood in the lounge of the house at Greenacres. In the corner, an artificial but incredibly realistic-looking tree stood on a festive mat, its branches adorned with small white lights that twinkled in the afternoon gloom.

'Take a seat.' Holly gestured at the sofa, so Fran sat down next to Glenda.

'Hello Fran, dear.' Glenda smiled. Her long white hair was coiled into its signature bun and her pale green eyes glowed in her weathered face. She was wearing makeup, and had clearly made an effort, as her cheeks were rosy with blusher and her eyebrows drawn on with a dark blonde pencil. Her familiar scent, Lily of the Valley, made Fran think of the days she'd spent at the vineyard as a child, when Glenda had baked with her and Holly and when life had seemed somewhat simpler. Sometimes, Fran thought she'd love to return to that simpler time, but then she also knew that she'd have to go through everything again, and witnessing Holly, Glenda and Bruce losing Holly's mum, Sarah, and her grandad, Henry, again was not something Fran wanted to see. Their pain had been unfathomable and although they had made it through that difficult time, Fran knew that they all missed Sarah and Henry Morton.

Bruce was sitting on a chair near the TV with Luke on his lap and his girlfriend, Janine, a local carpenter, was perched on the arm of his chair. Holly and Rich were standing up, holding hands. It all felt very formal and quite unusual considering how comfortable Fran had always been at Greenacres.

'We have something to share with you all.' Holly looked around at them. 'We think it's the right time now as we had confirmation today.'

Glenda gave a small laugh. 'You're going to have the wedding abroad?'

'No, Granny.' Holly shook her head.

Just then, Holly's dog, Gelert, a scruffy grey lurcher, ran into the room and jumped onto the sofa next to Fran. She held out her hand and he gave it a lick, then he proceeded to sniff her wrist, her arm and her face, tickling her skin with his whiskers and making her giggle.

'He can smell my dogs.' She smiled. Gelert had come to her first then Holly had adopted him, or he had adopted Holly. He was a friendly dog and had settled in well with his new family and he was particularly protective of little Luke.

'We're not going to get married anywhere other than here,' Rich said, smiling at Glenda. 'But we do have some slightly different news.'

'It was unexpected, but now we've had time to let it sink in, we're delighted.' Holly looked at Rich and he nodded.

'I think I have an idea,' Bruce said, his Australian accent still evident even over thirty years after he'd moved to Cornwall to be with Sarah. In his mid–fifties, he was, Fran thought, still a handsome man. Being in a relationship with Janine, who had been one of the senior carpenters involved in the vineyard's restoration, had also given him a new spring in his step.

'Ooh!' Glenda put down her knitting and clapped her hands. 'Are we having another dog from Fran?'

'No, Granny.' Holly shook her head. 'We're not having another dog, but... Today we went to a hospital appointment... We didn't want to say anything until it was confirmed but... I'm pregnant. Around twelve weeks along.'

'Goodness!' Glenda gasped. 'That is a truly wonderful surprise.'

'Congratulations!' Bruce stood up and balanced Luke on his hip. 'Fabulous news!'

'Congratulations, Holly and Rich.' Fran had known that they were going for a scan but she hadn't wanted to ask how it had gone until they were ready to share the news.

'There's something else, too.' Holly met Fran's gaze and raised her eyebrows slightly. 'It's twins.'

Fran's jaw dropped. That meant that Demelza, the bridal boutique owner, had been right. If she'd been right about that, then perhaps she was right about other things...

'Twins!' Glenda turned to Fran and grabbed her arm. 'Oh, my Henry would be overjoyed about this news. Three great-grandchildren at Greenacres. How exciting!' Her eyes glistened, so Fran shuffled over and gave her a hug.

'This is the best Christmas gift you could have given me,' Bruce said as he hugged Holly. 'Luke is incredible and now he'll have some brothers or sisters or both to play with.'

'Congratulations!' Janine said as she hugged Holly and Rich.

'We don't know the genders yet,' Rich said, 'but we'll find out at the next scan.'

'I think this calls for champagne, don't you?' Bruce said as he handed Luke to Holly.

'Good idea, Dad, but just juice for me.' Holly patted the curve of her belly, which could easily have been missed, but now that she'd drawn attention to it, Fran was convinced that it was actually quite a pronounced bump.

Fran handed Glenda a tissue from the box on the coffee table then she got up and went over to Holly.

'I'm so happy for you.'

'Thanks. It's a bit scary but also quite exciting.' She leant closer to Fran. 'We decided to tell Dad, Janine and Granny today so that they don't have to wait any longer to find out. Plus… after you rang to tell me you'd told Ethan the truth, we thought it would be best to let them know just in case the news leaked out.'

'I really don't think Ethan would say anything,' Fran said. 'He was surprised, but he does have integrity. He knows why I didn't tell him the truth straight away.'

'As long as you're all right.' Holly gave Fran a hug. 'At least the truth is out in the open now. Perhaps there's a chance for you two…'

Fran shook her head and swallowed hard. This was a happy occasion and she had to put on a brave face and show her best friend how delighted she was for her. 'We're just friends. Ethan has a complicated life and I'm better with animals. That's just the way it is.'

Holly smiled sadly. 'I don't think that's true at all, but whatever happens, Christmas is nearly upon us and before we know it, the wedding will be here then… twins!'

'Eeek!' Fran giggled. 'I can't wait to babysit.'

'I'm going to need all the help I can get.' Holly grimaced but she was glowing with happiness.

'You know I'm here for you.'

'And I am here for you. Always.'

And Fran did know that, because she and Holly had always been friends and always would be. Holly was starting another chapter of her life and Fran would be there to support her through it, because that's what friends were for.

–

Ethan placed the last gift he'd wrapped under the tree then he sat back on his heels and looked at his handiwork. He'd hurried into town yesterday to finish his Christmas shopping and had managed to pick up gifts for his aunt and uncle and his cousins, as well as to get some more gifts for Tilly. It hadn't been the jolliest of outings, but in spite of his low mood, he had found the hustle and bustle of shoppers in Newquay along with the carollers and the general upbeat mood had lifted his spirits somewhat. Of course, it would have been nice to have company, to have Fran's company in particular, but it just wasn't going to happen, so he pulled up his collar, put his head down and did what he had to do. Sometimes, it was all he could do.

One of the gifts under the tree was for Fran. He'd had to buy it when he'd seen it at the Christmas market because it had made him think of her. And even after everything that had happened between them, he still cared about her and still wanted to be her friend. They were due to spend Christmas Day together at the tea shop, so having a gift to give her might be the perfect way to let her know that he had no bad feelings towards her and that he hoped she had none towards him.

The tea shop hadn't been very busy today, in spite of it being Christmas Eve, but Audrey had told him that it was because most people would be last-minute shopping or visiting their relatives. They had, however, had more enquiries about tomorrow and seemed to be fully booked. Ethan was glad, because it meant they they'd be busy and there would be lots of people around benefitting from the generosity shown by his aunt and uncle. As for him, he found the prospect of not being alone on Christmas Day, just him and Tilly, or him, Tilly and his dad, quite exciting. Christmas should be about sharing food and laughter, about being with others and not being alone, and that was what they were aiming to do by opening the doors of the tea shop.

Ethan had enjoyed a dinner of Christmas ham, chutneys and homemade chips with Tilly, Audrey and Gary – as his cousins had been out with their partners – then he'd brought a tired, but very excited, Tilly back to the cottage, hoping that she'd go to sleep at a reasonable hour as he had wrapping to do. After a bubble bath and some warm milk, Tilly had finally submitted to sleep and Ethan had downed a very strong coffee then set to work. And now it was all done. His neck and shoulders ached from leaning forwards to wrap things and his fingers were sore from breaking off sticky tape, but at least he had managed to wrap everything. All he needed to do now was to take Tilly's stocking up and put it at the end of her bed then try to grab a few hours before she woke up and it all started again.

He stood up and switched off the tree lights then went to the front door and opened it. He gazed out at the yard and across to the tea shop. Frost sparkled on the ground and on the roofs of the tea shop and the farmhouse, the barn and the cattle sheds. The sky was black, the stars tiny diamond pinpricks, the moon a silver crescent. It was a beautiful night and he breathed in the icy air deeply, filling his lungs with it and savouring how fresh and clean it was out here in the countryside. The quiet was also soothing; no cars or emergency vehicles like in Bath, no drunks on the way home from the pub or mobile phones ringing.

The perfect peace penetrated him to his core and he released a deep sigh. Things didn't always work out as he hoped, didn't always happen as or when he would expect, and yet… things always worked out. He had a lovely home in a stunning location, he had a beautiful daughter and he had family around him. He had a job that he enjoyed and he would be able to watch Tilly grow up surrounded by love and laughter. He had a lot to be thankful for and he was very conscious of all the good things in his life.

And that included Fran, because she'd done what she'd done for what seemed like good reasons, and she didn't deserve to be punished for that. She was a good person and what she did deserve was respect, friendship and support. Ethan had had time to think about what had happened and time to calm down, and in retrospect, none of it seemed as bad as it had done at first. Sometimes, emotion clouded judgement and taking time to cool off, to let things sink in, could offer a new and more rounded perspective.

Perhaps it was the Christmas spirit getting under his skin, perhaps he was healing and opening up to new possibilities, perhaps it was Fran herself, so different from anyone else he'd ever met, but something had shifted inside him and the old fear that had gripped him no longer had so tight a hold on his heart. Like the bud of a snowdrop in the spring, his heart was opening slowly, and he found that it was no longer filled with as much pain as it had been. He was letting go, moving on and healing.

He took one more gulp of the delicious air then closed the door, picked up Tilly's stocking and climbed the stairs. Tomorrow would be a new day, a special day, and a day filled with possibilities, and Ethan intended on making the most of every single one.

Chapter 18

'Daddy! Daddy! Wake up... it's Christmas!'

Ethan opened an eye to find Tilly bouncing on his bed. He pulled the duvet over his head but she immediately pulled it back down.

'Get up, sleepy head, Santa has been! No staying in bed today, Daddy!'

He laughed and allowed his excited daughter to drag him out of bed and into her room, where the contents of her stocking lay scattered all over the floor.

'What happened here?' He acted surprised.

'Look at what he brought me.'

Tilly showed him every gift, then placed them all on her bed, before grabbing his hand again.

'Shall we go downstairs?'

'You think there's more down there?' he asked.

She nodded, her eyes wide and her tiny body trembling.

'Are you cold?' He frowned.

'No, Daddy, just excited!'

'Okay! Let's see what he brought you.' He laughed then allowed her to lead him to the top of the stairs.

'Daddy?' Tilly gazed up at him.

'Yes?'

'I love you so much. Merry Christmas.'

He crouched then opened his arms and she hugged him tight then showered chocolatey kisses all over his face.

'You found some chocolate coins then?'

'Yes, Daddy, they were in the bottom of my stocking. Want one?'

'It's a bit early for me. Maybe later.'

'It's never too early for chocolate, Daddy.' She grinned. 'Come on then.' Tilly tugged on his hand and he trotted down the stairs, the biggest smile on his face as they ran into the lounge and Tilly squealed with delight.

—

Fran had seen to her animals, given the cats and dogs their Christmas treats and eaten a breakfast of scrambled eggs and toast washed down with plenty of tea. She'd then Skyped her parents and Nonna before showering and dressing in jeans, boots and a red smock top with a Christmas tree on the front, complete with a flashing star at the top. She moisturised her face, added some mascara and red lipstick, put on her red-framed glasses and ran her hands through her hair. She was ready to do Christmas at the tea shop!

She went to the small tree in her lounge and picked up the gift bag she'd put next to it yesterday, then made a fuss of her dogs, including the small Westie that was settling in better by the day, before grabbing her car keys.

Her life was pretty good indeed. She had furry companions, no one expecting anything of her and she got to sleep in rather than wake up at silly o'clock because someone had forgotten to defrost the turkey or because Santa had forgotten to leave the gifts under the tree. She was free to do as she wanted, when she wanted.

That was all good, wasn't it? She wasn't missing out on a thing, was she? She shook her head as doubts tingled at her edges. This was not the day to wonder about what she didn't have; it was the day to treasure all the good things in her life.

She locked the front door behind her and headed along the path. The air was crisp and clear and frost sparkled on the grass of her lawn and crunched under her soles. She paused in front of her car and sighed. The windscreen was completely iced up and would take a good ten minutes to clear. But that was also part of living alone; there was no one here to defrost the windscreen while she made another cup of tea, no one to enjoy that lie-in with and no one to say Merry Christmas to along with a morning kiss.

She'd had several doggy kisses of gratitude as she'd opened the final doors on the dogs' Christmas calendars and handed them the various treats from inside, but as much as she appreciated the dogs' affection, a human kiss would have been rather nice too. Especially one of those gorgeous kisses from Ethan. That would have made her Christmas morning perfect.

Her life was good, but it didn't mean that it couldn't be better if she had someone to share it with, someone to be there for her as she would be for him. Someone to love and care for and to put her cold feet on in bed at night. Someone like Ethan. No... if it was going to be anyone, it could only ever be Ethan.

She opened the door and got in the car, wincing at how cold the seat was, carefully placed the gift bag on the passenger seat then started the engine. Lots of people didn't have a special someone and that was what today was going to be about – making the lives of others that little bit better, even if only for one day of the year.

And Fran was happy to be a part of such a day. She was also looking forward to seeing Ethan and Tilly, Audrey, Gary and their daughters and sharing in their Christmas cheer.

–

Ethan splashed some cologne on his cheeks then stood back and checked himself in the bathroom mirror. His jeans and green Christmas T-shirt combo were fine considering that he'd be in the kitchen for most of the morning, and he was glad he'd picked up the T-shirt because in a jumper, he'd end up too warm as he cooked. The T-shirt had a large snowman on it wearing an apron and a chef's hat. It seemed appropriate for him and for the day. He'd showered and washed his hair and felt fresher, although he was exhausted after his five thirty a.m. wake-up call. However, he'd had a lot of fun with Tilly and she had been delighted with her gifts. He had told her to pick her favourites so she could take them to the tea shop with her this morning and she was still deciding when he went back downstairs.

'Right, Tilly, what's it to be?'

'Glitterbug wants to take the Lego castle and the bumper book of fairy tales.'

'Okay, but you must take care not to lose any of the Lego pieces, and I'm not sure that anyone will have time to read the stories to you, but you can take it anyway.'

'Daddy, it has beautiful pictures inside and anyway, I can read it to myself.'

'Of course you can. Now run up and get dressed, then we can get Aunty Audrey or Scarlett to do your hair.'

'Scarlett said she might be late coming to the tea shop because she was going out with her boyfriend last night and they would probably feel a bit... what did she say... a bit... breakable this morning.'

'Breakable?'

'Yes... no... It was something like that because I asked her what it meant and she said like when you use one of Aunty Audrey's crystal glasses and they're easy to smash so it means they're...' Tilly poked out her tongue as she tried to think of the word.

'Do you mean fragile?'

'Yes!' Tilly pointed at him. 'That word.'

'Well perhaps Audrey will do your hair for you.'

'She will.' Tilly nodded with the confidence of a six-year-old.

'What time is it?' Ethan pulled his phone from his pocket. 'Your mum will be calling soon.'

Tilly wrinkled her nose.

'Just to say Merry Christmas.'

'She'll be busy or... *fragile* herself probably.'

Ethan suppressed a snort. Every year, when Melanie Skyped on Christmas morning, or weekend mornings, come to think of it, she was usually nursing a champagne hangover and Tilly had clearly noticed.

'Let's get the laptop on and you can have a quick chat before we go.'

'Okay, Daddy, but I'm not talking for long. I want Aunty Audrey to do my hair and I want to see all the lowly people.'

'Lowly people?'

'Yes... Scarlett said all the lowly people are coming for dinner.'

'I think she meant lonely people, Tilly, and lowly means something completely different.' He took a deep breath. 'They are people who don't have friends or family to spend Christmas Day with.'

'Like we used to be before we moved to Rosewood?'

'Yes.'

'But we're not lonely now, are we, Daddy?'

'No, we're not. Now go and get dressed!'

Tilly hurried upstairs and Ethan set the laptop up on the coffee table. He turned it towards the tree so Melanie would have a view of the Christmas he had put together for their daughter. In the past, he'd have experienced a pang of regret and sadness that Melanie wasn't with them, and sometimes he had felt jealousy, especially when it was clear that she was spending the holidays with some businessman or colleague, but this year, all he felt was pity for Melanie. She was the one missing out on Tilly enjoying the festivities; she was the one missing out on the love and joy that Tilly brought with her, and Ethan knew all too well that these days with Tilly as a child would not last for ever. Each day with her had to be treasured and each memory stored because all too soon she'd be grown up and maybe even have children of her own.

He just hoped that he was doing a good enough job of making Tilly's childhood special, because he couldn't change the fact that Melanie wasn't here, but he could try to ensure that Tilly didn't feel her loss too deeply.

The familiar tinny tone rang out on the laptop and he accepted the video call.

'Hello Melanie.' He smiled at the image on the screen. 'Merry Christmas.'

—

'Hello, Fran!' Audrey bustled over and hugged Fran then kissed her cheeks. 'Merry Christmas, love! Let me take your coat.'

Fran handed it over then looked around the tea shop. The tables had been arranged to create a circle with an opening at the centre – presumably so it would be easier to serve everyone. Each place setting had a festive napkin, a Christmas cracker, a water glass and a wine glass and red-handled cutlery. Carols drifted down from the speakers and the mouth-watering aromas of turkey and vegetables filled the room.

'Would you like a drink of something?' Audrey asked.

'It's still a bit early for me so I'll have something later.'

'Well let me know when you want something because I have champagne, sherry, Buck's Fizz and more. Although...' Audrey's eyes went to Fran's middle. 'You might prefer juice?'

'Audrey... I'm not pregnant.'

Fran had checked with Holly and confirmed that it was okay to clarify that she wasn't expecting now. Holly's scan and the fact that she had told her family meant that Fran was free to share that it wasn't her.

'Oh...' Audrey's eyebrows rose. 'Are you all right?'

It was clear that Audrey suspected that Fran had lost the baby.

'It's a long story, so I'll explain another time, but it wasn't actually me who was pregnant. There never was a baby.'

'Okay, my love. I won't pry but you know I'm here if you need me.'

'I do, and thank you. I'm really looking forward to a lovely day.'

'We all are.' Audrey nodded. 'Have you spoken to your parents this morning?'

'Yes, and Nonna, and they're all enjoying a lazy breakfast. They said to tell you Merry Christmas.'

'Ah, thank you. Lovely to hear.'

Behind Audrey, Scarlett and Harper were counting out chocolates on the counter and Audrey nodded towards her daughters. 'Stinking hangovers, the pair of them, but they're here so I'm not complaining.'

'Where do you want me?' Fran asked.

'The kitchen would be fabulous, thank you. Ethan could really do with the help in there while we see to things out front.'

'No problem.'

Fran went through to the kitchen and smiled at the sight that greeted her. Tilly was sitting at the kitchen island peeling sprouts and Ethan was basting an enormous turkey that sat in a large baking tray on the cooker top.

'Merry Christmas!' Fran said as she set her gift bag down in the corner where no one would fall over it.

'Fran!' Ethan glanced at her before setting the tray back in the oven. 'Merry Christmas to you too.'

'Merry Christmas!' Tilly jumped down and ran to Fran and wrapped her arms around Fran's waist.

'Hello, sweetheart. How has your morning been?'

'Amazing!' Tilly grinned. 'I had lots of lovely gifts from Santa and from Daddy and from Aunty Audrey and Uncle

Gary and from Scarlett and Harper and... and... it was all wonderful.'

'I'm so glad.' Fran smiled down at Tilly. 'I have something for you too. Do you want it now or after dinner?'

Tilly looked over at her father then back at Fran. 'After dinner would be nice, thank you, because I need to get those sprouts ready. I don't like them one bit but Daddy said we have to do them because other people like them.'

'Of course you do.' Fran giggled. 'Ethan, what can I do to help?'

He gestured at a pile of potatoes sitting on the worktop. 'Fancy tackling them?'

'Absolutely.'

'Here's an apron to protect your clothes.' Tilly handed Fran a white apron and Fran put it on.

'Let's get peeling then, shall we?' Fran perched on a stool and got to work, listening to Tilly as she listed all of her lovely gifts and to Ethan as he replied to Tilly's many questions.

The kitchen was warm and cosy, it smelt wonderful and Fran could just do her job and relax. It was a lovely way to start Christmas.

—

When the potatoes had been peeled and parboiled then set in hot oil and put in the oven, Fran had started on the carrots and parsnips. She worked quickly and quietly, allowing Ethan to focus on the rest of the jobs he needed to complete. The morning rolled on with food preparations and after Tilly had finished peeling the mountain of sprouts, she started to get a bit fidgety, so Ethan told her to go and sit in the tea shop with Audrey. When Tilly had gone, Ethan was left alone with Fran.

'How are you?' he asked.

'I'm okay.' She smiled.

'No... I mean... after the other day. How are you doing?'

'I'm okay,' she repeated. 'Just getting on with things.'

'Fran...' He put down the green bag he'd been filling with sprout peelings. 'I wanted to tell you that I'm sorry.'

'What for? You haven't done anything to apologise for.'

'Well... I think I have.' He gazed at her flushed cheeks, at her pretty indigo eyes behind her red-framed glasses and at her shiny hair. 'See... what you did covering for Holly was a good thing. She's your friend and you care about her and you protected her by doing it. I... I have issues because Tilly has to be my priority. Her mum has hurt her a lot with her absence and her almost apathetic attitude towards her and I just can't bear to think of Tilly being hurt by another woman.' He shook his head. 'The thought of being in a relationship again scares me for me, but mainly for Tilly because she's been hurt enough by Melanie's behaviour. She deserves better. And you... you're so nice and warm and so different from Melanie and Tilly thinks the world of you, but the whole pregnancy debacle confused and scared me and I needed time to think it over.'

'I really am sorry.'

'No, it's okay. I understand why you did what you did. I wish I could be tougher about things and not care quite so much, and if it were just me, then things would be different. I feel any rejection deeply because it's not just me being rejected but my daughter too.'

Fran put the peeler down. 'Ethan… I didn't reject you.'

'Not directly perhaps, but finding out that you'd deceived me was difficult because Melanie… my ex-wife… well, our whole marriage was a sham. It was never what she wanted and it ended up hurting me, hurting her, and if Tilly had been any older then it might well have been harder for her to accept and adapt. She was so young that it didn't impact upon her as it could have done but even so… I never want her to go through that again or to see me hurt. You and me… well, we were becoming friends and yet there was something more there… for me at least.'

Fran nodded.

'Did you feel it too?'

'Of course I did. Ethan, you're kind, funny, a loving father… you're a great cook and you're really good company. Plus… you're absolutely gorgeous and yes, I had feelings for you. I mean… I *have* feelings for you. I can't and won't deny that. Like I told you before, though… I'm not good at this stuff. I'm romantically inexperienced.'

'Me too.' He smiled.

'What a pair we are, eh? Plus… there are things that are different about us. Like… I love animals and you're not a dog person.'

'That's something I could learn to overcome though, isn't it? My fear of dogs. People overcome phobias like a fear of spiders and snakes and flying and they're far worse than a cute little puppy.'

'That is true.'

'I'd like to become a dog person. Do you think you could help me?'

She smiled. 'Definitely.'

'That would make Tilly very happy too as she loves dogs.'

'She can come and spend time with my lot whenever she likes.'

'That would also make her happy as she loves you.'

Fran glowed with pleasure.

'Perhaps we could... be inexperienced together?' he asked, holding his breath.

'What would that involve exactly?' Fran asked.

'Well... we could get to know each other better and...' He sighed. 'I would really like to be able to trust again, Fran. I'm sure I'm missing out by being so reserved, so... tightly coiled and so scared.'

'You could be right.'

'Okay you two...' Audrey marched into the kitchen. 'Let's get this out of the way so you can focus on feeding the five thousand.'

'The five thousand?' Ethan's eyes widened.

'Yes. There are more people out there than we expected but we can hardly turn them away, can we? So peel every potato and use every stock cube. But first... have a snog under the mistletoe, won't you?'

Audrey pointed at the mistletoe above the doorway that led to the office out back.

'I won't stay and watch but you'd better do it, then we can get this dinner ready. You've got five minutes so get snogging!'

Ethan watched his aunt leave the kitchen, then he turned his attention to Fran. She was blushing furiously and he felt heat creeping into his own cheeks.

'We don't have to...' He shrugged.

'Audrey is a scary woman when she gets her mind set on something and I'd hate to get on the wrong side of her.' Fran chewed her lip, but something flashed in her eyes and Ethan made up his mind.

He strode over to her, grabbed her hand and whisked her over to the mistletoe, then he cupped her face gently in his hands. His heart was racing and he felt breathless, but he knew he had never wanted anything more.

'Excuse the cooked-dinner aroma on my hands and clothes.' He laughed.

'It's fine.' Fran covered his hands with hers. 'You smell just like Christmas.'

'Is that a good thing?' he asked as he moved his face closer to hers.

'Oh yes.' Fran pushed up onto her toes. 'I happen to love Christmas.'

Then their lips met and their eyes closed and they kissed, and Ethan felt his fears drift away, and trust and love settle into their place.

–

'If I could just have your attention for a moment, please.'

Audrey stood at the opening to the circle of tables, a glass of champagne in one hand and a golden paper crown on her head. The tea shop fell silent and everyone looked in her direction.

'This is our first ever Christmas dinner at the tea shop, but it won't be the last. Looking around this room at people I have known for years and at new faces, it is clear to me that this is something that we in Penhallow Sands need. I have always been lucky enough to enjoy Christmas with my family, starting with my own dear parents and grandparents then moving on to celebrate with my wonderful husband and children. This year, I was excited to know that my nephew, Ethan, and his beautiful little girl, Tilly, would be with us. Then... one evening over dinner, Ethan suggested that we open the doors of the tea shop and provide a free dinner to all who would like to come and have company. It was a truly wonderful idea.' Audrey raised her glass. 'So to everyone here today, we at Rosewood Tea Shop and farm would like to wish you a very Merry Christmas. We hope that you enjoy your dinner and the company and that you will feel welcome to come and join us next year.'

Every glass in the room was raised and 'Merry Christmas' echoed around the room along with the clinking of glasses.

Fran sniffed, overcome by the emotion of the moment, and next to her, Ethan took her hand under the table. She smiled at him, then a glow rushed through her as she recalled their kiss in the kitchen. It had been so sweet, so tender and the start of something wonderful. Audrey wasn't the only one who was glad that Ethan and Tilly had come to the village; Fran was delighted. They still had things they needed to discuss and issues that wouldn't go away overnight, but now they had admitted their feelings for each other and agreed that they had a foundation to build on. Love was a complicated emotion and everyone had a past. In this case, Ethan had a child too, so they would need to consider Tilly every step of the way. However, Fran was glad to do it because Tilly was a lovely child and she deserved to be happy and to see her father happy.

'I'd like to say something too, if I may.' Ethan released Fran's hand then stood up. He cleared his throat. 'I would like to thank my Aunty Audrey and Uncle Gary and my cousins Harper and Scarlett for welcoming me into their home and their world. Tilly and I spent a lot of time alone before we came here. There were some very lonely dark days in amongst the good ones, but being here, I feel that I'm no longer alone. Part of it has to do with my family and part of it is because of the wonderfully warm community of Penhallow Sands. I feel that I'm a part of something here and not just on the periphery, which is something I felt in my former life. Tilly and I intend to stay here and we're both very happy about it.' He smiled at his daughter and she grinned back. 'Our hearts belong here now and we are excited about what the new year will bring.'

As he sat down, he leant closer to Fran and whispered, 'Thank you, Fran, for wanting us.'

'Ethan... it's me who should be thanking you.'

'I guess we can settle on thanking each other?' He raised his eyebrows. 'Perhaps... we can show each other at some point too.'

Fran smiled and blushed, then she nodded. 'Absolutely. I'm looking forward to it.'

She reached for his hand under the table and gave it a squeeze.

'Just give her a snog, Daddy.'

'What?' Ethan's eyebrows shot up his forehead.

'I said snog her. I'll get you some mistletoe if you're too shy to just do it.'

Ethan started to laugh. 'Tilly... Fran is my friend.'

'I know, Daddy. Fran's your very special friend. I'm six not four, you know.' Tilly rolled her eyes and Fran started to giggle.

'Okay, I guess that told me.' Ethan nudged Fran and he gave her a quick peck on the cheek.

'How's that, Tilly?'

'It'll do for now, I guess, Daddy, but it's not how they do it in the movies so next time try harder.'

'Yes, Tilly.' He whispered into Fran's ear, 'Let's eat so we have an excuse not to snog in front of my bossy daughter! Next thing we know she'll be rating us out of ten.'

Fran snorted then gazed down at the plate in front of her. It was piled high with buttered turkey, bright green sprouts fried with bacon, carrots and parsnips cooked in herbs and white wine, fluffy, brown roast potatoes, purple cabbage, herby apple stuffing, dark red port and cranberry sauce and lashings of Ethan's special thick gravy. It looked incredible and as she started to eat, she found that it tasted even better.

'Ethan,' she said in between mouthfuls.

'Yes?'

'You're a keeper.'

'Am I?'

'For many reasons, but especially for your culinary skills.'

'Why thank you. So my Christmas dinner has won your heart.'

'Oh, you already had my heart but now you have my stomach too.'

'Score!' He high fived the air.

'Thank you, Fran,' Tilly said as she laid the stationery out on the kitchen island. 'It's all so beautiful.'

'My pleasure, Tilly. I know that you like drawing and thought that I could help you some time.'

'I would love that!' Tilly grinned. She was rosy-cheeked after eating their Christmas dinner and she had a splodge of gravy on her top; she was the cutest thing Fran had ever seen.

'I've another gift for you too.' Fran reached for the square package she'd tucked in the bag.

'Really?' Tilly looked at Ethan. 'Daddy, I'm so lucky.'

'Yes you are.' He smiled. 'Fran, you shouldn't have.'

'Well... your daddy said that you'd always wanted a dog and although I couldn't just give you a real dog, I thought that dog-print stationery and then this gift might help.'

Tilly accepted the parcel and gently removed the tissue paper.

'Oh...' Her eyes widened. 'It's amazing, Fran. Did you do this?'

'Yes.'

'Look, Daddy.'

The three of them gazed at the pencil drawing of the small white Westie. He lay in his basket in front of the Aga, his chin on his paws, his eyes warm and trusting. At his side was a small toy dog with patches on its face and body.

'That's Glitterbug!' Tilly exclaimed. 'How did you draw Glitterbug?'

'From memory.' Fran chewed her lip. 'I hope I got it right.'

'Perfect,' Ethan said as he squeezed her shoulder. 'Tilly, don't you have something for Fran too?'

'Yes!' Tilly jumped down from the stool and ran through to the office then returned holding two small gifts wrapped in shiny red paper. One had a gold bow and the other a silver one. 'Here, Daddy.' Tilly handed Ethan the one with the silver bow then climbed back onto her stool.

'Thank you.' Fran accepted the gift with the gold bow from Tilly. Her throat was aching with emotion but she didn't want to cry so she swallowed hard and focused on undoing the bow then peeling back the Sellotape. Inside was a tiny charm. She picked it up and peered at it. 'Oh… it's wonderful, thank you.'

'It's a dog.'

'Yes, I can see that.' Fran leant forwards and hugged Tilly. 'Thank you so much.'

'Daddy, give her your gift.'

'Right.' Ethan nodded then held out the red parcel. Fran took it from him and opened it as carefully as she had the one from Tilly.

She lifted the lid of the box and found a silver chain bracelet. There was one charm already on it and she sighed as she ran a finger over the tiny silver heart.

'The symbol of friendship,' Ethan said. 'And more…'

'Merry Christmas,' Fran said as Ethan fastened the bracelet around her wrist then added the dog charm from Tilly. 'The first of many?'

'Yes, Fran,' Tilly said. 'We've got you now and you're not getting away from us.'

Tilly jumped down from the stool and wrapped her arms tightly around Fran's waist and Ethan slid his arms around Fran's shoulders. The three of them stood that way for some time as the Christmas music from the tea shop drifted through the air and something special settled into place, warming Fran right through.

It was love for this man and his child, and she knew for certain that she would never hurt either of them or let them down again.

–

'What's with all the secrecy?'

Fran glanced around her as Ethan led her across the yard to the tea shop. She was reminded of the wonderful Christmas Day they had enjoyed there. After enjoying Christmas dinner, along with fat puddings laced with brandy and served with clotted cream, as well as exchanging gifts in the kitchen – just Fran, Ethan and Tilly – it had taken several hours to tidy up the tea shop and to get things back to normal. Audrey had then closed the tea shop for the days immediately following Christmas Day and planned to reopen tomorrow for the last few days of December.

Fran had then gone home to let the dogs out and to check on them all and Ethan had gone with her. He had helped her feed the dogs and made a fuss of the small white dog and both of them had seemed to take quite a shine to each other. Before leaving, Ethan had asked if it would be okay to bring Tilly to meet the dogs after Christmas, which had really pleased Fran.

Now, three days later, Fran had come to Rosewood to have dinner with Ethan and Tilly and the rest of his family. They had made her feel very welcome and although she was keen to give Ethan space to deal with his feelings and to spend time with Tilly, she was also glad to see him again.

'I have something I want to show you.' Ethan opened the door to the tea shop and let them in, then closed it behind him.

'In here?' Fran giggled. 'Couldn't you have done it earlier?'

They had kissed in her kitchen on Christmas afternoon and again when she had arrived at Ethan's (while Tilly was upstairs getting ready) but done nothing more, aware that they wanted to take things slowly as they got to know each other better. Ethan was still vulnerable and he needed the time to feel fully secure before things moved on between them. Fran was happy to take her time because she liked Ethan so much that she felt like she was dating for the first time and she was excited but nervous around him.

'Not really… Anyway, there was no point moving it from here.'

'Moving what?'

'You'll see.'

In the kitchen, he turned on the lights and patted a stool.

'Sit here and I'll get it. Actually, close your eyes.'

'Okay.' Fran sat down then closed her eyes and waited.

She heard Ethan open a cupboard then carry something across the kitchen and place it on the island.

'Now then… open your eyes.'

She did and she blinked as they adjusted to the bright strip lighting overhead. Then they settled on the large cake on the island in front of them. The three circles were covered with white icing and decorated with tiny flowers in pink, purple and blue and small marzipan and icing wine bottles. Bright green vines wound around the flowers and wine bottles and on the top tier stood a H and an R, joined together with more of the vines and two silver rings.

'It's beautiful.' Fran shook her head. 'Absolutely perfect. When did you find the time?'

'A few late nights.' Ethan smiled shyly. 'And early mornings. And… Audrey helped with the icing and the decorations. She's quite talented with icing.'

'I'll have to thank her too. Let me know how much you want for it because I told Holly I'd get it as part of their wedding present.'

'No you won't.'

'Pardon?'

'It can be a gift from both of us.'

'I can't ask that of you, Ethan.'

'Fran.' He took her hands. 'I'm asking it of you.'

She opened her mouth to say more but the look in his eyes told her that she didn't need to. He wanted to do this, to give her this, and if she argued it would hurt him and that was the last thing she wanted to do.

'You're amazing.' She leant to him. 'I've never met anyone like you, Ethan.'

'Same here.'

He lifted her arms so they rested on his shoulders, then he lowered his head and kissed her, and Fran knew that this man really was a keeper.

The keeper of her heart.

Chapter 19

Ethan's stomach rolled as he knocked on Fran's door. He wasn't sure if this was the right decision or not, but Tilly had wanted a dog for as long as he could remember and he wanted her to be able to spend some time with Fran and with her dogs so he could see how they got on.

Fran opened the door and smiled at them.

'Come on in.'

They entered the warm hallway and Ethan sniffed appreciatively.

'Something smells good.'

'It won't be anywhere near as good as the things you make but I've baked a cheese and mushroom quiche and a chocolate cake.'

'Fran, just because I'm a chef doesn't mean I don't enjoy things that others bake. In fact, it's wonderful to have things made for me for a change.'

'Well, I hope you enjoy them anyway.'

She smiled at him and his heart soared. She was breathtaking and cute, an attractive combination, in a silky purple tunic top with a long black cardigan, leggings and fluffy slipper boots on her feet. Her hair was pulled back from her smooth forehead with a purple headband and it made her look even younger. There was a chickenpox scar just under her hairline and he had an urge to touch it.

Instead, he stuffed his hands into his pockets, not wanting to set Tilly's tongue wagging again by touching Fran in front of her, because then she might start insisting that they kiss again like she had on Christmas Day.

'I like quiche, Fran, and chocolate cake's my favourite,' Tilly said as she removed her coat.

'Everything's your favourite.' Ethan laughed. 'I've heard stories about children who are fussy eaters and whose parents worry but I've never had that problem with Tilly. She loves her food... except for sprouts.'

'I don't like some other things, Daddy, but I never wanted you to worry.' Tilly looked up at him and his heart melted.

'What don't you like?'

Tilly wave a hand dismissively. 'Well, I didn't like sprouts but Uncle Gary made me try on one Christmas Day and it wasn't that horrid with bacon. I guess that tastes change all the time.'

Ethan met Fran's eyes and they grinned at each other. The things Tilly came out with would never cease to amaze him.

'Where are the dogs, Fran?' Tilly asked.

'I closed the kitchen gate so they wouldn't rush at you.'

'You have a gate inside?' Tilly frowned.

'It's a stair gate. I have them everywhere.' Fran gestured around the hallway at the gates on the stairs and in doorways.

'It must take you ages to open and close them all.' Tilly's mouth was open as she gazed around.

'I don't always close them... mainly when I have visitors or a new dog staying.'

'Daddy said you have a new dog here now.'

'I do.'

'Can I meet him?'

'You can, but be calm and gentle with him as he's still a bit nervous and he can't hear anything.'

'He's a deaf dog?'

'He is.'

'I will treat him like a newborn baby. That's what my teacher said you have to do when someone's nervous. Newborn babies cry a lot, especially if you're loud around them, so you have to be quiet and speak softly like this...' She whispered the final words.

'Perfect! Come on then.'

Fran led them to the kitchen and she opened the gate then told the dogs to sit.

Ethan followed Fran and his daughter, realising that his nerves were melting away with how easy it was to be around Fran and at how well she got on with Tilly. They were quite similar in many ways with their sensible approach to things and their quirky sense of humour and he had a feeling that they were going to get on very well indeed. One thing that had crossed his mind recently was whether Tilly might be jealous if he became involved with another woman, but she had made several comments recently about him needing to kiss Fran and about what it would be like to see more of Fran and at no point did she seem at all negative. Fran had promised to teach her how to draw and paint and to let her walk the dogs and learn how to care for them and Tilly was nothing but happy and enthusiastic about Fran. Of course, Ethan knew that it could change if he didn't deal with things sensitively and ensure that Tilly had as much of his attention as she'd always had, but then he was starting to realise that his love wasn't limited. There wasn't a cap on it that meant he only had a certain amount to give. He didn't love Tilly any less since he'd met Fran and yet, he had feelings for Fran that were growing and evolving by the day. It was different to his love for Tilly and he could tell that it wasn't limited in any way, that he could love and care for them both, if things worked out between him and Fran that was. Who knew, there could even be an addition to their family unit at some point – whether human or animal – and he would still have more love to give. Being around Fran was helping him to learn more about himself and he was enjoying the experience. Whereas in the past he'd felt sad, trapped even by his negative emotions such as loneliness and hurt, he now felt that he was moving on from that and growing, that he had more to give and to learn and to achieve.

Ethan was healing and moving on in ways he'd never expected and it was the best feeling in the world.

–

Fran sat on the kitchen floor with Tilly as the little girl talked to her dogs. They were all being very well behaved and even the little white dog, which had initially hidden under the table, had now come out and was giving Tilly his full attention. Fran watched as the dog inched his way closer to Tilly until he was sitting right in front of her, then, as Tilly explained how she was going to learn to horse ride in the summer, the dog raised its paw and patted Tilly's hand.

'Did you see that?'

Fran turned to Ethan. He was sitting at the table sipping his coffee. He nodded.

'He gave me a high five,' Tilly said.

'He likes you.' Fran smiled. The dog could tell that Tilly was sweet and gentle and that she could be trusted. 'Right, I'll get our lunch ready.'

She went to the sink and washed her hands, then she sliced up the quiche and took it to the table along with a bowl of potato salad she'd made earlier.

'What can I do?' Ethan asked.

'Relax. You're my guest.' Fran squeezed his shoulder.

When she'd brought everything to the table, Ethan told Tilly to wash her hands and they all sat down to eat. The dogs wandered off to their beds, except for the new one, and he stayed right by Tilly's feet with his chin resting on her toes.

'I think he wants to come home with me, Daddy.' Tilly smiled.

'That may well be, but I think it might be a bit early to think about taking him home, don't you?'

Tilly pouted. 'Why?'

'Well...' Ethan forked a potato. 'A dog is a big responsibility.'

Tilly nodded. 'So is a child.'

Ethan spluttered. 'Tilly, I don't know where these things you say come from.'

'I told you before, Daddy, I listen to people.'

'She's a good listener.' Fran bit her lip.

'Isn't she just?' He shook his head.

'If we adopted this boy it would help Fran.'

'It would?' Ethan asked.

'Yes because she has lots of dogs anyway and she would have space for one more if there's one out there in need.'

Fran lowered her gaze to her plate. She didn't want to get in the middle of this conversation but Tilly was making some good points.

'But what about when you go back to school?'

'Then you can pop back in the day and let him out.'

'I can?'

'You always go home at some point, Daddy, and if not, then Scarlett or Harper can go.'

'Tilly, we can't rely on other people to let our dog out.'

'Daddy...' Tilly sighed. 'That's what families are for. They help each other out.'

Ethan leant on his hand and put his fork down. He looked defeated, but Fran knew that he had to be sure before he gave a dog a home. It was a big responsibility and something to think very carefully about.

'Look, Tilly, why don't I have a chat with your dad about this after lunch and see if we can sort something out? Even if you can't adopt this little one, perhaps you could think of a name for him and come and visit him lots.'

Tilly's eyes moved from Ethan to Fran and back again, and she frowned then shrugged. 'Okay. Whatever you think is best.'

Fran nudged Ethan under the table and he nudged her back. Tilly was a highly intelligent child and she knew how to be persuasive, including how to back off at the right time to let someone think. Fran was very impressed and amused and she could see that Ethan had his hands full. She hoped that she could be there for future discussions like this to offer him support because as Tilly got older she would likely run rings around him.

Poor Ethan!

276

Chapter 20

'I think that's everything,' Fran said as she looked around Shell's Shack. There were gold foil banners pinned to the counter, the fireplace and the windows announcing *Look Who's Getting Married*. On the tables were pink plastic champagne flutes, bottles of Prosecco and bottles of non-alcoholic fizz. Shell had put together a buffet, which was spread out on the counter, and there was a large lemon drizzle cake also courtesy of Shell.

'You've done a great job,' Shell said, peering out at Fran from behind a large pink tiara complete with feathers and rhinestones.

'She deserves a good hen party. I'm hoping she's only going to get married once.' Fran crossed her fingers.

'Holly and Rich are made for each other.'

'They certainly are. I would struggle to imagine either of them being with anyone else.'

The door opened and along with a gust of ice-cold wind came laughter and the mixed aroma of several perfumes.

'Wow, Fran, this looks amazing!' Holly hugged her. 'You didn't have to do all this.'

'Of course I did. You're my best friend.' Fran smiled at Holly, who looked gorgeous in a loose red shift dress with sheer sleeves and knee-high black boots.

'Are we having bubbly?' Glenda asked as Shell helped her to a chair.

'Of course, Glenda,' Shell replied. 'I'll pour you a glass right away.'

'Wonderful!' Glenda clapped her hands. 'I do love a drop of fizz. My Henry used to say, "Glenda, you can't beat a glass of the good stuff." Of course, he was usually referring to Greenacres wine, but then that was Henry! He was so proud of our wine.' She gazed out through the window, lost in her memories, and Holly caught Fran's eye and smiled. They had discussed Glenda's frequent comments about the past and both hoped that Glenda's happy memories of her husband were helping her to deal with her grief at losing him earlier that year. 'And now we're going to have twins to help out too!'

The cafe fell silent and Shell looked from Glenda to Holly to Fran, then at Lucinda Turner and Catherine Bromley, who had just walked in. Rich's mother, Lucinda, was pink-cheeked and bright-eyed as if the cold had given her a boost, but Catherine was shivering and blowing on her hands.

'Oops!' Glenda grimaced. 'It's meant to be a secret.'

Holly shrugged. 'It wouldn't have been for much longer anyway. Yes, I am pregnant and yes, it's twins.' She held out her hands.

'That's wonderful news!' Shell hugged her then stepped back and Catherine did the same.

'I knew.' Lucinda nodded. 'They told me on Boxing Day. Gave me a scan photo in a frame.' She hugged herself. 'I'm so excited that I'm going to have three gorgeous grandchildren!'

'Anyone mind if I sit down?' Holly asked. 'I'm exhausted and I need all my energy for tomorrow. I know this won't be the wildest hen do you've been to, but I am grateful to Fran and Shell for arranging it and to you all for coming.'

Shell filled glasses, though Holly opted for the non-alcoholic fizz, and then they got stuck into the buffet. Stories were told, there was a lot of laughter and Fran was glad that she'd persuaded Holly to have a hen night. Or hen evening, rather, but it was something. Rich had gone out with a few friends but only to the village pub and he'd promised not to drink much, and Bruce was at home with Luke and Janine. It might not be the crazy hen night that some women enjoyed before getting married but for pregnant Holly and for their social circle, it was just right. She hadn't invited more people because Holly hadn't wanted a big affair but Lucinda was family and Catherine had become close to Holly since her boyfriend rented a cottage on the Greenacres land. None of them were big into clubbing or those event-style hen nights that involved escaping from a prison van or being kidnapped. All of that seemed too much like hard work.

When they'd polished off the food and Holly couldn't stop yawning, Fran looked at the clock and found that it was only just gone eighty thirty.

'I think I need to go home to bed,' Holly said. 'Tomorrow will be a long day. We have the caterers coming early and the band to set up and Fran and I have hair and makeup and... well, it'll be a busy one.'

'And a wonderful one,' Lucinda said, hugging Holly. 'I'm so happy that you and Rich will soon be married and will complete your little family.'

'Thanks, Lucinda. I'm really happy too.'

'Look!' Fran pointed at the window and all heads turned. She hurried to the door and pulled it open and they all gasped.

In the past two hours, the village of Penhallow Sands had had heavy snowfall and they hadn't even noticed, but now everything was white and snow was still falling. They put their coats on and went out into the street and looked around. The icy air was still as big fat snowflakes fell to the ground. The road already had a good covering and if it kept snowing it would soon be deep.

'I'd better get us home,' Holly said to Glenda.

'But I haven't finished my fizz,' Glenda said.

'Bring it with you, Granny. We need to get back to Greenacres. I'll call Rich now because he can come with us.'

Holly pulled out her mobile and waked back inside and Fran helped Glenda to button her coat.

'I think we all need to get home,' Fran said to Shell. 'I'll give you a hand to tidy up first then—'

'No you won't, Fran! You get back to your dogs and cats. I can clean up here. There's not much to do anyway.'

'As long as you're sure.' Fran didn't fancy walking home in her boots, which were fashionable rather than practical. If she'd only checked the weather forecast, she'd have worn her snow boots and good gloves. She had to get back for the animals, even if she did have to hike there.

'Come on then, Granny.' Holly took Glenda's arm. 'We need to go and collect Rich from the pub then get home. Fran, will you be okay?'

'Of course. Text me later, Holly.'

'Will do.' Holly helped her granny to the car then turned to Fran. 'What if it keeps snowing? We'll have to cancel the wedding.'

'No you won't.' Fran gently squeezed Holly's arm. 'It will be fine either way. We'll sort something out and even if your guests and caterers and band can't make it… we'll sort something. I promise.'

'Thank you, Fran. I don't know what I'd do without you.'

Fran gave her a reassuring smile. 'Go on, get home. Drive carefully.'

They hugged then Holly got into the car and drove slowly away.

'We'd better get home too,' Lucinda said as she took Catherine's arm. 'Our menfolk will be wondering where we are.'

'Mark's coming down to meet me,' Catherine explained.

'Take care,' Fran said, then she turned back to Shell. 'Thanks for this evening.'

'My pleasure. Now… if you need me to do anything tomorrow, Fran, just call. I have some things in the freezer that I can throw in the oven and I can easily whip up some cakes. Let's make sure that Holly and Rich have a wonderful day, snow or not!'

'Thanks, Shell.'

Fran got into her car and started the engine, but as she drove away, her heart was in her mouth. The sky looked full of snow and it was a challenge she hadn't anticipated. However, it was one that she'd readily accept to ensure that Holly had a wonderful wedding, even if it was a white one!

'Right, have we got everything?' Audrey asked Ethan for the tenth time that minute.

'I think so.'

He looked from one of Gary's Land Rovers to the other. They were packed with Tupperware boxes filled with food that he and Audrey had been baking since five a.m. Thankfully, they'd had plenty of supplies at the tea shop, so when Fran had called him last night in a panic because of the snow and the forecast, he'd been able to reassure her that he would help out. Fran had called again at eight a.m. this morning to say that the caterers Holly had booked for her wedding reception couldn't make it from Newquay because the roads were so bad, so Holly had been frantic. Luckily, Ethan had predicted it might happen and had got as much food together as he could do. It would mean that Holly and Rich would have a buffet instead of a sit-down meal, but it was better than nothing. Besides which, he'd put together some of his speciality finger food and Audrey had been so impressed that she'd already said she would add some of them to the tea shop menu.

Now all they had to do was to get Tilly, Audrey, Harper and Scarlett into the cars and drive over to Greenacres. Looking at the sky and the way the snow was still coming down, though, Ethan was worried that not many guests would make it. His Uncle Gary had gone over to Fran's earlier and picked her up and taken her to Holly's, so at least Ethan knew she was already safely there. Audrey had insisted on packing extra clothes, flasks of hot chocolate and blankets just in case they got stuck in the snow, but Gary had laughed at her and reminded her that he had years of experience driving across the land in all weathers, often to rescue animals, so a bit of New Year's Eve snow wasn't going to stop him going anywhere.

Soon, they were on the roads, Gary driving one vehicle and Harper the other, the four-wheel drives managing the snow no problem at all. Tilly chattered excitedly to Audrey, telling her (again) about Fran's dogs and how she was allowed to go and visit them at any time. When they reached the sign for the vineyard, Ethan released a breath he hadn't realised he'd been holding. He really wanted the day to go well for Holly and Rich and felt privileged to be a part of it. Gary parked over by the barns and they started unloading everything.

'Ethan, right?' Rich emerge from the barn. 'Thank you so much for this.'

'Yes, that's right. Good to meet you.' They shook hands. 'And it's no problem at all. I'm glad I could help.'

'I can't believe we haven't been introduced yet, but with the wedding planning and so on, it's been a chaotic few weeks.' Rich shook his head. 'I can't believe I'm actually getting married today.'

'I know what you mean. It was really busy up at Rose-wood too. Fran said the same about the wedding, that she couldn't believe it was finally here.'

'Right...' Rich rubbed his hands together as if steeling himself. 'Shell is bringing some food from her cafe but we're so grateful that you were able to bring some too.' Rich peered into the Land Rovers. 'Looks like you brought enough to feed an army.'

Ethan laughed. 'I'm sure it won't go to waste.'

Rich frowned, his dark brows appearing below the rim of his hat and framing his brown eyes. 'We've already had most of our guests ring to say they can't make it.' In his wax jacket, bobble hat and snow boots, he didn't look as though he was getting married in two hours. 'Holly's so disappointed.'

'I'm sorry, Rich.' Ethan patted his arm. 'It must be upsetting. However, and I'm not in any way dismissing how important guests are, but... at least you and Holly are here and your nearest and dearest will be. You'll have the most important people around you to celebrate your special day.'

Rich nodded. 'You're right. Thanks so much. And I told Holly that we can always have a big party in the new year for all the people who couldn't make it today.'

'That sounds like a good idea.'

'And...' Rich smiled. 'We'd be very happy if you... and the tea shop, of course, would do the catering.'

'I'd be delighted!' Ethan nodded. 'I've already suggested something similar to Audrey about the tea shop branching out into catering for events and this would be a great start.'

'Fantastic. Who knows... we often have events like weddings here so it could be a regular thing.'

They shook hands.

'Now, shall we get all the food inside and get everyone settled so we can see how many... or how few... guests we'll have for the wedding?'

'I hate to ask this, but can the registrar make it?' Ethan asked as they walked into the barn.

Rich nodded. 'Friend of a friend, and she has a Land Rover too, so she said she'll be here, no problem at all.'

'Wonderful. If not, Gary already offered to go and collect her.'

As Ethan's family, including Tilly, started to carry the Tupperware boxes into the barn, Ethan's tension ebbed away. Even though it might not be the day that Holly and Rich had imagined, it would still be a good one, with the support and friendship of local people.

–

The registrar had arrived and spoken to Rich and Holly separately, the guests who could make it were seated in the barn with the heaters lit and mulled cider served and Fran and Holly had just finished getting ready. The makeup artist couldn't get through the snow, so Holly and Fran had done each other's makeup and Fran thought they'd done a good job. It was minimalist, natural and exactly how she thought they should look.

'I can't believe it's happening,' Holly said as she turned around and smiled at Fran. In her beautiful silver dress, she was stunning. Jamal had arrived early with Bradley and he'd put gentle waves into Holly's long blonde bob and pinned her veil and tiara in place. Holly was wearing a silver chain with a small heart locket that had been her mum's and she touched it now, making a lump rise in Fran's throat.

'She's with you, Holly. All the way.'

Holly nodded and blinked rapidly. 'My eye makeup.' She fanned her face with her hands.

'The mascara's waterproof.' Fran giggled. 'So we'll be fine.'

'I'm so glad you're here with me for this, Fran.'

'Where else would I be? You're my best friend and I love you.'

They hugged then and Fran thought her heart would burst.

—

Ethan knocked on the kitchen door at Greenacres. He'd been sitting with Tilly and his family in the barn, waiting for the ceremony to begin, when Tilly had whispered to him that she needed the loo. There were toilets in the barn, but because of the cold weather, there had been a problem with the pipes, so Audrey had suggested he take Tilly over to the house instead.

They'd trudged across the yard through the snow and Ethan had hoped that Tilly would be quick as he didn't want her disturbing the ceremony by walking back into the barn after Holly or right before her.

A man came to the door and opened it. 'Hello, can I help you?'

'Hi, I'm Ethan Clarke and this is my daughter, Tilly.'

'Yes, of course. Audrey's family. I'm Holly's dad, Bruce.'

They shook hands then Bruce stepped back. 'Come in, please.'

'I'm really sorry about this but Tilly needs to use the toilet.'

'No problem at all.' Bruce gestured behind him. 'Downstairs cloakroom is through that door.'

'Thank you!' Tilly rushed through, clearly more desperate than she'd let on.

'This is a big day for you.' Ethan smiled at Bruce, who looked petrified.

'Very big.' Bruce nodded. 'I can't believe my baby girl is getting married. I wish her mum was here to see it.'

Ethan nodded. He knew that feeling.

'I'm sure she knows, somehow,' Ethan said, offering the platitude that sometimes helped him.

'I hope so.' Bruce gazed out of the window. 'She'd love that it's snowing. Who knows, eh? Perhaps she sent the snow to make the day extra special.'

'Perhaps.'

'Right, I'd better get upstairs to finish dressing then bring my daughter over to the barn. I'll see you shortly.' Bruce smiled.

Ethan stood in the kitchen and waited. Tilly was taking a while so perhaps she'd needed more than a wee.

'Oh! Hello.'

Fran entered the kitchen and his jaw dropped.

'Wow!' He crossed the kitchen to her automatically and cupped her face. 'You look incredible.'

In a shimmering silver silk dress with chiffon sleeves and a headband in her short hair, set with pearls and diamantes, she looked like a princess. She was wearing silver-rimmed glasses and freshwater pearls in her ears.

'Really?' She laughed.

'Really. I've never seen anyone look more beautiful than you do right now.'

She held his gaze and his whole body tingled as his heart expanded with love. He lowered his head and kissed her gently, then sighed as he felt her lips part beneath his. He slid his arms around her and pulled her tight against him, kissing her deeply now.

When she pulled back gently, he sighed. 'Sorry.'

'Don't apologise. That was gorgeous but I came downstairs to find some crackers because Holly's feeling nauseous. I think it's mainly nerves making the morning sickness worse, but I'll have to get back because I don't want her vomiting over her wedding dress.'

'No you don't!' He shook his head. 'Quick, get back to her.'

'Can we finish this later?' Fran asked.

'I'd be very disappointed if we didn't.'

She grabbed a bag of crackers off the table, pecked him quickly on the lips then hurried from the room.

'Daddy!' Tilly emerged from the cloakroom. 'Sorry about that but I had a bit of a nervous belly.'

'It's okay, Tilly. Are you all right now?'

She nodded. 'Let's get back to the wedding.'

'We better had.'

He helped her put her coat back on then took her hand and they left the house and hurried back to the barn. Ethan's head was filled with images of Fran in her bridesmaid finery and his heart was still pounding from the promise he'd felt in that kiss.

–

'Here.' Fran handed Holly a cracker and she munched on it slowly.

'Thanks, Fran. I think if I have a few more, it should pass.'

'You'll be fine.' Fran rubbed Holly's back gently.

There was a knock at Holly's bedroom door so Fran went and opened it.

'Is there a beautiful bride in here?' Bruce asked. In his charcoal-grey suit with white shirt and silver tie, he looked very smart.

'There certainly is.' Fran stepped aside and Bruce gasped.

'Far too beautiful.' His voice wavered and he walked to Holly and hugged her. 'How're you feeling?'

'I'm okay, Dad. A bit nauseous – hence the crackers – and a bit emotional… missing Mum and Grandpa… but glad you're here.'

'What about those little ones?' He nodded at her belly, which gently curved under her dress.

'They're safe and warm and can't wait for the buffet.'

'I've seen what Ethan, Audrey and Shell have put together over in the barn and they've done you proud, Holly. It's a fabulous-looking feast.'

'I'm so grateful.' Holly's eyes glistened.

'Hey, don't cry. Not yet anyway. Let's get you over to the barn, shall we?' Bruce held out his arm and Holly slid hers through it.

'What about our shoes?' Fran asked, eyeing the delicate silver heels that sat in their open boxes on the bed.

'I vote for boots.' Holly pointed at a pair of white snow boots in the corner of her room.

Fran nodded. 'Mine are downstairs and I think that's a very wise decision. No one will see them under our dresses anyway.'

They made their way downstairs then pulled on their coats and gloves.

'One moment!'

Fran went through to the kitchen then returned with Gelert, Holly's grey lurcher. He had a silver bow on his collar and was wearing his own coat.

'Your pageboy is ready.'

Holly leant over and rubbed the dog's ears. 'Come on then, boy, let's get to a wedding.'

'A white wedding indeed!' Fran said as they left the house at Greenacres and crossed the yard, using the path that Gary and Ethan had dug through the snow.

The air was cold and fresh, snowflakes drifted down, settling on their heads and shoulders, and the house and outbuildings looked like a scene from a Victorian Christmas card. Then the barn doors opened before them and the glow of thousands of fairy lights inside welcomed them, along with the warmth emanating from the heaters and the love of family and friends.

–

As Holly and Bruce entered the barn, Ethan found himself straining in his seat to see Fran. Next to him, Tilly was doing the same, and he smiled. They both had it bad for the beautiful artist.

The barn doors were closed and a hush fell inside as Holly and Bruce prepared to walk down the aisle that had been cleared in the centre of the barn and led right up to the far wall where the registrar and her assistant waited behind a desk. In front of them stood Rich, in a dark grey suit with a silver and red patterned tie – a nod to the time of year, he'd told Ethan earlier. Ethan glanced at Rich's face, and his expression said everything: Rich loved Holly with all of his heart and always would do.

It was magical in the barn, with fairy lights wound around the beams and the wooden posts that supported the roof. The space smelt of cinnamon and vanilla from the oil burners on the tables and the heaters made every-thing cosy and warm.

Then the music began, an instrumental version of Christina Perri's 'A Thousand Years', floating from the speakers set high on the barn walls. The band hadn't been able to make it, but Rich said not to worry because they'd had a good music system installed.

First along the aisle came Fran with the dog, Gelert. Ethan had never seen anything more beautiful. She seemed to glide rather than walk and even when she reached the front and stood to one side, Ethan couldn't drag his eyes away from her to watch Holly's progress along the aisle. But he watched Fran gazing at Holly and in that moment, he knew for certain that Fran had done what she had done for her best friend because she loved her. She was a loyal person, a caring friend, and that filled his heart with nothing other than admiration and respect for her. How many people would pretend to be pregnant just to protect their friend's secret, even when it wasn't that bad a secret to disclose in the first place? Fran had integrity, she had dignity and she would, he knew, never let anyone she cared about down.

And that included him and Tilly.

—

Fran smiled as Holly arrived at her side and Bruce kissed her cheeks then placed her hand in Rich's. They didn't have fresh bouquets because the florist hadn't made it, but it didn't matter, because Glenda had given Holly a pink silk rose bouquet that her husband had given her years ago. The flowers were slightly discoloured but Holly hadn't cared and had said it was her something borrowed, along with her mum's necklace, which was her something old; the dress was her something new and in her ears were tiny sapphire studs as her something blue.

There were twenty-four people sitting either side of the aisle, not as many as Holly and Rich had invited, but more than they'd expected to make it with the weather being so bad. Rich's parents were there with baby Luke, along with Ethan and his family, Jamal and Bradley, Janine, Catherine and Mark and a few others from the village.

As Holly and Rich said their vows then exchanged rings, Fran glanced sideways and met Ethan's gaze. The intensity in his eyes made her heart race and her stomach clench. He was looking at her as if seeing her properly for the first time and she wondered what he was thinking.

Then the music began again and the guests applauded as Holly and Rich embraced and Fran made her way over to Ethan.

It was time for the celebrations to begin.

Epilogue

One year later...

'I can't believe it's still snowing,' Fran said as she peered out of the tea shop window. It was Sunday but they'd come across from Fran's cottage because Ethan was putting together some ideas for his new venture as events caterer.

'I do wonder when it will stop.' Ethan wrapped an arm around her shoulders and pressed a kiss on her head. 'Thank goodness for Gary and his Land Rovers.'

Fran leant against him, enjoying his warmth and his familiar scent as she looked out at the leaden sky. It was snowing so heavily that she could barely make out the farmhouse and the buildings behind it.

'Can we build a snowman?' Tilly asked, taking hold of Fran's hand.

'When it stops.' Fran smiled down at Tilly. 'We wouldn't be able to see what we were doing out there at the moment.'

'And I don't want either of my girls getting cold,' Ethan said. 'Talking of being cold, I'm going to get us cookies and hot chocolates.'

Tilly grinned at Fran as Ethan went behind the counter. 'How long does pregnancy last?'

'About nine months.'

'Nine months is a long time.' Tilly frowned. 'Why does it take so long?'

'Well, a baby has to grow strong enough to be able to survive when it's born.' Fran turned and led Tilly over to the table near the log burner and they sat down. Tilly picked up the pencil she'd been using earlier and started to sketch an outline.

'How does it get born?' Tilly asked without looking up.

'A baby has to come out of its mummy's tummy.'

'How does it do that?'

'Uh...' Fran chewed her bottom lip. 'It comes down the... birth canal.'

'There's a canal inside a mummy?' Tilly paused in her sketching and raised an eyebrow.

'Kind of.' Fran glanced around, hoping to find some inspiration. Explaining exactly how a baby was born was not on her to-do list for today, but it was something she should have expected at some point. After all, it came with the territory of being around a young child.

'Okay.' Tilly nodded. 'That's interesting.'

Ethan arrived at the table with a tray. He placed three mugs of hot chocolate topped with whipped cream and marshmallows on the table, then a plate with three giant chocolate chip cookies.

'They look amazing.' Fran picked one up.

'Freshly made to cater to your healthy appetite.' Ethan winked.

'You spoil me.' Fran smiled at him as she nibbled on her cookie. It was fresh and crumbly and the chocolate chips were rich and dark. 'Delicious.'

'Good.'

Fran shifted on her chair.

'Are you okay?' Ethan reached for her hand.

'Just a spot of backache.'

'Do you want a cushion?'

'No, I'm fine. I must have slept awkwardly.'

Fran finished her cookie then sipped her drink. The hot chocolate was silky as it filled her mouth and she chewed on the tiny marshmallows. There were definite advantages to being in a relationship with a chef, although she was putting on some weight, but then Ethan said he loved her curves.

The door opened and Holly and Rich entered with a gust of wind and a scattering of snowflakes that drifted across the floor. Rich pushed the pram inside and set the brake.

'Hi,' Ethan said as he hurried to close the door. 'Glad you could make it.'

'I wouldn't have missed trying this new taster menu you've been talking about just because of a bit of snow.' Rich helped Holly out of her coat and hung it on the back of a chair then did the same with his.

Holly sat next to Fran and peered at the cookies. 'They look good.'

'You want one?' Ethan asked. 'And a hot chocolate?'

'That would be wonderful, thank you.' Holly nodded. 'I need the extra calories at the moment.'

'Of course you do.' Fran smiled. 'And how is everyone this morning?' She peered at the pram as Rich removed the wind cover.

'They're doing well.'

'Where's Luke?'

'Insisted on staying with my dad to help him.'

'With what?'

'Dad was clearing the snow from the yard and Luke is his shadow at the moment.'

'That's so lovely.'

'It's very cute seeing a boy not yet two years old trying to shovel snow.'

'And how are the twins?'

'Thankfully sleeping.' Holly slumped in her chair. 'I'm exhausted.'

'I can't believe they're almost six months old.' Fran peered at the sleeping girls lying next to each other in the twin pram; they were identical in every way. Their pale eyelashes fluttered on their cheeks and they both sucked on their dummies as they dreamed.

'Me neither. I thought Luke's first year flew by but with three children, it's going even faster.'

'I guess I have all this to come.' Fran gazed across the table at Tilly, who was sketching again, her tongue poking out of her mouth.

'She's grown up so much in a year.' Holly leant closer to Fran. 'I can't believe it's been almost a year since we got married.'

'I know!' Fran exclaimed. 'It'll be your first anniversary in days.'

'And the first anniversary of the tea shop opening its doors on Christmas Day.'

'We're looking forward to that this year. Ethan's got a big delivery coming next week so let's hope the snow's gone by then.'

Holly nodded. 'I hope so. People still talk about last year and it's important to a lot of the villagers in Penhallow Sands.'

'Okay...' Ethan returned to the table and set down two more hot chocolates for Holly and Rich. 'Enjoy those and I'll start bringing the food through. I've put together some ideas for weddings based on the success of the ones we've already tried, as well as some different ones for birthdays, but we can mix and match for your clients and see what works.'

Over the past year, Ethan and Rich had worked together to calculate costings and menu ideas to expand the catering side of the tea shop with Greenacres as a prime client, using Rich's accountancy skills and Ethan's creative flair. They had become good friends and Fran was happy to see them getting along so well. It meant that the four of them, along with their children, could spend more time together.

Since last Christmas, Fran and Ethan had become really close and in the autumn, Ethan and Tilly had moved into Fran's cottage. They'd considered staying at Rosewood, but the cottage there was too small for Fran's animals and she also had her studio and her work to think about, although she had cut back a bit on that recently. They had taken their time to get to know each other and ensured that Tilly felt comfortable with their relationship before even considering moving in together, but since they had, everything had been perfect. The three of them got along so well and Fran had gone from thinking that she didn't need anyone in her life to enjoying having a ready-made family. Her dogs also loved it, especially the small white Westie, who Tilly had named Snowy. The lucky dog got to sleep at the bottom of Tilly's bed and he followed her everywhere when she was at home and waited at the door for her every afternoon to greet her when she got home from school.

As Ethan set out the food he'd prepared for Rich and Holly to try, Fran gazed at the sleeping twins. Holly had gone from fleeing Penhallow Sands, believing her life would never be the same again, to being happily married to a man she adored. After their wedding on New Year's Eve, as Fran and Ethan had danced at the reception, he'd told her that she was everything he'd ever wanted in a partner and that as long as she felt the same, he wanted them to be together. It had been a big step for him after going through such heartbreak and knowing that he had to put Tilly's welfare first, but it turned out that he believed what Fran had done for Holly by pretending to be the one who was pregnant had opened his eyes to how amazing he thought she was. Having a man look at her the way that Ethan did, having him hold her the way he did and having his trust had allowed Fran to fall deeply in love with him, and she was happier than she had ever been.

'Will you have two babies?' Tilly snapped Fran out of her daydream.

'Pardon?'

'Will you have one baby or two like Holly?'

Fran smiled. 'I'd like to think that I have you so I don't need to have a baby—'

'Can you choose how many you want?' Tilly cut her off, her enthusiasm for the topic clearly making her mind race.

'Not really.'

'It would be better if you could.' Tilly held out a hand and counted on her fingers. 'Like when you go to the

298

supermarket and buy a… coconut. You can buy one if you don't want a lot of coconuts or two if you want more.'

'That's true. But I don't think it applies to babies.'

'I will have one. Perhaps.' Tilly frowned. 'But then perhaps I won't because I want to be an astronaut and I don't think you can take babies into space.'

'Not yet at least.'

'Hmm.' Tilly returned to her drawing. 'There! All done.'

'Can I see it?'

'Of course you can, silly, it's for you.'

Tilly carefully tore the page from her sketchpad and handed the drawing to Fran. As she gazed at it, her vision blurred and she had to blink hard to see it properly.

Tilly came round to Fran's side and pointed at the picture. 'See, there's Daddy in his chef's hat.'

'Is he holding a cake?'

'Yes, it's your favourite chocolate cake.'

'Yum.'

'And there's me.' Tilly pointed at a shorter figure holding what looked like a ball.

'Are you playing football?'

'No!' Tilly rolled her eyes. 'That's my space helmet.'

'I see.' Fran swallowed her laughter. The drawing was very good but a few things still needed some definition.

'And that… is you.'

'What's this?' Ethan came up behind Fran and leant over to see the picture.

'It's us three, Daddy,' Tilly said. 'Can I go and taste the food now?'

'Of course you can.' Ethan gestured at the table where Holly and Rich were sampling pastries.

'Thanks, Daddy.' Tilly went over to stand with Holly and Rich.

Fran pointed at the big belly she had on the picture. 'Do I look that big in real life?'

Ethan wrapped his arms around her and kissed her cheek. 'You're perfect, angel. I think that's just Tilly's proportions being a bit off again.'

Tilly returned to them. 'Do you like my drawing?'

'Yes, Tilly, it's very good.' Fran held it up.

'Do you like your big belly?'

'Why is it so big?' Fran asked.

'It's not really that big.' Tilly shook her head. 'I just thought it might be like that if you had a baby like Holly did.'

'Oh.' Fran met Ethan's eyes. 'Right. But you know I'm not having a baby, don't you?'

'Of course I do, silly. But you could be. One day.'

'That's told you.' Ethan squeezed her hand.

They hadn't really talked in detail about having a child, but had decided to see what happened in a year or so. It would mean that Tilly had a sibling, and although it was something Fran had never given much thought to, she found that she was warming to the idea. She loved being a mum to Tilly, and although Melanie would always be Tilly's biological mum, Fran knew that she'd have a place as Tilly's stepmum. Maybe they would add to their family, maybe not. Time would tell.

'Do you want to try some of the food now?' Ethan asked. 'You can tell me what you like best because I always trust your judgement.'

'I'd love to.'

And as Ethan led her over to the table where her best friend and stepdaughter were now chatting about whether cheese or cheese and onion tartlets were better, Fran's heart soared.

Her heart was full, her life was wonderful, her family was complete, and all because Ethan and Tilly had come to the Christmas tea shop at Rosewood.

Acknowledgements

My thanks go to:

My husband and children, for your love and support.

My warm and wonderful agent, Amanda Preston, at LBA.

The fabulous team at Canelo – as always, your enthusiasm and hard work are deeply appreciated. Special thanks to my amazing editor, Louise Cullen, and to the real (and absolutely gorgeous) Fran, for allowing me to use your name.

My very supportive author and blogger friends.

All the readers who come back for more and who take the time to write reviews and share the book love.

Cornish Hearts

The House at Greenacres
The Cottage at Plum Tree Bay
The Christmas Tea Shop